The Woman with the
A mafia romance

―

Jessica Gadziala

Copyright © 2021   Jessica Gadziala

All rights reserved. In accordance with the U.S Copyright Act of 1976, the scanning, uploading, and electronic sharing of any part of this book without permission of the publisher is unlawful piracy and theft of the author's intellectual property. This book or any portion thereof may not be reproduced or used in any manner whatsoever without the express written permission of the author except for brief quotations used in a book review.

"This book is a work of fiction. The names, characters, places and incidents are products of the writer's imagination or have been used fictitiously and are not to be construed as real. Any resemblance to persons, living or dead, actual events, locales or organizations is entirely coincidental."

Cover Design: Jessica Gadziala

The Woman with the Ring

1

Isabella

The olive oil spilled while I was preparing lunch. Generations of women before me would have seen it as a bad omen. I, however, just saw it as a minor inconvenience to be wiped away while I was already running late for work.

I should have heeded the warning, called out of work, ordered in a pint of salted caramel gelato, got back into my comfy pajamas, and spent the day watching movies.

I mean, who was to say that the exact same fate still wouldn't have found me. In my room. In my bed. That may have even been even more traumatizing, having my comfort zone invaded.

I probably never would have given the olive oil a second thought if the day had gone like it was supposed to. Work, a short walk to the coffee shop, and then the subway back home.

It was the first thing I thought of, though, when hands came out of nowhere, one slapping over my mouth, and the other going around my waist, lifting me up and off my feet, leaving me peddling the air for a horrifying, soul-stopping moment before I found myself pushed toward a waiting black utility van. The kind without windows. And, I noticed with horror as I was shoved into it, padding glued up the walls. To muffle the sounds of screams. To prevent anyone from banging frantically on the metal to attract attention.

How many women had they snatched off the street to require them to outfit their vehicle for kidnapping?

"Just get in with her," a man barked from the front seat. He was nothing but a black woolen hat and a puffer jacket to me. "You're going to be seen," he added. "If you cost us this job, I swear to God..." he went on as the man jumped inside the back with me, and slid the door closed.

He'd said "cost."

But it came out like "cawst."

Cawst.

That was more Bronx than Manhattan.

What the heck would a couple of guys from the Bronx come to Manhattan to kidnap a woman for? They had plenty of women in their own backyard.

Unless...

No.

Nope.

I wasn't going to let my mind go there.

I'd spent way too many hours of my life worrying needlessly that my family's *Family* business would end up hurting me in some way. And it never did. So there was no reason to believe it would now.

Besides, the mafia didn't deal in women. They left us out of it.

Or, at least, they always had in the past.

"Fucking Christ," the man in the back with me growled, narrowly missing the heel of my shoe as I kicked out my legs.

I should have listened to my cousins when they'd encouraged me to take martial arts instead of dance. What the hell good did dance do for me? It certainly didn't help me fight off a kidnapper, that was for sure.

The guy in the back with me was thoroughly average in the looks department. Dark hair, dark eyes, with a somewhat soft chin and a bit of scruff. I put him around five-ten and on the thin side, but still a lot stronger than me.

"Bitch," he growled as my hand shot out, my fingernails scratching down his face.

"Just fuckin' tie her up or somethin'," the man from the front demanded. "We got a fuckin' forty-minute drive. She's gonna pop your eye out at this rate."

"At least she's not—" the man with me started to say just as I sucked in a deep breath, harnessed my inner horror-movie-girl, and screamed at the top of my fucking lungs. "Shit," he hissed, body dropping down on mine, straddling my chest, and slapping his hand over my mouth, fingers bruising in. "Shut the fuck up," he growled in a tone that suggested he didn't understand why I was making such a big fuss.

"Hold on. I think I got some duct tape, man," the driver said, reaching over to rifle through his glove box, then tossing back a giant silver roll of tape.

I didn't want to know why a man had a need to drive around with duct tape in his glove box. All I knew was it couldn't be good, right?

The man on top of me dropped the tape down beside my head before lifting up one knee, using it to pin down one of my arms. And then the next. Until I was helpless to do anything but try to writhe around like a fish pulled from a line and tossed on the dock.

"Tell me when," the man on me demanded to the driver who had slowed to a stop.

"Hold on. Let me turn down the side street," the driver called. "Okay," he said a moment later. "Get it done," he added.

And just like that, the hand lifted from my mouth.

But before I could draw in a breath to scream again, duct tape was being taped across my mouth.

"There. Done."

"Do her arms, man. Then you could ride up here with me."

"Yeah," the guy on top of me said, scooting back, then tossing me onto my stomach. Pain shot through my cheekbone as my face slammed against the hard floor.

"Easy, man," the driver growled. "We bring her in all fucked up, and boss man is gonna be pissed."

But he'd already wrenched my arm back and up to wrap a layer of tape to it, the stickiness nipping at my skin. His weight shifted, yanking up my other arm, then securing it to the other.

Then just like that, the weight was lifted as the man climbed off of me and moved between the front two seats to drop into the passenger one with a groan.

"She fucked up my face," he growled.

"You were ugly before, you're ugly now," the driver said, tone light and teasing. "Don't see the problem."

"Dick," the other guy grumbled as I threw myself onto my back.

"Turn the music on or somethin' in case she starts knocking around," the driver said.

I was considering trying to kick the walls or doors.

But, clearly, they had all their bases covered.

The music started thumping from the speakers, making it impossible to hear my kidnappers, though I was vaguely aware of the timbre of their voices.

Gagged and bound, I had nothing to do but think.

For several horrific moments, I thought about all the typical things women thought about in situations like this. About all the ways a man could hurt a woman.

It wasn't long, though, until I remembered that I wasn't the average woman.

Which meant I had to look at this whole situation as more than a snatch and grab kidnapping and potential rape by random, strange men.

See, they'd said something about their boss.

Their boss.

From The Bronx.

A low, pathetic whimper escaped me as the name flashed across my mind.

It couldn't be him.

But, also, it couldn't be anyone else, could it?

Primo Esposito.

The boss of the Esposito family.

A man that had, as legend went, sliced his father's throat during a Family sit-down, wiped the knife off on a napkin, then sat down to finish cutting his steak with it.

He was a brutal, cold-blooded, homicidal maniac.

The word was that the entire Esposito Family was vicious and unpredictable.

It was why the new *Capo dei Capi* of all the New York City organized crime families had been trying to step lightly around them. Anytime my brother, Emilio, came to Sunday dinners, he was always griping to the cousins about the Espositos not respecting the Costa Family, not paying their dues, not following the rules.

But as far as I could remember, there hadn't ever been any word about Primo or his men kidnapping women. That being said, my brother and the rest of the Costa Family tried to keep the women out of the businesses as much as possible so none of us could get in trouble with the police.

For all I knew, Primo Esposito kidnapped and abused women all the time.

A low, pathetic cry escaped me, muffled by the duct tape.

Frustrated tears burned my eyes.

Because there was nothing I could do.

I was gagged and bound. There were two of them. And if I knew anything about the soldiers in the mafia, it was that they were always armed.

There was no way out of this for me.

Except, maybe when the van stopped. Maybe I could possibly make a run for it. Dance had at least given me some stamina. And I somehow doubted these guys were the 'spend endless hours at the gym working on calisthenics' type. Besides, I wouldn't have to run far. Just far enough to get around people, to get inside a store, or anywhere that someone might help me.

No one was going to stand by and let a bound and gagged woman be dragged off by kidnappers. People were better than that.

Plan made, I spent the entire ride trying to keep my breathing slow and even, trying not to let my mind run away with me. It wouldn't do me any good to get worked up by the possibilities of what might happen if I didn't get away. It was just going to psych me out, make me second guess my instincts.

It felt like an eternity of bouncing around in the van before it finally pulled to a stop where the engine cut, the music turned off, and the passenger got out.

Just him.

That was good, right?

I had a better chance of evading just him. And the driver would be slow to get out of the car and lead in the chase.

I could actually do this.

Taking a deep breath, I let the passenger open the door. I even let him yank me toward it because I didn't want the driver to suspect anything before it actually happened.

The sounds of people met my ear and I felt a flood of relief so strong that I nearly cried out.

But then my feet were hitting the ground outside the van.

I guess my kidnapper didn't expect for me to try to run because the hand he had on my arm was weak, easy to break away from. And that was just what I did.

I yanked and I bolted.

And there were people.

And they saw me.

I even observed wide, surprised, and upset eyes.

But no one helped.

No one helped.

They turned their backs.

They went inside the buildings.

Heart slamming in my chest, I screamed against the duct tape gag as I ran up to a young guy who was walking trash out of the deli to the street.

His body stiffened.

His hands even started to raise.

Until an older man from inside the deli rushed out, grabbed him, and yanked him back inside the store, locking the door.

No.

No no no.

People were good, damnit.

They didn't stand by while innocent women got chased down by gangsters.

With a sob catching in my throat, I turned to run again.

And ran straight into a brick wall of a person hard enough that it knocked what was left of my breath from me.

A scream rose through me, thinking it was one of my kidnappers.

But when my gaze rose, I realized it was much, much worse than that.

I'd never seen him before. He was elusive by nature. And I wasn't exactly a part of the *Family* per se, just related by blood to it. So I didn't know all the players. That being said, you just knew a boss when you spotted one. They carried themselves differently. Everything about them commanded attention and respect.

This was Primo Esposito.

Boss of the Esposito crime family.

I don't know what I expected of him. Bosses came in all shapes and sizes and ages. But from what everyone said about his nature, I guess my mind filled in the gaps to make him short and stout with a receding hairline and evil black eyes.

I was completely wrong on three points and halfway wrong on the fourth.

Primo Esposito had to be about six feet tall with a strong, but wiry build—like that of a swimmer. He had a full head of inky-black hair and the kind of bone structure you saw in Hollywood, not standing on a street corner in the Bronx wearing a black suit with an understated gold cross necklace.

The eyes, though, that was where I was partially right.

They weren't black, but rather a deep chocolate brown and framed with thick lashes.

But they *were* evil.

Those were evil freaking eyes if I'd ever seen any.

"You see that, little lamb?" he asked as his strong hand grabbed my arm, using his other hand to wave at the street where everyone had disappeared. "No one cares about you being led off to slaughter."

2

Primo

Two kidnappings in twenty-four hours.

It was a record.

I didn't like snatching women off the street. But the Costa Family had made it impossible to negotiate any other way.

I knew it was going to come to something like this when the previous *Capo dei Capi* had died and been immediately replaced by his son. I couldn't claim to have any love lost when the old boss died, but after years of negotiations and renegotiations, we'd managed to come to an agreement that both our Families were content with.

But then Lorenzo Costa got the position and undid all the shit his father and I had ironed out years before. Was Lorenzo a better boss than his father? Probably. His old man was a narcissist with a fragile ego who kept yes-men at his beck and call, instead of having impartial parties around to tell him when shit wasn't going right.

That didn't mean that I was going to be brow-beat into a deal that didn't work for my men or me.

Maybe Costa managed to get the Morelli and the D'Onofrio families to come to heel, but the Espositos were no one's fucking bitch. I would get the deal I wanted by whatever means necessary.

Which, at the moment, meant taking the woman who belonged to Lorenzo's brother, Santi. To draw them into my neck of the woods for a long-overdue sit-down.

It also meant snatching Isabella Costa as well.

Not to draw the Costas out per se, but to finally put an end to the feud.

It was a two-part plan.

Was it primitive and borderline heinous?

Probably.

But no one had ever accused me of being a good man.

I didn't tell my men this, but I'd chosen Isabella Costa for more than just her connection to Emilio, her brother, who was high ranking in the Costa Family hierarchy. There were plenty of other Costa women.

But I'd caught sight of Isabella leaving their mother's house after Sunday dinner once. And the decision had been made.

Isabella Costa was a slip of a woman. Short, slight, but when I'd seen her, she'd been putting her brother in his place over some disagreement, shoving her finger in his face and stabbing it into his chest until he was backing away from her and holding his hands up in a defensive gesture.

If a woman was going to survive inside my world, she had to be strong.

From the looks of things, Isabella Costa was that.

She was also beautiful with her soft, rounded, feminine face with plump lips, deep-set light brown eyes, and long, wavy black hair.

I might have been making the deal to bring peace between warring Families.

But I wasn't going to shackle myself to a wife I didn't find attractive in the process.

I'd just been getting out of my car in front of the warehouse when I'd seen the van with two of my soldiers in it pulling up.

You could say I was pleasantly surprised to see the tiny woman break free from their hold and attempt to run for her life.

She probably thought that people were inherently good.

That was her mistake.

No one was going to save her.

No one was going to get in the middle of my business.

She was in my neck of the woods.

Which meant she was completely at my mercy.

She was even smaller up close and personal. Her arm felt a little too breakable when my hand closed around it to drag her back toward the warehouse, giving my men a hard look that had them shrinking into themselves, likely worried about the repercussions of making me finish a job I'd hired them to carry out.

I'd have to punish them.

I was not the kind of man who ran his organization based on trust and understanding of mistakes.

I reigned with rules and ruthless consequences.

So while I knew that my neighborhood would not fuck around and get in my business, no matter what their moral compass was saying, I couldn't look the other way when some of my men aired my business out like dirty laundry either.

I led the woman around the warehouse toward the back service entrance, taking her up to the third floor where the conference room and offices were. If this day went like I planned for it to go, she would end up on the top floor. A floor where only close personal friends and high-ranking men in my Family were permitted to go.

My home.

Where I planned to keep her.

Indefinitely.

Maybe reluctantly at first. But, eventually, willingly.

But until the deal was made and the vows were exchanged, she wasn't a wife, she was a prisoner. Which meant she got tossed in the empty storage room that served as a cell when necessary.

"Here you go," I said, yanking open the door to a room that had a small cot, a bottle of water, and nothing else.

When her feet refused to move forward, I grabbed her other arm, pushing her into the small space.

"I'll take this off," I told her, reaching for the end of the duct tape. "You can scream as much as you want in here. No one will hear you. And if they do, they won't save you," I said, taking an uncharacteristic level of gentleness when removing the tape from her lips. Those were lips I would need to have a first kiss with if or when the plan was in motion. I'd prefer they weren't all ripped up. "We can do better than this," I added, gesturing toward her duct-taped wrists.

I watched as her eyes widened when I reached into my pocket for a set of handcuffs I almost always kept on me. Experience told me that you never knew when you might need a set.

I clipped the bracelets on her wrists before removing the duct tape. If she struggled against the tape, she could fuck up her wrists. And this deal wasn't going to happen if her Family thought I was harming her.

Finished, I took a step back.

"Sit tight. We have a meeting to attend in a few hours' time," I said, making my way to the door.

"Please, don't," she begged, voice choked, like it was killing her to do it. But there was something inside that was stronger than her pride. "Please, don't leave me in here. I won't try to escape again. *Please*," she cried, voice taking on an edge that hinted at tears.

I wasn't a gentle man.

But I felt the unfamiliar urge to go back on my word, to take her out of the room, to keep her from continuing to panic like she clearly was.

Which was exactly why I couldn't do that.

"It will all be clear in a few hours," I told her, then closed and locked the door. "You," I called, snapping at one of my soldiers that was standing around. "You guard this door. No one goes in, or they answer to me," I told him, the threat clear in my tone. "And she does not come out, either, unless it is cleared with me first."

"Got it, boss," the soldier agreed, nodding like his life depended on proving to me he could handle the job.

It did.

Alright.

That was one prisoner down.

Now it was onto the next. And, arguably, the much more difficult one. Though, luckily, she was only around temporarily. She was just the bait to draw the wolves out into my neck of the woods.

Alessa Morelli wasn't the typical mafia sister and daughter and cousin. Meaning she didn't stay at home and cook and raise kids or just live a normal, working life. No. She was actually *in* the Family. Which was surprisingly progressive for the Morellis. Though they didn't officially give her any sort of position; they just hired her out to do jobs. She did the work with none of the respect. It fit with how I was currently feeling about the Morelli men.

The men who'd made my brother disappear.

I wasn't a fool.

Men in our business didn't simply *disappear*.

They got killed.

And their bodies were disposed of.

In this case, my brother, Due, got killed by Alessa Morelli's brother who had been in hiding ever since. Which was why I needed Alessa on top of Isabella Costa.

With Isabella, I would get her brother, Emilio, and the *Capo dei Capi*, Lorenzo. But to get the Morellis to the meeting as well, I needed something of theirs.

Alessa was all I had to work with.

And she was a fucking spitfire. Trained and capable with a hell of a fucking mouth on her.

I liked her spirit.

Even when she was trying to stab me with a knife as I fetched her from my office, taking one of her cuffs and attaching it to my own wrist, dragging her along with me while I worked, not sure I trusted any of my men fully with her.

Men in our businesses tended to underestimate women.

Not me.

I knew there was nothing more fierce than a woman in a male-dominated industry. Of any sort. They were not to be underestimated. They would slit your throat and then step on your bleeding-out body to get a step higher in the organization.

I gave that ambition the kind of deference it deserved.

So I kept her at my side.

Even as she berated me about being a neanderthal for my plan to form an alliance between the families with an arranged marriage.

Was it old school?

Sure.

But it worked.

History had shown it again and again.

They wouldn't come at me because I had one of their loved ones in my camp. And I would have the peace of mind knowing I had Isabella as a bargaining chip.

"They're never going to go for it," Alessa Morelli said as I dragged her around the conference room.

It wouldn't be long.

Pretty soon one of my scouts would get word back to us that the Morellis and Costas were on their way to come pick up Alessa.

They didn't know about Isabella yet. That was the part I was going to go ahead and keep to myself until the right moment. Until we got shit ironed out with Alessa's family.

"I heard you the first five times, babe," I said, rolling my neck. "I think you overestimate how good of men your family and the Costas are."

"Better than you," Alessa shot back, full of fire and spit. When we'd made the video call to her loved ones, she'd attempted to slice my throat. I had to give her credit for the attempt, even if she ultimately failed.

"Yes, well, that goes without saying," I agreed.

From my position near the windows looking down on the street, I could just barely make out the first whistle. Then the second. Then the third. I got to watch as my soldier out front reached for his phone just a moment before mine buzzed in my pocket.

"Just the Morellis and Costas," I reminded him.

They wouldn't come alone. But their men had to stay on the street with most of mine.

Alessa and I watched as the cars pulled up, the men filed out, and the rules were laid out.

In the end, it was Alessa's father and her brothers who were allowed up. Then there were the Costa *Capo dei Capi*, Lorenzo, his brother (and Alessa's man) Santiago, as well as Isabella—in the storage room's—brother, Emilio. Then, of course, because this crew never went anywhere without their rabid dog, was a man by the name of Brio. Brio was the kind of cold and vicious that gave even me pause at times. I'd never seen a more capable torturer or killer. In my opinion, he'd been born into the wrong Family. He would have been a great Esposito.

"Let her go!"

Those were the first words spoken during this important meeting. They were spoken by Alessa's brother, Ricco. The same man who had murdered my brother.

"Maybe," I said, waving toward the conference table. "We will see about that." I watched as they all took their seats before taking my own. "Want a seat, baby?" I asked Alessa, waving at my lap. Really, I just wanted a rise out of her Family by the comment. And I got it.

"Not if you were the last man on Earth, Primo," Alessa said, getting a small smile out of me. You had to appreciate all her fire.

"You didn't have to take Alessa," Lorenzo, the Five Families new *Capo dei Capo*, said a few moments later after some tense hellos. "And shoot my man in the process," he added.

Yes, well, things had gotten a little messier picking up Alessa than they had when grabbing Isabella.

"Relax. Salvatore will live. And I did need to take Alessa if I wanted to smoke out Ricco," I said, gaze sliding toward the man who'd shot his brother.

"All the proper channels were gone through to order the hit on Due," Lorenzo said, meaning a mission with the whole Commission. Except it wasn't the whole Commission since I hadn't been present. And if I knew anything about the Lombardi Family, they wouldn't have been present at the meeting either, since they were having just as many issues with the new leadership as I was. If not worse. "If I'm not mistaken, your father had gone through the same channels in his day to have a member of my Family hit," he added.

Just the mention of my father had my blood boiling and my spine straightening.

"Don't compare me to my father," I demanded, voice a harsh whisper.

"I'm simply proving that this system works in favor of all the Families with legitimate concerns. Yours included. This wasn't done in a shady or unfair way."

"It was my *brother*, Lorenzo," I insisted. It was one thing to get some random made man taken out. But a boss's brother? That shit was serious. I was *taking it* seriously.

"And you know The Commission only approves the hit of men as high up in the hierarchy if there is just cause."

"What just cause could you have possibly had?" I snapped.

"Ricco," Lorenzo said, nodding toward Alessa's brother who pulled a rolled-up folder out of his bulletproof vest, spreading it on the tabletop, and pulling individual pages out, then passing them across the table toward me.

I could feel myself straightening as I took the folder. Because if there were documents or pictures of any sort, then it was entirely possible I was mistaken about the situation. The Commission might well have had their reasons.

I never could have anticipated those reasons, though.

A muscle in my jaw ticked as I clenched it hard enough for pain to shoot up my mouth and to my temples as I looked down at the pictures in front of me, not sure I wanted to believe them, but not being able to deny them either.

"Your brother was caught soliciting minors," Ricco explained, making my stomach drop, even as I looked at the proof of it before me. "Online, as you can see from the messages," he went on. "But also in person. We got word from someone in your community whose son said Due tried to get him to get in his car and come back to his place for ice cream. He was nine years old," Ricco finished.

Rage, a familiar and old friend, burned through me, a fire that caught and spread until it engulfed me entirely.

My gaze rose.

"And you just shot him in the back of the head?" I asked.

"He was a fucking pedophile," Ricco snapped.

"Let me rephrase that," I said. "You *only* shot him in the back of the head?" I asked. "Men like that should be taken apart piece by piece," I added, barely able to get the words out, my jaw was so tight. "No matter who they are. If you didn't have the stomach for it," I went on, "you should have brought this to me. I would have done it."

I wasn't putting on some sort of show for them.

I meant that.

I meant it down to my bones.

Yes, I believed in family.

But I did not believe that your blood should be protected at all costs, no matter what.

If I believed that, my father would still be alive and running the Esposito Family.

On a growl, I reached into my pocket to produce a handcuff key, freeing Alessa whose Family I no longer had any issue with.

"It was fun, baby, but go back to your man," I said, and she didn't even pause.

"This isn't over," she said as she got to him. "He has a plan," she added.

"No no," I said, waving a finger at her. "No spoilers."

"Spoilers for what, Primo?" Lorenzo asked. "We dealt with the issue."

"We dealt with one issue," I said. "We still have many to contend with. And they all come back to the utter lack of trust between our Families."

"I don't disagree," Lorenzo said, nodding. "Which is why open and honest sit-downs are important."

"No," I said, shaking my head. "We're beyond talking. You and I both know it would never be enough."

"What then do you propose?" Lorenzo asked, giving me a dubious look.

To that, I raised a hand in the air, a cue to my man to knock on the door. And for the man inside to bring out Isabella.

"What the fuck is this?" Lorenzo asked, body going tighter than ever before.

"My proposal," I said, shrugging. "We could fuck around with this war. We could each lose dozens of men and millions of dollars. Or we can end it all right now. With an act of good faith."

"With a fucking sacrifice," Alessa snapped, practically vibrating with rage.

"Alessa here doesn't approve of my plan," I said, shooting her a barely-there smirk. "Called it out of the Dark Ages, if I recall correctly," I told them.

"No," Emilio, Isabella's brother, said, quicker to figure out what was going on than I was.

"I understand your hesitance," I agreed, nodding. "She is your little sister, after all," I said, waving the guard and his sister closer.

"I said no, Primo," Emilio ground out, his gaze going to his sister. "If you hurt her…" he added, voice tight.

"She isn't harmed," I insisted. I'd been clear with my instructions. She would be no good to us if she was covered in bruises. They would never believe I meant well with my plan then.

"She's been crying," Emilio insisted.

My gaze shifted toward his sister. She'd been pleading for me not to lock her in the room the last time I'd seen her. At that point, though, she hadn't been crying.

She'd clearly been doing so since I'd left her, though. Black mascara ribbons were dried on her pretty face. Her eyelids were swollen, and her eyes and cheeks red from the tears.

"I imagine it was startling to be snatched off the street," I said, shrugging. Women had a lot to fear from strange men, after all.

"Bell..." Emilio said, voice apologetic as he looked at his sister.

To that, Isabella merely shrugged. She'd been born into a mafia Family. At some level, she knew that shit like this went down, no matter how much her family likely tried to shield her from the reality of it.

"No," Emilio said again.

"War it is then," I said, moving to stand. "Shall we start now?" I asked, reaching for my gun as my men appeared from their hidden positions, surrounding the table as well as the men gathered there.

I didn't want a massacre.

I understood how unstable that would make the mafia not only in the city but all across the United States. But I was done being treated like shit by the current administration. I was willing to fight my way back up to the top with my fists and teeth if necessary.

"No!" Isabella shrieked suddenly, a shrill, animalistic sound that had everyone pausing. Her gaze went to her brother, then the rest of the men there, as well as Alessa, assessing and understanding the damage that could be done with one word from me. "No," she repeated, looking at her brother, then turning her attention toward me. She struggled to hold my gaze, but I had to give her credit for doing it. "I'll do it," she announced, even if her lower lip trembled as she did it.

"This is fucking ridiculous," Alessa said, getting to her feet.

"It has always been a way to secure alliances between feuding clans," I said, shrugging, keeping my gaze on Isabella as the tremble moved from just her lips to her whole body.

"Yeah, but we're not fucking warring clans in the middle ages. We're a progressive fucking modern society," Alessa insisted.

"Of criminals," I said. "We all believe we can't trust one another. If one of yours was in my organization, that would force the trust."

"Then take me," Emilio said. "Take me on. I will work for you."

"No." What the fuck use would I have for him?

"You're not taking my sister," Emilio insisted, his body going stiff at the sounds of guns cocking all around as my men prepared for violence.

"It's okay. It's okay, Milo," Isabella insisted, trying to be brave, willing to be a sacrifice to keep the peace. As a part of me knew she would. Women were often better at that than men. Being selfless. Taking the burden upon themselves.

"It's not okay. You're not marrying this fucking monster," Emilio growled. And, to be fair, it wasn't an inaccurate descriptor.

"To save your life, and the lives of everyone here," Isabella said, holding up a hand as if to say there was no real choice in the matter.

"Do you even understand what you're saying?" Emilio said. "You'd have to live with him. For-fucking-ever. And other things," he added, face twisting up in disgust at the idea of his sister in bed with me.

Isabella's cautious gaze slid to me, guarded, but needing answers.

"I do want an heir," I confirmed. "It is non-negotiable."

"No," Emilio said again.

"It's... it's fine," Isabella said, though nothing about her said it was. "If you promise that you will not be the reason any harm comes to my Family," she added, looking at me, chin lifting.

"I will," I agreed. That was the whole point.

"I will slit your throat in your sleep if you go back on your word," she told me, voice shaking, but delivering the threat regardless. I liked that. But the guard holding onto her, well, he yanked her hard, making her wince.

"Don't touch her," I snapped, making the man shrink back, and Isabella's brows draw together. "Any wife of mine will be protected and will want for nothing," I said, looking over at Emilio. "She won't come to harm by my hand, or by anyone in this Family. It's the right decision," I added, looking over at Lorenzo.

"You can't be considering this," Alessa insisted, shooting daggers at Lorenzo Costa, our *Capo dei Capi*.

"It doesn't sound like the decision is mine," Lorenzo said, giving Emilio an apologetic look.

"You can stop it," Emilio insisted as he looked at his boss and longtime friend, tone desperate.

"Milo," Isabella said, drawing her brother's attention with the nickname. Once she had it, she waved her arms at the dozens of armed guards around. "This is the only way you walk out of here alive today," she reminded him.

"So you have to lose your life?" Emilio asked, voice getting rough.

"I'll *live*, Milo. And I will see you. Right?" she asked, looking at me, gaze desperate.

To that, I shrugged. "After a few months to make sure they are abiding by the truce, yes."

"Then it's settled," she said, shoulders straightening a little.

"You—"

"You heard her," I said. "It is settled. Now go."

"We can't go. I can't just leave her here with you," Emilio said. I understood his protectiveness. But it was over. It was settled. She'd *agreed*. They couldn't say I was forcing her per se. It didn't matter if she liked the choices, she still made a decision.

"That is exactly what you are going to do," I insisted as my men moved closer toward them.

I waved at Isabella, my soon-to-be wife, waiting for her to approach, then reaching to undo her handcuffs.

She avoided my gaze, but stayed by my side as she watched her loved ones make their way toward the door, having no further say in the matter.

Though Emilio's gaze said he was going to do whatever it took to see his sister got away from me.

"I, ah, what now?" Isabella asked, gaze downcast.

"Are you asking your shoes or me?" I asked, waiting for her to gather her courage to look at me.

"You," she said, voice tight.

"Now, we marry," I told her, shrugging, and waving toward one of my men who approached, making her shriek and jump away.

"No. Please. No. Don't put me back in that room, please," she begged, eyes welling up and pouring over before she could even attempt to save her pride and blink them away. "I won't try to run. I won't. I said I am going to stay. And I will. Just don't lock me up in there," she cried, pressing a hand to her throat, making me aware of two things at once.

One, she clearly had issues with claustrophobia.

Two, she didn't fully grasp the deal she'd just made.

"I am not your warden, Isabella," I said, watching as she blinked up at me through watery eyes. "I am your fiancé," I added, reaching into my pocket to produce the ring.

3

Isabella

He was my warden, though, wasn't he?

Because I couldn't leave. Not without him seeking out and slaughtering everyone I loved. I could never let that happen.

I actually felt a little whiplashed from the whole thing. It didn't help that I'd been locked in that teeny room with no window or hope for escape. Each moment inside there had the walls closing in tighter and tighter until it seemed like all the air had gotten sucked up, making my chest heavy and my throat tight.

That was when I finally broke down and lost the battle with the tears. I didn't want to shed them. I didn't want to be that weak. But I'd had issues with small spaces ever since I'd gotten myself trapped inside a shed at my Great

Aunt's farm once. I'd been stuck there for almost twelve hours and had been almost out of my mind with fear by the time the family found me.

It had been an issue ever since.

I actually felt like I was choking a bit when I had to step into my closet to find something in the corner of it.

So being in that little rooms for hours had set my anxiety through the roof. Then to be dragged out to see my family there, to hear that I was being used as some sort of white flag in their war, and to realize that if I didn't let myself be used that way, my loved ones would die, well, yeah, it was no wonder I literally felt a little unstable on my own two feet. And as for my head, well, it kept shooting off in a dozen different directions every second.

I needed to focus.

Even as I thought that, though, a ring was what I first saw.

And, God, what a ring.

I didn't want to like it. It was a fancier version of the cuff he'd taken off my wrist. It was a symbol of my imprisonment, of his ownership of me.

But the part of me that had always loved unique jewelry was a little fluttery at what the man who was going to be my husband had picked out.

It was a large kite-cut black rutilated quartz on what looked like a platinum band. On each side of the main stone was a trio of black stones that my gut said were black diamonds.

It was oddly fitting.

For a man as dark as him.

It was a symbol of that darkness.

And my attachment to it.

For life.

My stomach sloshed at that realization, immediately spoiling my enjoyment of the ring itself. How could I like it when I knew what is symbolized? A life with a monster in a man's clothing. The loss of all my hopes and dreams for my future. Having to endure spousal *attentions* from a man who plucked me out of my life like fucking Hades taking poor Persephone from a field of flowers and pulling her down into his underworld and forcing her to rule with him.

Persephone eventually fell for Hades, though.

I couldn't fall for Primo Esposito.

Even if he was, objectively, attractive. Darkly attractive, if that was a thing.

He was a psychopath who used his position and power and money to bend people to his will. I had absolutely no doubt that the reason no one helped me on the street was because he ran his neighborhood with an iron fist. He kept good, normal citizens terrified of him and what he might do to them if they stepped into his business.

That was the kind of evil bastard I was marrying.

The kind I would need to share a *bed* with.

"Isabella," Primo's voice snapped, the sound like a whip cracking in the oversized, silent space, making my head whip up to find him looking down at me, those dark eyes unreadable.

"What?"

"Your hand," he said, tone impatient.

"You're being snippy with me?" I asked, but I raised my hand. "This was your plan," I reminded him.

"Yes," he agreed as his hand grabbed mine.

And it didn't, it absolutely did not, make a strange spark ping off my nerve endings. If it did, it was because I was revolted that he was touching me. That was the only logical explanation.

"But you are the one being difficult," he told me as he slid the ring on my finger.

"Just the words a woman wants to hear while getting an engagement ring," I grumbled, trying not to wonder how the damn ring fit me perfectly.

"If you were expecting romance from a man like me, Isabella, you were very much mistaken."

"I don't want romance from you," I insisted, snatching my hand back, crossing it over my chest, tucking the hand under my other arm, hiding the ring.

"Good. Then you won't be disappointed."

"Every single thing about this situation is disappointing," I corrected him, feeling my jaw quiver.

I had a temper. Everyone knew that about me. But I almost always ended up crying when I was angry. It was frustrating and embarrassing and something my brother had teased me about a lot when we were kids. Even well into adulthood, though, it wasn't something I could shake.

Primo's mouth opened as if he was going to snap back at me before he shut it again, thinking for a moment. When he spoke, his voice was calm, patient even.

"You will learn that there are benefits to being with me."

"Your probable early death, you mean?" I asked, watching as one of his dark brows rose. I couldn't decide if he was surprised or annoyed. Or maybe both. "I am banking on that. I imagine there are at least a dozen men who want you dead."

"A thousand or more," he said, shrugging it off.

"So I will just bide my time then."

"Perhaps you should wait until the marriage is official and the papers are signed before you hope for my death, little lamb. At least then you'd be entitled to it all."

"I don't want anything from you," I hissed, wrapping my arms around myself more tightly.

"An inexpensive wife. How unexpected," he said, reaching for his phone as it buzzed, taking a second to check the screen. "I have some business to attend to. Terzo will see you to my apartment. You have a few hours to clean up for the wedding."

That soon?

I guess he didn't want there to be any chance of me sneaking out of the deal. Or for my family to figure out how to get me out of it.

"Terzo?" I asked, stiffening, not wanting one of those guys who'd kidnapped me near me again.

"My brother," Primo said, waving toward the side of the room where another tall—but not quite as tall—, dark, and handsome man with an unmistakable resemblance to Primo, but younger by a good eight or so years. "Terzo. You know the schedule?" he asked, not sparing his brother a glance as he shot off a text.

"Yeah."

"Good. She stays in the apartment until I tell you to bring her."

"Oh, but I'm not a prisoner or anything, right, warden?" I griped, getting his gaze to lift, that brow quirked up again.

"Just do what you're told, Isabella."

"If you thought that was the kind of *wife* you were going to get, you chose the wrong woman, *Primo*." I spat out his name like it was sour on my tongue. He kept using mine, so I wanted to use his. Even if I said it like it was a curse.

"You're only going to make things harder on yourself with that attitude," Primo said, shrugging. "But whatever sets your panties on fire, baby."

"Don't talk about my panties," I snapped, jaw tight.

That got his full attention, though. And I knew from the way he slowly tucked away his phone and stalked toward me, leaning down as he held my gaze, something dark and wicked in his eyes, that I'd fucked up.

"I will talk about your panties anytime I want, Isabella. Or have you forgotten that you will be my wife in all ways a woman is a wife?" he asked.

That flip-flop in my stomach, that was absolutely disgust. Right?

It was a moment of pure insanity that had me lashing out. And I mean *lashing* out. I cocked my arm back and slapped him across the face. Hard enough that the sound ricocheted around the empty room.

Oh, I'd fucked all the way up that time.

Because the men in the room all stiffened and reached for their weapons.

"One, little lamb," he said, running his fingertips across the red mark on his cheek. "You get one of those. Now get your ass up to the apartment before I drag you there myself. Terzo," he called, keeping unnerving eye contact the whole time it took for his brother to move in at my size.

"Ready?" Terzo asked, tone lighter, like he was trying to deescalate the situation.

"Yeah," I agreed, gaze moving away from Primo, looking at his little brother who seemed like a more friendly face at that moment. "Sure," I added, falling into step with him as he led me away from the boss of the Esposito crime Family.

My soon-to-be husband.

"Why are we going up?" I asked when we walked into the oversized elevator in the warehouse.

"Primo lives here," Terzo said, shrugging.

"He lives in a warehouse?"

"The top floor," Terzo confirmed. "The lower floor is for the trucks to back up into and the workers to load in and out. The second floor is the meat processing and packaging center. We are leaving the third floor. And the top is Primo's place."

"He lives above a meat packaging facility?" I asked, nose wrinkling.

"Primo likes to be close to work if or when something is going down," Terzo said as the elevator came to a stop.

The doors opened to a, well, metal box.

My stomach immediately dropped at the tight space.

"Half-inch steel wall, a layer of Kevlar, then another half inch steel wall," Terzo explained. "It's bulletproof," he told me when I didn't respond. Not because I wasn't interested but because I felt like the air was suddenly very thick in the small space as the doors behind us slid closed.

Terzo pressed a button on the wall, making a drawer move out. He pressed his finger into a screen there, then ran his fingertips over a number pad, typing in a passcode.

Then, finally, what felt like a lifetime later, the box opened, and I felt like I could take a proper breath again.

I don't know what I thought the home of a man like Primo Esposito would be like. But this definitely wasn't it.

It was, well, homey.

I guess I figured a cold man like him would be all about that awful, industrial look.

But no.

The whole space felt warm and inviting, if a bit masculine, but not in an oppressive way. The walls were exposed red brick, the floors dark hardwood, and the ceilings were exposed wooden beams stained to match the floor. Except for in one area where there was a closed-off loft. The bedroom, I figured. And there was only one.

I tried not to focus on that. It wouldn't do me any good.

I focused on the space instead.

It was huge.

I'd seen the warehouse from outside, but I'd been a little too busy running for my life to take in the size. But it must have been a big warehouse to make such a roomy space.

Windows lined the whole front of the building, letting in a fair amount of light, but there was some kind of film on them that didn't let it come in completely.

In the center of the room was the living room with a giant brick fireplace that seemed to separate the living room with its framed flatscreen, brown leather couches, and a long, low table behind the couches filled with what looked like a huge collection of records with the player perched on top.

When I took a couple steps to the side, sure enough, I saw more exposed brick and windows, but also an all-black kitchen. The cabinets and cupboards, the countertop, and all the appliances looked to be black stainless steel. It was a big kitchen, too, but all standards, not just New York City ones.

I loved to cook.

But I'd be damned if I ever cooked for him.

"You're free to roam around," Terzo said, walking over toward the couches and dropping down, reaching for his phone. "It's yours now too," he added, and his words were like a kick to the stomach.

It was mine now.

Because I would never see my own apartment again.

Okay, admittedly, this one was much nicer than mine, but mine was full of the love I'd put into it. It was my safe space. It was the one place in the world I had to go to when everything felt like it was falling apart, and I could bundle under the covers and recover.

I would never have that again.

This would be my home.

This warehouse apartment was owned by a man who'd forced me into agreeing to marry him.

A pathetic whimpering sound rose up my throat.

My gaze shot over toward Terzo, not wanting him to hear if I was about to have another weak, emotional moment. I opened my mouth to say something to him about exploring the upper level before I remembered his words.

This was mine now.

I didn't need to explain myself to him.

Squaring my shoulders and lifting my chin, even if my insides felt like they were shaking, I made my way across the apartment toward the staircase that led up.

It wasn't that I wanted to be in Primo's bedroom. In fact, it was the last place I wanted to be. But it was the only place I could see that I could escape for a little while.

I needed to get myself together.

I might have been stuck in an impossible situation, but I was not going to let Primo see that he was getting the better of me. I needed to wash my face. I needed to give myself a pep talk. And then I needed to slip behind a shield of cold indifference.

It was the only way I was going to make it through this sham of a wedding.

And whatever might come afterward.

Primo's bedroom was, essentially, a brick-walled box. No windows. But the anxiety didn't build as I made my way toward the door that looked suspiciously like the same material the metal box we'd stepped into from the elevator. Because the bedroom stretched the entire width of the warehouse and about a third of the length.

There was a moment of hesitation as I reached toward the handle, a part of me worried it wouldn't open without a code, and some prideful part of me not wanting to have to ask Terzo Esposito to give it to me.

The matte black knob turned in my hand, though, and I felt a trip in my heartbeat as I pushed it open. Some twisted depth of my mind had me wondering if this was going to turn into some cheesy erotic fiction movie, and I was going to walk into a full-on sex dungeon complete with whips and chains. He already carried handcuffs on him, after all.

But I simply walked into a bedroom.

Like the floor below, the walls were all exposed brick. There was the same dark wood floor and the same exposed wooden beam ceiling. The bed was enormous. A California King, perhaps? It was impossible to know since any apartment I'd ever been in was lucky if it could hold a queen, let alone anything bigger. It had a sturdy wood frame stained the same color as the floor and all-black bedding. Two nightstands flanked it in a matte black color. Each had a lamp.

It was clear that Primo slept on the side nearest to the door judging by the discarded coffee cup on the nightstand and a pair of cufflinks left sitting close enough to the edge to fall off.

I had the asinine urge to go over there and push them back so they didn't fall. What did I care if he lost one of his fancy cufflinks? I wasn't supposed to be helping the man who'd ripped me off the streets and out of my old life. Hell, I should have been walking around the house, breaking all his mirrors and spilling all his olive oil, hoping to bring some bad luck into his life. The kind of bad luck that would make me a young widow, and free to get back to my old life.

I took a slow, deep breath, then let it out on a sigh.

That was likely a pipe dream.

The reality was, I was probably stuck with this man forever.

"At least my prison is pretty," I mumbled to myself as I moved past the bed to the far wall where Primo had another—smaller—record shelf set up with a wooden player on top with a clear plastic cover.

The man clearly liked his music.

Across from the bed was a dresser. Above was a framed piece of art in reds and blacks that made me immediately feel unsettled when looking at it, so I didn't spend much time with that.

Finished with the bedroom, I walked through to the master bath.

A low, whimpering noise escaped me. Because it was the bathroom of my dreams with its glass shower enclosure with multiple shower heads as well as a rain shower head above. The tile in it was a muted black that gave it a sexy look I'd only ever seen in movies. The large soaking tub to the side of the space was a similar black color. As were the double sink vanities. Even the sinks themselves and the toilet were black.

It should have been oppressive, but it just looked sleek and sexy and way too inviting.

I guess it was a good thing I liked it since I would be using it day in and out. And it was damn sure an improvement from my shoebox, outdated bathroom in my apartment.

Curious, I moved toward the vanity it looked like Primo used, picking up the little black bottle of cologne sitting there, and taking a sniff.

"Damn him," I grumbled as my body responded to the spicy scent.

It was right about then that I finally caught sight of myself in the round mirror above the vanity, though.

It wasn't good.

I guess I figured I must have looked rough, but the reality was worse than expected. Dried mascara clung to my cheeks. My eyes were puffy from my panic attack crying. And the skin of my cheeks was raw from the tears.

It shouldn't have mattered. I didn't want to be pretty for him. But some internal vanity reared its ugly head, having me grabbing for one of the washcloths—black, and I felt it was safe to assume it was Primo's favorite color—wet it, and went to work on my face with cold water until I got all my smeared makeup off, leaving me looking younger than I did with it on.

Reaching up, I pulled the tie out of my hair, shaking the long strands out over my shoulders as I took a few deep, steadying breaths.

It was pointless to freak out, after all. It wouldn't change my fate.

What I should have been focusing on was how to work this situation to my advantage. There had to be a way, even if nothing was coming to me at the moment.

Dropping the washcloth in the—yep, black—hamper, I moved toward the only other door, opening it, and finding myself in a mini hallway that went off in both directions.

Giant, walk-in, his & her closets.

The left side was filled with Primo's wardrobe that seemed to consist of nothing but black. The man didn't own a single item of white clothing. The one to the right, though, was empty save for the built-in shelving units. It was a closet I wouldn't have a panic attack about entering.

Small wins.

I had to count them.

They might be few and far between.

I moved back out of the closet and bathroom to go stand in the bedroom, unsure what to do with myself for however long it was going to take for Primo to return to drag me to my fate.

I found myself pacing the room for a few useless moments, needing to spend my nervous energy. Once it was gone, I found myself dropping onto the edge of the bed. For all of two minutes before unwanted images flashed through my mind.

Of me in that bed.
Of Primo in it as well.
He wanted an heir.
It was non-negotiable.
Which meant I was going to need to endure sex with him.
Would he take it if I wasn't willing?
Of course he would. Because I was never going to be willing.

On a choked, dying animal noise, I moved off the bed, dropping down on the floor over near his record player instead, leaning back against the wall, closing my eyes, and trying to escape from the warehouse in my mind.

My mind went right where it always went.

To my family.

Emilio would blame himself. And I had no way of reaching out to remind him that it was my choice, that I would do anything to save him and all our loved ones. My mother. God, my mother was going to be a wreck. An absolute wreck. Same went for my other siblings, for my cousins. Especially because it was going to be weeks or months before Primo would let me reach out to them to let them know I was okay.

"There's a bed right there," the loud, smooth, deep voice said, making my whole body jolt as my eyes shot open, finding Primo standing just inside the doorway.

"Your bed," I said, voice rough.

That damn brow rose again and I decided it was a condescending movement. And I hated him even more for it.

"Your bed now too," he said, shrugging.

"I'd rather sleep on the floor," I grumbled.

Primo ignored that.

"Are you going to dress or what?" he asked, making my brows draw together.

"This is all I own right now," I said, waving down at my work outfit—slacks and a blouse. Nothing special. And more than a little wrinkled and dirty from the events of the day.

"The dress in the closet. I'm assuming you've thoroughly inspected the space."

"There was nothing in the closet," I said, chin lifting.

"There is a dress. And shoes," he said.

"There's not," I countered.

"There is."

"Go see for yourself if you're so damn certain," I invited, waving toward the closet.

Primo turned and moved through the bedroom to the bathroom.

And because I knew I was right and was just a teensy bit competitive that way, I got up to follow, standing in the doorway with my arms folded.

"See?" I said, jerking my chin up when he whipped around to face me.

"No. It is here," Primo insisted, moving into the closet that would eventually be mine.

"Really? Where? Is there a secret compartment in the wall?" I asked, tone dry, getting a glance from him, but I couldn't read what I found in his eyes.

"She must have put it in my closet," he grumbled, storming past me into his own closet, taking a moment to find a garment bag and a shoebox.

"She?" I asked, watching as he moved into my side of the closet, hanging up the bag and putting the shoebox down on the ground.

"The housekeeper."

"You have a housekeeper?"

"Do you think I have time to wash my own dishes?"

"Well, she missed the coffee cup on your nightstand," I told him. "What?" I asked, seeing something flash across his gaze.

"She was otherwise distracted," Primo said, moving out of the closet.

There was something in his tone.

"Distracted how?" I pressed.

I regretted it when he turned on his heel, giving me a devilish smirk.

"You fuck your housekeeper?" I asked, only just realizing that I might not only have to sleep with this man, but also endure his relentless cheating.

God, my pride. It would be in tiny pieces.

I didn't tolerate cheating. Ever. It was an immediate cause to dump a guy.

Not only because they'd betrayed me and my trust and the relationship we'd started to build, but because he'd made a fool of me as well.

That, well, that wouldn't stand.

But what choice would I have here?

None.

I would have none.

"I fuck whoever I want," he said, shrugging. "But if you must know, I don't fuck her. She just sucks me off on occasion."

Gross.

"That is not going to happen again," I informed him, chin raising, back straightening, hoping I could at least fake the strength I wasn't feeling.

"Is that so?" he asked, watching me.

"You've made a fool enough of me," I told him, hoping my jaw didn't look as trembly as it felt. "I will not have you doing that to me too."

"You think you can tell me what to do?" he asked, stalking forward, towering over me, making me need to crane my head up to keep eye contact. "Just who do you think you are?" he asked, tone low, threatening.

But if I backed down now, I would be backing down my entire life. I'd rather not live at all than live like that. Bowing and kowtowing to this monster of a man.

"Your *wife*," I said, clenching my teeth to keep my lips from quivering.

His hand rose at my side and it took a lot of strength not to wince, to jerk away.

But he wasn't going to strike me.

No.

Instead, he grabbed the back of my neck, fingertips digging in.

"That's right," he agreed, nodding. It was a borderline painful pressure, and the gesture was unmistakably possessive. Which I didn't want. Not at all. But there was a weird tightening between my legs at the feeling regardless. "Now get dressed, so we can make it official."

4

Primo

I wasn't the most moral of men. Anyone would tell you that. My sins were as dark a shade as they came in. But I had some beliefs in life, shit I held sacred.
   Like family.
   Like the Family.
   Like taking care of my neighborhood.
   And the sanctity of marriage.
   I had no delusions when it came to the situation. Isabella's consent to the marriage had been coerced. She didn't truly have a choice in the matter. No halfway decent person would save themselves by sacrificing ten or twelve others. That wasn't how things worked.
   It also meant that she hadn't exactly agreed to fucking me either.

And I might be a bastard in many—if not most—ways, but I didn't rape. That was one place where I drew a line.

I wasn't going to force myself on Isabella.

I trusted that in time she would learn to feel a connection toward me. And the physical part of the relationship would start.

But because I believed in the sanctity of marriage, in the vow you made to not only your partner but God, it meant I couldn't fuck around anymore.

I had a feeling my balls were going to be blue before I got any relief.

But that was the choice that I'd made.

It was also why I'd gone ahead and let the housekeeper suck my dick that morning before the plan was officially in motion. It was the last release I would get for a while that wasn't done by my own damn hand.

That shit I'd said to Isabella had just been to see how she would react.

I wasn't disappointed.

Sure, the motivations might have been selfish, not wanting other people to think she was someone not worthy of the respect of her husband, but I liked to hear the possessiveness in her tone.

Even if it had nothing to do with me.

I figured that one day it might.

"Is that the flowers?" I asked, coming down the stairs to see Terzo standing in the kitchen with a box on the counter.

"I haven't opened it yet," he said as I made my way into the space. "Why are you bothering with flowers anyway?" he asked.

Young.

And therefore a little bit stupid.

"Because she will be my wife," I said, pulling the top off the box to reveal the peach peony bouquet I'd ordered.

Because when watching Isabella while planning the whole situation, I'd noticed she only ever picked up peach peonies to keep at her apartment.

"But it's not a real marriage."

"It will be a real marriage," I told him. "It might not be traditional, but it is real. And because it is real, she will be afforded at least the smallest of gestures that convey how seriously I take the institution. So my wife will have a bouquet. Just like she has a dress and shoes and a ring."

"I'm not getting married," Terzo said, shaking his head.

"That's exactly how you should be thinking at your age," I agreed. "Until you are mature enough to give marriage the consideration it deserves. Are our brothers almost ready?" I asked.

"They are waiting downstairs."

"Good. And the church is ready?" I confirmed.

"The priest is waiting."

"Good," I said, going through the list in my head, not wanting to miss anything. "Do you have the other box?" I asked, watching as my brother shook his head as he reached into his breast pocket to produce the black jewelry box. "I could get another best man if you have a problem," I reminded him. "I'm not short of any brothers to choose from."

Aside from Terzo. And Due.

Who was hopefully being sodomized with cacti in hell.

Love and loyalty were never given blindly. There were always rules. There wasn't such a thing as unconditional anything in this world. And there shouldn't be. Everything should come with conditions. Everyone should have lines that others are not allowed to cross.

I don't care if you're my soldier, my best friend, my brother, or my damn son. If you messed around with kids, I would disembowel you without hesitation. I was genuinely pissed off that I didn't get a chance to confront Due myself over his actions. That was something that never should have needed to go before The Commission. I would have gladly taken care of it myself had they approached me with their information.

That was the whole point of this alliance. They would feel comfortable coming to me with issues now that I had one of theirs in my life and world. All this moving behind one another's backs shit would stop.

"The fuck is taking so long?" I grumbled, checking my watch when it felt like an hour passed. She only had a dress and shoes to get into. It's not like she had makeup to put on or anything.

In fact, I decided I liked her even better without it. She'd wiped away all the evidence of it from earlier. Which made her face seem more open. More, I don't know, vulnerable and readable.

I was going to go right ahead and not mention that to her, though. If I did, she would probably wear makeup day and night, even to sleep, just to spite me.

I had no delusions about how she felt about the arrangement and me.

She'd managed to suppress the flinch when I'd reached for her, but there was no mistaking the fear that crossed her eyes. I'd seen that look too many times on countless numbers of faces. There was no mistaking it.

"Here we go," Terzo said as, sure enough, there was the sound of heels on the platform outside the bedroom. "Damn," he said before I even got a chance to turn.

It took a lot to impress my persnickety brother, though, so I turned immediately, watching as Isabella came down the steps in her wedding dress.

It was a dress, not a gown.

I'd gotten the impression that while she did like her fashion, that she seemed to prefer simple and sleek styles, timeless designs.

So I'd chosen a simple creamy pearl-colored silk dress with a hem that nearly made her shoes disappear entirely. I'd underestimated just how short she was, it seemed. The bodice of the dress was demure but not prudish, and the straps were thin, leaving her tanned shoulders bare.

She'd tamed her hair, too, and it fell in soft waves down her back.

Her chin was high.

Like a queen walking to the guillotine. Aware of her fate, but refusing to reduce herself on the way to it.

I'd chosen well.

There had been no shortage of women in the Costa Family to select, but something about Isabella just called to me. As if something within me recognized that she was the one who could navigate this future with me. Whether she liked it or not.

Before I could open my mouth to give her a compliment, she was coming to a stop and dropping the skirt of her dress that she'd gathered in her hands, letting it fall to spill all over the floor.

"This is way too long," she told me. Not a thank you for the dress. Not a comment on the style. A complaint about how it fit.

I liked that more than I should have.

"I will note your measurements for future reference," I said, holding out the box.

"What is this?" she asked, immediately suspicious.

"What does it look like?"

"I don't want it."

"Too bad," I said, flipping the top open. "You will wear this," I told her as she stared at it, her gaze downcast so it was impossible to read her feelings about it.

It had thirty-nine round-cut black diamonds, each of them set in a ring of normal diamonds. A total of one-hundred-and-twenty karats with a white gold band.

"I said I don't want it," she said, still looking downward.

"That's a fifteen-thous—" Terzo started to say, getting cut off by one gesture before I snatched the necklace out of the box, opened it, and moved behind Isabella to drape it over her skin.

"I said I don't want it."

"And I said too fucking bad," I said, clasping it into place. "Are you going to be a pain in the ass about the bouquet as well?" I asked, grabbing it off the counter.

"Are those peach peonies?" she asked, gaze shooting up to me.

"They are."

"How did…" she started then trailed off as realization dawned on her. "You've been stalking me?" she asked, face twisting.

"I was deciding which Costa woman to choose," I said, shrugging.

"That's really creepy. Just so you know. Lurking in the shadows like some basement-dwelling incel."

"Such love words on our wedding day," I said, shoving the bouquet toward her. "Let's go. The priest is waiting," I said, waving toward the door.

I noted that when we got in the elevator, she took several slow, deep breaths, further confirming my suspicions about her issues with small spaces.

She was silent the ride down, and as we approached with my other brothers.

"Isabella, this is Dawson and Dulles."

"Dawson and Dulles," Isabella repeated, brows knitting. "Primo, Due, and Terzo. First, second, and third," she said, making it clear she had at least a cursory knowledge of Italian.

"Dawson and Dulles had a different mother," I told her, leaving out the gory, ugly details that surrounded that truth.

They looked different from myself and Terzo as well. They were tall, but where Terzo and I were of a slimmer build, they were naturally stockier, and many hours in the gym made them wider still. Where my and Terzo's hair was black, theirs was a dark shade of brown. And where our eyes were brown, theirs were a bright, almost unnatural shade of green. They were identical twins, but a youth spent getting scrappy on the streets left them with scars that helped you tell them apart.

"Everything clear?" I asked, looking at them, relaying the silent question.

The Costas haven't shown up to stop this, have they?

"Everything is set."

"Let's go then," I said, nodding toward the door that led outside.

"Where's the car?" Isabella asked when noticing the empty alley beside the building.

"We're walking."

"We're *walking*?" she snapped. "It is thirty degrees out. I'm wearing a freaking silk sheet," she added, waving at herself.

"It is across the street, baby," I said, shaking my head, pressing a hand to her lower back, and pushing her out the door.

"Easy for you to say with your suit on," she grumbled, shrinking into herself as the cold bit at her skin.

I figured I'd thought of everything.

I'd missed the jacket or wrap or shawl.

Or perhaps a part of me had purposely omitted it. Because I wanted the neighborhood to see her in her wedding dress, walking alongside me willingly.

There would be no mistaking who she was, what her connection was to me.

It was worth three minutes of exposure to the cold.

Her hatred should keep her warm enough. And make no mistake, she was fuming as she lifted her skirts and tried to keep up with my pace as I led her down the alley, onto the street, and then across it.

I could feel my neighborhood leaning against their windows to watch. Those on the street paused to offer me tight smiles and nods, silent congratulations on my nuptials.

The church was an old, familiar building that had served as a solace for me as a boy when my homelife became intolerable. Something about the cut fieldstone rock that had been worn by several lifetimes of weather to a soft, muted gray, the stained glass windows, the red accents in the interior, it all made the world fall away when I entered.

"What?" I asked when Isabella pulled to a stop just outside the round wooden doors with their cross emblems.

She was trembling from the cold and I only barely refrained from slipping out of my jacket and draping it over her shoulders.

"I'm afraid that I will burst into flames if I enter a church with you," she said.

Gaze forward, she missed the smirk that tugged at my lips.

"Come," I said, reaching down to grab her hand, feeling her whole body stiffen at the contact. "We need to make this official."

5

Isabella

I'd dreamed of my wedding day countless times in my life.

My family used to tease me when, as a girl and even a teen, I used to buy wedding magazines and cut out my favorite dresses or flower arrangements or cakes.

It had all always been very clear to me.

A big church wedding with my family and friends followed by a reception in a sprawling room somewhere. Something beautiful, but understated. Not trying too hard.

I imagined my mom getting tipsy at the open bar and getting on the dance floor to make memories that would be put to film that she would later regret. I pictured the menu, the band, the smiles on my loved ones faces.

But I'd never pictured the man.

I figured he would become clear to me when the right one finally crossed my path. I never wanted to sully my daydreams of my wedding with the faces of the guys I actually dated. A list of men who'd never meant anything close to important to me.

I was a romantic, though. I believed he would find me if I gave him enough time.

I should have settled for one of the other random guys I'd dated. It would have saved me from this fate.

If I'd done that, though, would it be one of my female relatives instead? I couldn't imagine a single one of them being condemned to this fate. Maybe it was better that it was me.

In all the times I pictured my wedding day, though, I never imagined being dragged out in the freezing cold in what was no more than a slip. Without my mom. Or my brother. With absolutely friggin no one that loved me around.

At that thought, I felt the sting in my eyes again, needing to blink the tears back as Primo kept leading me down the aisle of pews and up toward the altar where the shrunken form of the priest stood waiting for us. Waiting to seal my fate.

He seemed clueless to my being forced into the situation, at least. He gave me a tight smile that spread when it shifted to Primo.

Strange.

But okay.

From there, things were a bit of a blur.

Words were read from the Bible.

Then Primo was being prompted to recite his vows.

I watched as he produced the wedding ring that was clearly designed to go with my engagement ring. It was made of black diamonds in a shape that had it cupping the shorter point of the kite-shaped stone on my finger.

I was more distracted by Primo's warm hands on my frigid ones as he said his words. Maybe he looked at me. I didn't know. I had my gaze downcast, a part of me so disassociated that the priest needed to prompt me twice to start repeating after him.

And then we got to the words.

Those two words.

The ones that would seal this whole deal.

"Miss?" the priest prompted again, making me shake my head, snapping out of my stupor.

"I... do." I'd barely managed to choke the words out.

But they came out and they were heard.

And it was all over.

"I now pronounce you husband and wife. You may kiss the bride," the priest invited.

My stomach twisted at the words.

But before I could even think to respond to them, Primo's hand was grabbing the back of my neck with the same pressure and possessiveness that he'd done back in his apartment. This time, though, he was dragging me forward until my chest crushed to his. I had one short moment to feel the hard line of him before his lips were crashing down on mine.

Hard.

There was nothing soft or sweet or even formal about this kiss.

It was rough and primal, borderline painful.

Before I could even count to five, though, it was over, and Primo was thanking the priest, saying he would see him soon, then turning to go down the aisle again.

"Are you coming?" he asked, turning back to me, brow raised. "Mrs. Esposito?" he added, and the title was like a kick to the gut, knocking out all my air.

"This isn't... this isn't official," I said, looking up at him.

"In the eyes of God, it is."

"Yeah, well, the state of New York weighs in on these matters too. And if I'm not mistaken, for this to actually be official, there would need to be a marriage license."

"There is," he said, shrugging.

"There can't be."

"And yet, there is."

"I would need to be present. There are no proxy licenses."

"There are a lot of things you can get in this world if your pockets are deep enough," he said, making a shiver course through me.

Primo mistook the tremble for an outward chill instead of an inward one, though. And just like that, he was shrugging out of his suit jacket and moving toward me to slip it over my shoulders.

The material was still warm from his body, heating up my cold skin even as I could smell that damn intoxicating cologne of his clinging to the fabric.

"Are you ready?"

"Ready for what?" I asked, hearing the defeat in my own voice.

"To go back to the apartment," he said.

I was proud of myself for holding it together until that moment. Aside from the whole storage room freak out which would have happened no matter the circumstances. But I hadn't broken down over my fate.

But right then, standing in the middle of a church with a wedding ring on my finger, alone with the man who was now my husband, who would now want... husbandly things from me, I was losing my grip of control. And fast.

Tears flooded then spilled from my eyes before I could even try to blink them away. As if that wasn't bad enough, a hiccuping cry escaped me, a sound that had Primo's head jerking back a bit.

"What?" he asked, moving a step closer as his brothers hung several yards away by the doors, letting in the cold.

My hand rose, closing over my mouth to keep in another humiliating whimper. And failing.

"Isabella, what?" Primo growled, taking another step toward me, towering over me, stealing all the air.

"I don't want to," I choked out, blinking another flood of tears down my cheeks.

"Don't want to do what?" he asked, tone sharp, impatient.

God, I didn't even want to say it.

"I don't want to sleep with you tonight," I told him, lower lip quivering, and I never felt more pathetic than I did right then.

"I see," Primo said, jaw tight.

And I really, really didn't want to piss off a man who was expecting to consummate his marriage. The repercussions of that...

"I know the deal I made. I know," I said, tears flowing freely. "I won't go back on that," I added, sniffling. "Just... don't make me tonight," I pleaded, hating myself a little at having to beg.

"Do you know what you are saying, what you are implying?" he clarified.

"What?" I asked.

"What is sex without consent?" he asked.

"R...rape," I answered because it was the only way to describe it.

"Do you know what we do to rapists in this community?" he asked, voice dark.

"No."

"We kill them, Isabella," he said, and there was no doubt in my mind that he was telling the truth with how fierce his voice sounded. "I don't abide rapists. And I do not tolerate being called one either. Let's go," he snapped, grabbing my wrist and all but dragging me through the church, leaving me tripping over my skirts since I was trying to hold the jacket on my shoulders.

Before I could even wrap my head around what we'd just discussed, we were across the street and in the elevator on the way back up to the apartment.

Our apartment.

That was going to take some adjusting to.

Terzo, Dawson, and Dulles rode back up with us, and I found myself oddly comforted by their presence. It meant, at least, that I wouldn't be alone with Primo. For a while anyway. Eventually, that was something I was going to need to come to terms with. But until then, there were other people for him to pay attention to.

No one spoke to me, though, as we made our way into the apartment. The men made their way toward the kitchen and I spotted Dawson making coffee.

God, I could use a cup. It was the longest day of my entire life. Physically and emotionally. Coffee had always been a comfort drink to me instead of a stimulant. I drank it to unwind after work.

I could use some unwinding.

But I didn't want to have to ask for a cup.

Instead, I made my way back up the stairs to the bedroom, going into the closet to kick out of the heels that, while very expensive judging by their red bottoms, pinched my toes.

Unsure what else I could do, I went to the bathroom door, locking it, then turning back to the bath.

If I couldn't unwind with some coffee, I could at least do so with a bath.

A part of me was terrified to strip naked in a house full of mafia men. But something in the firmness of Primo's voice had me believing that he wasn't a man who would touch me without my consent.

There was that at least.

So I stripped out of my wedding dress. I grabbed a fluffy bath towel that was more like a blanket, and hung it beside the tub before climbing in.

I don't know how long I stayed in there. But when I finally climbed out, the water had a chill to it and my fingers were thoroughly pruned.

I dried off, but had nothing to wear but my dirty work clothes or the wedding dress I'd worn for all of half an hour. Decision made, I climbed back into it, then made my way toward the door, pulling it open, and nearly tripping over the mug of coffee set on the floor.

He'd brought me coffee?

No.

That didn't seem like something a man like Primo did.

Maybe one of his brothers, then.

Dawson and Dulles seemed a little friendlier than Primo and Terzo.

It wasn't the fancy latte I might have gotten for myself, but it had milk and sugar which made it completely drinkable.

I drank it while flipping through Primo's records, finding no real rhyme or reason to his collection. He had everything from Sinatra to some pop-punk band I remember some of my friends liking in high school.

Finding myself too interested in that, I left the vinyl alone and made my way back down the stairs. The men were all still in the kitchen, but this time, there were smells. Heavenly smells.

Food.

God, I was so hungry.

I didn't even know what time it was, but it felt like I hadn't eaten in days.

"Isabella," Primo called, making me jolt, not thinking he could even see me from his position. "You need to eat," he added when I didn't respond.

"What did you order?" I asked, though it really didn't matter what he'd ordered. I would eat one of his ties if it was smothered in enough red sauce.

"Order? No," he said as I moved into the kitchen, finding him standing there with his sleeves rolled up, revealing strong, tanned forearms and a very pricey-looking watch.

But what was more off-putting than seeing him looking casual was the fact that he appeared to be scooping something out of a pot.

A pot.

Like he'd cooked.

No.

That wasn't possible.

I was pretty sure none of my male relatives even knew how to turn a stove on. The women made sure of that. I came from a traditional Italian family that way. The women showed their love with food. Mountains of food for the men and children. I'd been making ravioli with my mother since I was three years old, standing on a chair at her side and putting the ricotta mix into the center of her rows of rolled dough.

"Sit," he demanded, waving toward the dining room table toward the side of the kitchen.

I think I was too shocked to object to sharing a meal with them. My legs just led me over to the table and lowered me into a chair.

Not two minutes later, Primo was pushing a plate in front of me.

"Penne vodka with pancetta and fried ricotta," Primo said, in the self-assured, rehearsed way of someone who made and served food frequently to guests. Which didn't fit the image I held of him at all in my head. "There would be garlic bread if my brothers could be responsible enough to pull it out before it burned," Primo said, shooting said brothers a hard look. "White or red?" he asked, making me look up to find him holding bottles of wine.

I slow blinked at him for a moment before I found my voice. And it was pure sass that came out of me.

"Don't you know the answer to that from all the stalking you've done of me?" I asked, getting a snicker from one of his brothers. Dulles, I think. The one with a scar splitting his lower lip.

Primo's insufferable brow lifted at the comment. "You drink them interchangeably," he informed me. "And often incorrectly," he said, grabbing a corkscrew and opening the red.

"Incorrectly," I repeated as he reached for a long stem glass.

"You had lunch with your brother a week ago. You ordered some pasta with red sauce and ate it with white wine," he informed me as he placed the deep red wine in front of my plate. "Pinot Noir would have paired better," he told me, motioning toward the glass he'd left.

Admittedly, I wasn't all that versed in wine. I just knew that I liked it. White, rosé, red. It didn't matter. And since my family had always been more casual about that kind of thing, I never really learned about what went with what. We drank whatever we had on hand for family dinners.

"Eat," Primo demanded, walking back toward the kitchen to plate dishes for his brothers. Who each slowly joined me at the table as I went ahead and ducked my head as I started to eat.

Maybe I shouldn't have been antisocial. These men were, whether I liked it or not, related to me now. I would have to learn to interact with them or it was going to be a very tense life. But I just didn't know what to say right then. Hell, there wasn't even a voice in my head talking like it constantly did on a daily basis. I just felt blank.

Luckily, the men went on without me, discussing things from sports to something about organic turkey that I didn't even begin to understand.

The food, though, God, the food was impeccable. I was actually a little jealous that Primo could cook that well. I suddenly felt like every dish I ever made was crap.

Terzo was the one to clear the table.

And then, suddenly, everyone was gone.

Including my husband.

I had no idea where they went. And I honestly didn't care. I was too exhausted to be curious about their operation.

Alone, I made my way to the living room, turning on the TV because the quiet in the apartment was deafening, then curling up on the couch.

I was out cold before the show could go to its first commercial break.

I don't know how long I was asleep, but I know what woke me.

Strong arms sliding under my back and knees, then lifting me up off the couch.

My entire body jolted hard. Disoriented, a little slow to take in the details, my immediate instinct was to get away.

"Sh," a male voice said as I found myself pulled against a strong chest. With a newly familiar spicy cologne clinging to the fabric of his black shirt. "We're going to bed," he added as he started walking through the apartment toward the stairs.

"I want to sleep on the couch," I insisted.

"No."

That was it.

No.

And his tone brooked no argument.

Too bad for him that I was always up for one.

"Yes. I was comfortable," I insisted even if I was wondering how to get the crick out of my neck.

"You won't be sleeping on the couch."

"Why not?" I asked as Primo's arms held me tighter as he started up the stairs.

And it didn't feel a little bit good.

I repeat: it did *not* feel good.

But if it did, it was only because it had been a long, long time since I'd felt a strong man's arms around me.

"You are my wife. You will sleep in my bed."

"Why? No one is here to see me sleeping on the couch."

"My men come and go at all times when they need me."

"So, you care about appearances?" I asked, rolling my eyes at him. "That's pathetic."

"In this life, Isabella," he snapped, and I tried not to notice the unique way he said my name—Issa-bella instead of Is-abella, "appearances matter. It is why we dress well. It is why we have codes and rules. Anytime you stray from the appearances that outsiders come to expect from you, you open yourself up to speculation, you make yourself weaker. A man whose wife does not share his bed is weaker if other men find out. And this room is bullet-resistant," he added as he lowered me onto what would be my side of the bed.

"Wait, no," I said, sitting up on the bed, watching as he walked around the foot of the bed. "You don't just toss around phrases like that and not expect follow-up questions."

"What questions could you have, baby? How bulletproofing works?"

"I'm not an idiot. And Terzo explained the steel and kevlar thing."

"Then what is the question?" he asked, taking off his watch while standing on his side of the bed. Next came the cufflinks. And I was pretending not to notice that it was a very intimate thing to see a man going about his nighttime routine.

"Why would I need to sleep behind a bulletproof wall?" I asked.

"Because, whether you like the situation or not, you are now a mafia wife. No, more than that. A boss's wife. A mafia queen. You are a high-value target to anyone who wants to fuck with my Family."

"Gee, that's just what a girl wants to hear right before bed," I said, shaking my head.

"You asked," he reminded me, reaching for his belt.

"What are you doing?"

"What does it look like I'm doing?" he asked, removing the belt, then rolling it up in his hand and securing it before putting it in the dresser.

Then, ah, well then, he started to unbutton his shirt.

And I couldn't seem to make myself look away as he slipped off the black fabric and exposed the strong back beneath.

The strong back criss-crossed with scars. Old scars, faded to nearly skin tone with age.

What the hell had happened to him?

There was a tattoo on his upper arm that I spotted as he started to turn, but I couldn't quite make out what it was.

Then, well, then there was the whole front of him to see.

I knew he was strongly built thanks to being yanked against him for our wedding kiss and then being carried against his chest. But I don't think I was fully prepared for just how well built he was under that black suit of his. He had a lean build, but his eight-pack was something that could make a woman cry. And that Adonis belt, that deeply-etched V that disappeared into the waistband of his pants, that was the kind of thing that graced the covers of men's fitness magazines.

I didn't want to be impressed by his body.

But there was no mistaking the sheer perfection of it.

"Like what you see, baby?" Primo asked, making my stomach drop at being caught gawking.

"What is that tattoo?" I asked, trying to sound casual, unimpressed.

Primo's other arm lifted, rubbing over the tattoo. "Family crest."

"Family crest," I repeated. "Didn't you, you know, murder your father with a steak knife?" I asked, not understanding the idea of having a symbol of family pride on your arm if you went around killing members of said family.

"I will slit the throat of anyone not worthy of carrying the family name," he said, calm, casual.

The only kind of people who could pull that off were psychopaths.

And I was married to one.

Before I could say anything else, though, he was undoing his pants and letting them drop down his legs, leaving him in nothing but a pair of tight black boxer briefs.

My gaze slid away, not wanting to be caught looking at *that* particular part of his body. He might get the wrong idea. I didn't want to push him to test his belief in being the kind of man who didn't force himself on women.

He disappeared into the bathroom for a moment, brushing his teeth, making me all-too-aware of the fact that I didn't have one of my own.

"What?" he asked when he walked back into the room. I guess my gaze must have been on him, but my mind was far away.

"I don't have anything," I told him.

"Anything," he prompted, standing off the side of the bed.

"Clothes, personal care items, anything. I don't have anything."

"My men will get your old things eventually," he said, shrugging. "But you can shop tomorrow. Dawson and Dulles will take you."

"I thought I wasn't a prisoner anymore."

"You're not. You're my wife. Which means you need guards," he informed me.

"Oh. Okay."

"They will take you anywhere you need to go. You can get whatever you need. And then you will meet me for dinner."

"For dinner," I repeated.

"Yes. Food. Eating…"

"I know what dinner means," I said, rolling my eyes.

"Then why are you repeating the term like it makes no sense?"

"I didn't realize we would be spending so much time together."

"An hour out of your day is so much time?" he asked, yanking back the blankets on his side. "The community needs to see you, get to recognize you."

"Why?"

"So they know you're mine," he said, getting into the bed, flicking the covers over himself. "Are you done with the questions?" he asked.

My gaze moved forward, looking at the godawful painting across from the bed.

"One more."

"I'm waiting."

"Can I buy art?" I asked.

"Art?" he asked, turning his head on the pillow to look at me.

"I really hate that," I told him, waving toward the monstrosity across from the bed.

And to that, I got a low, rumbling noise that might have been Primo's version of a laugh.

"What?" I asked as he reached into the nightstand, grabbing something.

"It's not art," he said, making me aware he'd grabbed a remote when he clicked the button and made the ugly red screensaver disappear. "You can switch the image if you hate it so much. But to answer your question, you may buy whatever you want."

And with that, he flicked off the light, and it seemed like the conversation was over for the night.

He seemed to sleep.

I sat awake for a while, clicking through the images on the TV before I found one that reminded me a lot of my aunt's farm from when I was a girl.

You may buy whatever you want.

Those words came back to me as I was just starting to drift off to sleep.

Well.

That certainly gave me an idea, didn't it?

Sure, I might have been forced into this marriage. I lost contact with everyone who was near and dear to me.

He got everything out of this, and I got absolutely nothing.

Except an open invitation to spend as much of his money as I wanted.

And I suddenly wanted to spend a boatload of it.

6

Isabella

I woke up on top of him.

There was no nice way of putting it.

I was sprawled over him like he was the damn mattress itself.

Leg over hip, head on chest, arm resting on his shoulder.

His body was warm beneath me, his strong chest rising and falling rhythmically enough that I figured he was still asleep, that I could slowly and carefully move off of him before he noticed I'd climbed him like a damn tree in my sleep.

"Comfortable, lamb?" Primo's voice met my ear the second, the absolute second, I tried to lift my head.

Damnit.

"This is my side of the bed," I said as my leg shifted and I became intimately aware of Primo's cock pressing against me. Hard. And, well, big. And my body absolutely did not respond to that. Nope. Not at all.

"It's my side of the bed," Primo clarified. "I might not mind sharing," he added, his hand sliding down my spine. And because of the barely-there silk material of my dress, he might as well have been caressing my bare skin. A tremble moved through my insides at the soft touch, reminding me how long it had been since I'd felt that from a man.

"Well, it was my side of the bed in my old apartment," I told him.

"And the draping yourself over me part?" he asked as I pulled away, going as far to the other side of the bed as possible.

"I, ah, I had a body pillow," I told him, leaving out the part that I actually named the damn thing. "That's how I sleep...on the body pillow," I added. "I will have to add it to the list of things to pick up today," I added.

"No."

"No?" I asked, looking over as he got out of the bed.

"You heard me. No," he said as he got up and walked toward the bathroom.

Alone, I took a second to try to collect myself before getting up to rummage through his dresser, finding a simple black t-shirt. Eyes on the door, I quickly shrugged out of my wedding dress and pulled the shirt on. Once he got out of the bathroom, I would put on my pants I'd been abducted in then tie up the shirt in the front. It wouldn't be high fashion, but it would do until I could buy something more suitable to wear.

Feeling antsy to get out of the bedroom and away from the bed where I'd made a fool of myself, I rushed out, going down into the kitchen to make a pot of coffee, then look through the cabinets and fridge, finding eggs, mozzarella, and spinach, and making myself an omelet.

This is going to sound absurd, given that I wasn't exactly a willing member of this marriage, but as I heard Primo coming down the stairs after his shower, I actually felt a surge of guilt at making food only for myself. I couldn't help it. It was how I was raised. You never, ever cooked for just yourself if someone else was around. Hell, my mother never cooked for just herself even if she *was* the only person around. She always made extra and had it in the fridge just in case someone popped over. If they didn't, she would pack it up and bring it out to hand off to a homeless person.

Primo's gaze moved over me standing in his kitchen, his eyes lingering on my bare legs for a moment. He watched as I took my omelet and coffee toward the dining room table, but said nothing as he made his own coffee and eggs.

"Dawson and Dulles will be here within the hour to take you whoever you need to go."

"Okay."

"And then you will be meeting me for dinner."

"I remember. Where?" I asked. "I need to know what to wear," I added.

"I doubt you know any of the restaurants in the Bronx," he said, and he wasn't exactly wrong. "A dress is fine."

A dress was always fine. For literally almost every activity or venue. But there were different kinds of dresses.

"How formal?"

"Not formal."

I said nothing to that, simply focused on my food.

In turn, so did Primo.

In fact we said nothing else as we ate then took turns putting our dishes in the dishwasher.

It wasn't until his brothers showed up—all three of them and without knocking—that there was noise in the apartment again.

"Did you get the text I..." Terzo started, coming to a dead stop at seeing me there, like he'd forgotten completely about the whole kidnapping, meeting, and forced marriage thing just the day before.

Then his gaze slid down, taking in my bare legs the same way his big brother had.

"Yo," Primo called, voice a whip cracking in the space, making Terzo straighten and turn. "Don't look at her like that," he said. "Isabella, it's time to get dressed," he added. "You will need to get going," he concluded.

And because I was suddenly very aware of my half-nakedness, I didn't think twice about the command. I just rushed across the apartment. I was halfway up the stairs before I remembered to worry about their gazes on me as I went up the steps with nothing on but a pair of panties under the shirt.

But when I looked, Terzo, Dawson, and Dulles were looking at Primo.

It was only Primo whose gaze was on me.

That weird flip-flopping sensation in my belly had to do with, you know, the anxiety of carrying out my plan to spend a ton of his money without checking with him about it. It didn't make sense that it could be anything else.

By the time I came back down, Primo and Terzo were gone and Dawson and Dulles were waiting patiently by the kitchen counter.

"I hope you two are wearing comfortable shoes," I said, getting a smirk out of Dulles.

"That sounds like a threat, woman," he said, those green eyes of his brightening.

"It is," I confirmed, feeling my lips twitch at his chuckle.

"We are at your disposal," Dulles said, waving an arm.

"Do you have a jacket?" Dawson asked, looking at my short-sleeve outfit.

"I wasn't exactly given a chance to pack," I reminded them then waved down at my outfit. "This is all I have. Unless I want to shop in my wedding dress."

"Let me see if Primo has anything," Dawson suggested.

"Anything that fits that man would be a floor-length dress on me. It's fine. I will grab a jacket at the first stop," I said.

"What is the first stop?" Dulles asked as we made our way to the elevator.

"What is the closest, but most expensive store?" I asked, getting a chuckle out of Dulles.

"Oh, you're fixing to do some damage, huh?" he asked, sharing a strange look with his brother.

"I'm figuring my husband has earned it," I said, giving them a long look.

"You might be right," Dulles agreed, tone oddly firm.

After that, the day was a blur. My feet, even in expensive flats I bought at the first store along with my warm floor-length black coat with the bright red lining that made me feel fancy and chic.

All I knew was that by the time we stopped for lunch, the large trunk of the SUV was positively packed. And that was just with clothes and undergarments and shoes. We hadn't even gotten to the basic care items like shampoos, soaps, lotions, makeup, or perfume.

"Better?" I asked as the men with me slowly perked up as they ate.

Really, they'd been troopers. There hadn't been a single grumble loud enough for me to hear. But I watched as, like flowers left without water too long, they slowly started to shrink and wilt on me.

"Yeah," Dawson agreed over a mouthful of meatball parm sub.

"You could make shopping a sport, woman," Dulles said, shaking his head.

"In my defense, I actually never shop like this. Because, you know, I typically have all my basic care items and wardrobe and am just adding one or two things."

Despite myself, I decided I liked the twins. Maybe it was because they had a different mom from Primo and Terzo, but they were easier to get along with. Especially Dulles who had a boyish sort of charm and a pretty good sense of humor. Even when being made to carry three bags full of my bras and panties.

Dawson was a little quieter than Dulles, but had been a decent shopping companion as well.

"Yeah, I get that," Dawson said, nodding.

"I promise we just need like maybe two more stores. One box-type store where I can get just basic stuff like a toothbrush and such. And then a quicker trip to a makeup store."

"Primo said you look better without it," Dawson said, and I watched as Dulles's eyes closed and his head shook. Because he knew what was coming.

"Did he now?" I asked, a smirk pulling at my lips. "I guess I will have to make sure to get some setting spray."

"Setting spray?" Dawson repeated.

"Like a seal coat," Dulles said, getting a small laugh out of me. "So that shit never comes off."

"I fucked up, huh?" Dawson asked, sending me a sheepish look.

"Not at all. You've proven quite valuable."

"Shit," Dawson said, closing his eyes.

"Anything else about me that Primo likes?" I asked, reaching up toward my head. "My hair, perhaps?"

"Nope. No. Actually, he said he'd like you better bald," Dawson quipped and I couldn't help but laugh at that too.

"You know… you guys aren't so bad," I said, nodding.

"Be still my heart," Dulles said, pressing a hand to it. "Not so bad. What a compliment."

"Well, compared to Primo and Terzo, you're practically Mr. Congenialities."

"We weren't raised with the three of them," Dawson admitted. "We only became a part of the family when we were teens."

"So all this good you guys have going on is from your mother."

"Yeah," Dawson said, but his mood and face had gone dark. So had Dulles's.

I'd said something wrong. I didn't know exactly what. I guess maybe they lost their mom. In which case, my heart went out to them. I didn't know what I would do without my mom.

Well, I guess I was about to find out since I wasn't going to be allowed to contact her.

And just like that, any traces of a good mood vacated me as well.

We were a solemn trio for the rest of the shopping trip. I didn't even get a thrill when I dropped a couple grand unnecessarily at the makeup and perfume counters.

By the time we got to the box store to get my other essentials from conditioner and razors to tampons and a toothbrush, I was good and done with the day.

I just wanted to go back to the apartment and take a long bath before crashing hard.

I shouldn't have been so tired. Compared to my normal life which included work and often at least one family function of some sort, this was a tame, relaxed day. But I felt physically and emotionally drained as I helped the guys cart my bags up into the apartment.

I put some of my basic things away, but left everything else in the main living space for Primo to see when he got home. Hopefully it would make him check his credit card statement so he could see the dent I'd put into his bank account.

Though, now that the day was mostly over, the thrill over his reaction to the whole thing had waned.

I just wanted to sleep.

I just wanted to escape back into a world where I could see my family again since they always tended to pop into my dreams.

Dawson and Dulles retired to the living room with something on the TV as I went upstairs to squeeze in that bath I'd wanted before getting myself ready for dinner.

Did I put a full face of makeup on?

Damn straight I did.

And I put on a simple black dress that had cost nearly a thousand dollars, put on shoes that cost about the same, and spritzed on some of my personal favorite perfume. I'd debated buying one of the bottles that cost over five hundred dollars. They'd even smelled divine. But in the end, I'd gone with the perfume I'd been wearing since my sixteenth birthday when my mother had brought me to Macy's and told me that it was an important part of a woman's life to choose her signature scent, and that I should take as long as I needed to figure out what mine was. I had that afternoon. I'd worn the same scent ever since. It was a comfort thing. And it made me feel attached to my mom.

"Hey, Izzy, babe," Dulles called through the bedroom door, "I get that you are doing that whole making him wait thing, but you just aren't going to want to push it. Primo hates waiting," he added.

"And what do you think he could possibly do to me if I make him wait, that is worse than forcing me to marry him?" I asked, walking through the bedroom, grabbing a clutch that was empty save for lipstick and eyeliner since I literally didn't have anything else. No cell, no money, no ID, no credit cards. It just felt right to have it.

"Wow," he said as I pulled open the door. "You look good, woman," he said, nodding. "My brother is a lucky man."

"Your brother is a vicious bastard."

"Which is why he is lucky to get someone like you," Dulles said, eyes a little darker than usual before I started to follow him down the stairs.

"Is this another walking to the restaurant thing?" I asked, already feeling my shoes start to pinch. They were, as my mom would call them, 'sit down shoes.' I should have tried to stretch them out before wearing them.

"It's not far, but we're driving you and dropping you out front," Dulles said.

"Finally off duty, huh? You must hate having to play babysitter."

"It beats some of the other jobs," Dawson said, holding my jacket out for me.

And with that, it was back out of the apartment. I never thought I would rather stay in the home of my abductor, but within only one day, I was preferring that to leaving.

The restaurant Primo chose was intimate and seemed somewhere between casual and formal, which made my dress work perfectly.

I shrugged out of my jacket to hang it by the door, knowing it was too long to fold over the back of my chair, then offered the hostess a smile.

"I am meeting..."

"Yes, Mrs. Esposito," the hostess said, giving me a service-smile. "Your husband is..." she started, half-turning.

"Oh, I see him," I said, even if I was still reeling from being called Mrs. Esposito and having a stranger refer to Primo as my husband. That was going to take some adjusting to.

Primo's gaze found me right then, his eyes doing a slow once-over of me before he got to his feet. I swear he did it in slow motion. His hand rose to secure his jacket button. It was such an old-fashioned gesture that I found myself charmed by it despite myself.

He didn't approach.

Of course not.

He wanted me to come to him.

For appearances' sake.

And I had no choice but to do so.

I was just moving down the aisle toward him when I felt it.

A hand grazing my ass.

And, honestly, I was just going to keep on moving. I'd confronted handsy men in the past and things tended to get pretty scary when you stood up for yourself. I wasn't big or strong enough to take on a full-grown man, so I'd learned to bite my tongue and endure the indignity.

See, the thing was, I didn't really just belong to myself anymore, did I? I belonged, in a way, to Primo. And Primo was big and strong. And he was not someone who tolerated disrespect.

I'd gotten to the table only to have him bark at me to sit while he started marching up the aisle.

Really, I figured he would give the man a few harsh words, using his intimidating stature against the stranger.

Maybe even throw around a "do you know who I am?" sort of thing.

So I sat initially.

For all of five seconds.

Before there was the sound of women shrieking and silverware clattering, and something slamming down hard.

My heart leaped into my throat as I twisted around to see Primo's hand grabbing the back of the man's neck, yanking his face off of the table only to slam him down again.

People panicked and fled their tables while the staff stood back in shock, doing nothing. But of course they wouldn't do anything. This was the same community that hadn't saved a kidnapped woman, either.

I knew enough about the world I'd been born into—and now married into—to know that the mob still had a stranglehold on their communities. Whether they got that mind-my-own-business attitude from fear or respect was anyone's guess. But either one was equally effective.

And judging by the psychotic display Primo was exhibiting, I had to imagine he ruled with fear, not respect.

I watched with a twisting stomach as he slammed the man's head down a third time. He showed no signs of slowing down.

He was going to kill the man.

Right there in public in front of dozens of witnesses.

A part of me should have been thrilled. He'd go to jail and I'd be free. But I couldn't just let him murder a man for copping a feel. Knock a little sense into him? Sure. But this was too much.

"Stop," I demanded, getting to my feet.

My heartbeat was hammering in my chest, my pulse fluttering in my throat and temples. I wasn't the bravest of women. And I certainly wasn't brave in the face of fearsome violence. But everyone else seemed even more terrified than me. So I had to be the one to step in.

"Stop!" I yelled louder as I took a step forward. "Enough. That's enough," I demanded, but Primo was in his own twisted head. He wasn't hearing me.

Blood splattered over the tablecloth.

I couldn't bring myself to look at the man's face. I knew it wasn't going to be pretty. And I didn't have the kind of stomach that could handle that kind of thing.

"Stop," I tried again. "Primo, stop!" I demanded, pressing a hand to the center of his chest.

And that, that barely-there touch, managed to penetrate through his rage where my words could not. His hand held the man's head against the table as his gaze slid to me.

"That's enough," I told him, voice calm even if my insides felt like they were shaking. Because when I tell you that you could see evil in that man's eyes, I wasn't exaggerating.

His chest was heaving a bit but I watched as he unclenched his jaw, as he came back down into a more rational version of himself.

"Not quite," he said.

And before I could react, he was grabbing the man's hand in both of his, the same one he'd grabbed me with, and slammed it down on the edge of the table with a horrific cracking sound followed by the howling of the man.

"No one touches what is mine," he announced, loud enough for anyone who was listening—meaning everyone in the restaurant—to hear. His gaze slid back to me then—unreadable—as he wiped his hands down the sides of his stomach. "Come, sit," he said, waving toward the table.

"You expect me to sit at a table and share a meal with you after that?" I snapped, voice a whisper only he could hear.

"That is exactly what you are going to do," he said, one hand moving outward toward me.

"Don't touch me," I whispered to him again, watching as that brow of his quirked up.

He didn't snatch his hand back, but rather hovered it over my lower back as I turned and marched back to our table since it didn't exactly seem like I had much choice in the matter.

Back to the scene, I couldn't tell exactly what was going on behind me, but I heard voices and shuffling as, I imagined, the man's companions grabbed him and got him out of the restaurant.

"That was too much," I scolded him as he took his seat.

"I disagree."

"Because you're a monster," I told him. "You don't beat men to a bloody pulp in the middle of a crowded restaurant."

"Why not?"

"Because you just don't."

"That man put his hand on your ass without your permission," Primo said, resting an arm on the top of the table and my mind flashed back to him breaking the guy's hand, making my stomach twist again. "Or was I mistaken, did you give him permission to grab your ass?"

"Of course not," I said, chin lifting. "But that was an overreaction."

"Was it? In the old country, he would have forfeited his hand for that."

"That's barbaric."

"That's the life, Isabella. Were you not born and raised into it?"

"I guess my Family is just more civilized than yours."

"This is your Family now, lamb," he reminded me.

"Yeah, thanks for the reminder," I grumbled.

"So am I to assume you've never had your ass grabbed before. A perfect ass like that, just went un-groped your entire life?" he asked.

"No," I said, shaking my head. "Men always think themselves entitled to a woman's body when they like it."

"And your brothers, your cousins, no one has ever made them pay for it?" Primo asked, looking outraged by the concept.

"They were never around when it happened."

"But when you told them," Primo prompted.

"I didn't tell them."

"And why would that be, Isabella?" he asked, leaning forward a bit. "Because you knew they would react? Your old Family isn't more civilized than your new one. You just didn't give them the chance to show you how they conduct their business."

"Well, I would prefer not to have to witness how you conduct your business," I told him as a brave server finally started to approach the table.

Her hands trembled as she showed us the wine.

"That is good, yes," Primo said, nodding, barely sparing her a glance.

"Thank you," I added, giving her a soft smile that she couldn't quite bring herself to return. "See? That poor girl is terrified of you," I told him as she rushed away.

"Fear is good," Primo said, reaching for the wine to pour me a glass, then one for himself. "You should look at your menu."

"I'm suddenly not very hungry," I said, tone a little petulant, but it wasn't a lie. The blood still had me a little queasy.

"You're going to eat," he informed me.

"You might be used to getting your way, but not even you can command my stomach not to feel sick," I told him, watching as his gaze slid to me.

"Sick?" he repeated.

"I don't like blood," I told him.

"Blood, small spaces, any other irrational fears I should know about?"

"They're not irrational."

"They are."

"Just because you don't have the same fears doesn't make my fears irrational," I shot back, reaching for my wine because my nerves were frazzled and I knew the alcohol would help at least a little bit.

"No, the irrationality of your fears is what makes them irrational," he informed me, so damn smug when he said it, too.

"I have my reasons for being afraid of small spaces."

"No, you likely had one experience with small spaces that triggered an irrational anxiety response to it that you've never worked on since then."

"So, what, you're a boss *and* a shrink now? Where did you get your degree, Dr. Esposito?"

"Careful," Primo said, tone low. If I wasn't so riled, I might have called it scary.

"Or what?" I snapped, rolling my eyes. "Are you going to bang my head against the table and break my hand too?" I asked.

"I told you I wouldn't hurt you," he said, almost sounding offended.

"You said you wouldn't rape me," I reminded him. "There are other ways to hurt me."

"I won't strike you. I figured that went without saying."

"Gee, I feel so much better," I drawled. "I have to share a bed with a violent psychopath, but at least he won't hit me."

"Are you always so difficult?" he asked, sighing.

"Yes. Maybe you should have stalked me for a little longer and learned that about me before you decided to force me to marry you," I suggested, shooting him a saccharine smile.

He hissed something under his breath right then. It was too low to make it out. But it sounded frustrated and annoyed. And I felt a little thrill inside at getting the better of someone like him. Even in such a small way.

"You know what," I announced, mostly to myself as I picked up the menu. "I think I just got my appetite back."

7

Primo

It looked like she'd opened up a department store in my apartment. And judging by the names on the bags, she'd spent a small fortune acquiring it all. I almost didn't want to check my statement.

Not that the money mattered.

When you made millions each month, even if the shopping spree set you back a couple hundred grand, it wasn't going to hurt your bottom line.

I'd underestimated Isabella.

It was something new for me.

I was typically a pretty good judge of character.

But I hadn't expected as much defiance as I'd gotten from my new wife. And make no mistake, that was what the spending spree was. Defiance. Because, as she kept accusing me, I had watched her for a bit while I'd made my decision on which woman to choose. And in doing so, I'd seen her shop. Never once at any of the stores whose bags were scattered around my living room, though. So she'd gone to the designer stores just to stick it to me.

There was a flaw in her plan, though.

I *liked* that she was willing to do that. I appreciated her spirit. I even admired her fearlessness in doing something that no one else would feel safe doing.

Hell, it had all been worth every penny when she walked into that restaurant in that little black dress that hugged her soft curves just right.

It was masochistic of me to feast on her like I had when I knew I wasn't going to be able to touch her. But feast I did.

And so did every other man in the restaurant.

Which was fine.

I didn't mind if they looked, if they admired what was mine, if they envied me.

But they did not get to touch.

Ever.

The rage had been immediate. It was familiar in one way. I'd always had a temper. But it was unfamiliar in some ways too. Because I'd never felt quite as possessive as I had at that moment.

I would have killed that man.

And good riddance to him.

But I was never that out of control.

He absolutely would have lost his life if Isabella hadn't stepped in right when she had.

Then, this woman had the audacity to be pissed at me for defending her. For punishing a man for touching her without permission.

I didn't begin to understand her.

But, still, I found myself impressed with her balls. Because not many men in the damn *mafia* would stand up to me like she had, would have spoken to me like she did. It was impressive. And despite all her attitude and comments about how she thought I'd chosen wrong, I knew down to my core that I'd made the right choice.

She was the right woman to be my wife.

She had what it was going to take to live in my world.

Whether she'd accepted that yet or not.

"What is the word?" I asked after we got back home and my brothers showed up.

Isabella had stormed upstairs as soon as we'd walked in the door. Judging by the sound of water splashing on the tile floor, she was taking a shower. It took a fuck of a lot of self-control not to imagine her up there, stripping out of that dress, taking off her bra, sliding out of her panties, and stepping under that spray.

Fuck.

Apparently, it took more self-control than I possessed.

It was going to be more difficult than I realized to wait for her to get to a point where she was willing to sleep with me.

Maybe I shouldn't have married someone I was so fucking attracted to. I mean the woman had me hard and desperate as a teenaged boy when she'd climbed over me in her sleep. I felt ready to bust by the time she woke up and realized what had happened.

I don't know what compelled me to be so set on viewing my vows as sacred. Hell, I snubbed my nose at plenty of the other shit the bible told me not to do.

I guess maybe it stemmed back to watching my old man cheat relentlessly on my ma, and watching her shrink away little by little each time until there was nothing left of her.

As much as possible, I wanted to do things differently than my old man did. So when it came to settling down, getting married, and starting a family, that meant I had to be loyal to my wife, regardless of if our sex life existed or not.

It meant that I wouldn't scream at her or beat her. And while, of course, my mother never told her sons about such abuse, I had no doubt my father was the sort to force himself on my ma too.

I was going to break that cycle.

Among other ones.

But those would come further in the future.

"No one went to the cops," Terzo said. And that was about what I expected. It was why I typically stayed in my neighborhood. Where everyone knew who I was, and no one wanted to get on my bad side.

It helped that I'd paid for everyone's meals and gave the restaurant itself a nice stack of cash for the inconvenience. And to erase any of their camera footage.

Things are getting harder and harder these days. What with people and their nonstop use of their phones and tendency to record and post anything they found online for the world—and the cops—to see.

Luckily, I employed a lot of the street kids. So they kept their phones in their pockets.

"Good," I said, grabbing a cup of coffee.

"Where was my guard?" I asked, looking at my brothers.

Typically, one of them would be with me to act as a lookout. And to rein me in if I got out of control. Dawson and Dulles had been with Isabella all day, so I'd sent them home. But if Terzo had something to handle, he should have replaced himself with someone.

"My fault," Terzo said, shaking his head. "I got a call."

"From whom?"

"Vissi."

"Vissi," I repeated, spinning around. "He's in Italy. It would have been—"

"One a.m. there," Terzo agreed. "But he wasn't in Italy."
"Where was he?"
"At JFK."
"What? Why?"

Vissi was our distant cousin. He'd gotten into some shit a year or so back, prompting me to send him back to the old country to be with his relatives until shit blew over.

"He said it was time. Bitched that his grandma made him put on twenty pounds and was trying to marry him off. I didn't want him stranded at the airport. I should have sent someone else," Terzo said. "Won't happen again."

"Where is Vissi now?"

"He went to see his ma. You know how she is." I did. She was the strong Italian mom that my mother hadn't been given the chance to be. And she would break a wooden spatula across Vissi's head if he came to see me and work before he saw his mother. "He said he would be here in the morning for coffee and to catch up."

"Good. It's been too long."

Vissi might have been a cousin, but he was more like a best friend to me. He'd been closer to my age than Due and Terzo had been at the time, back in the day when the difference between twelve and thirteen and sixteen might as well have been a decade. So Vissi and I fucked around and got in trouble together while Due and Terzo stayed home.

Maybe that was why Due had turned out as warped in the head as he had. And why Terzo was as moody as he was.

I should have been around to protect them more.

Hindsight was twenty-twenty.

"He's going to want a party," Terzo said, rolling his eyes. "You know how Vissi is."

I did. He liked to be the center of attention almost as much as he liked food, friends, drinks, and fucking.

"Alright. Arrange it."

"When?" Dulles asked.

"Tomorrow night."

"Where?"

"Here. We're still not sure how safe it is for Vissi. Better to be safe than sorry."

"He's going to be shocked to meet your... wife," Terzo said, and I didn't like that pause. Was it a non-traditional situation? Yes. But she was my wife.

"Did you tell him?" I asked.

"No. I figured that was your place to explain."

"Probably for the best," I agreed. Vissi wasn't going to be overly accepting of the whole situation. Especially if he got the information from someone who didn't know how to break it to him. "Alright. I want you to put the word out to the capos about keeping an eye for any suspicious cartel movements. They're going to figure out Vissi is back eventually. I want us to have a heads-up if they decide they want to try to make a move on us."

"Got it," Terzo said, nodding.

"And what do you want to say about the party?" Dawson asked.

"Capos and wives, girlfriends, or fuck-buddies. No kids." It wasn't that I didn't like kids. But it would be late. And late-night parties and kids just meant a lot of whining and screaming.

"You don't think maybe you should, y'know, check with the missus before you plan a whole party?" Dulles ask.

"She'll be fine with it."

"Okay then," Dulles said, but there was something in his smirk that said he disagreed with me.

As it turned out, my brother knew my wife better than I did.

"That will be a no for me," Isabella told me later when I made my way into the bedroom after my brothers had taken off for the night.

"What? Why?" I asked, stopping short on my way to the bathroom to take a shower.

"For any number of reasons," Isabella said as she rubbed on some soft, feminine-smelling lotion as she sat off the side of the bed, her back to me.

I didn't know what to expect from her when it came to her bed clothes. I'd only ever seen her on her way to work or to see family or go meet up with friends before. And her style was modern, yet timeless.

What did this woman choose to wear to bed?

A fucking gown.

I mean, it was one of those floor-length silky nightdresses, but it might as well have been a gown with its fancy lace back and the sexy way it glided over her body. Something about the wine-red color of it went really well with her dark hair and tanned skin.

"Name one," I invited, leaning against the bathroom door jam.

"Okay. You didn't discuss it with me first."

"Fucking Dulles," I grumbled.

"What was that?" she asked, turning to face me, brows raised, daring me to repeat it.

"Nothing. I am not going to be the kind of husband who runs every little minor detail by his wife."

"And I am not going to be a wife who tolerates a husband who doesn't respect her enough to ask if she wants a bunch of strangers in her... home."

That word was hard for her.

I figured it would get easier as time passed.

"They're not strangers. They're Family."

"They're *your* Family," she shot back.

"They're yours now too. Whether you like it or not."

"I'm getting really fucking sick of that phrase. If you wanted someone who was just going to take whatever shit you shovel at her and thank you for it, you married the wrong woman. You could have ordered in a wife from some other country who would have been happy to live in your fancy apartment and spend your money. But you chose me. And I won't be a doormat that you walk all over, Primo.

"I get that you're an egotistical asshole and maybe it is going to take me putting my foot down a few times to get you to understand where I stand here. So this is me putting my foot down. I am not going to be paraded around your fucking family like a trophy of your cunning deal to get one over on the Costa Family. Entertain your guests by your fucking self."

With that, she whipped up the blankets, climbed under, and turned off the light.

She wasn't wrong.

I'd chosen her for her spirit.

And I couldn't exactly be pissed when she tossed all that sass at me, could I?

I made my way into the shower, still steamy and smelling of sweet, girlish scents. And my pathetic ass took deep breaths and felt my cock hardening again at the thought of her running the soapy luffa up and down her arms, her legs, over her breasts, her stomach, lower.

On a sigh, I reached down for my cock, stroking one out to the idea of my wife who was just one room away. But it might as well have been across the country or the world since she would rather roll around naked in a cactus patch than have my hands on her.

It was going to be a long fucking marriage.

And now I had to figure out how to tell everyone who knew and respected me why my new wife would not be attending a social function with me.

The whole mail-order bride thing was starting to sound better and better.

But it was too late.

I was stuck with Isabella.

And sometime in the middle of the night when she rolled onto me with a soft, mewling sleep sound, then let out a little sigh as she wiggled into place, liking me more in sleep than she did while awake, I realized that while she wasn't happy with the situation, and despite the frustration she was causing already, that I was satisfied with my choice.

Eventually, she would be my wife in every way that mattered.

I just had to be patient.

Admittedly, though, that wasn't a trait I was known for.

8

Isabella

I was being obstinate.

I recognized that about the whole situation.

I may as well have crossed my arms and stomped my foot about it when he'd told me.

There was even a chance that he wasn't a complete and utter asshole about it, that he just didn't realize that you were supposed to talk to your partner about things like functions, especially ones in what was supposed to be their home as well.

I couldn't shake the feeling, though, that he was doing it to parade me around. And I didn't like that. I didn't like what it said about how he valued me, or what it said about my Family.

On top of all of that, it would have just been incredibly uncomfortable for me. Everyone at the event would know I'd been, for all intents and purposes, forced into the marriage, that Primo had conned me into it. I didn't want them to sneer at me, or look down on me, or even to pity me.

I just didn't want to interact with them at all.

At least not so soon.

I was surprised, though, that he didn't mention it again in the morning as we each made our separate breakfasts, even though we both ended up making almost the exact same thing.

He did mention that his brothers would show up at six with the supplies for the bar, so I figured the party would be starting sometime around seven or eight.

It gave me the whole day to go about taking my bags upstairs, arranging everything where I wanted it in my closet and the bathroom cabinets.

It was an almost meditative day, especially after I found a record I liked and put it on the player. If I didn't think too hard, it almost felt like a normal day in my life. Slowly but surely, I saw myself more in the space, too.

My nightstand filled up with my lotion, a couple notebooks, books, and a small stash of candy for the little mood-lift it would provide.

My robe hung in the bathroom, my products sat in the shower, and I'd even hung a canvas I'd picked up on our travels the day before. It was some cheap print of Manhattan meant for tourists to pick up, but it was a small reminder of home for me.

"Alright," I said, grabbing my coffee, then moving toward the stairs. "You guys have fun," I said to Dawson and Dulles because, despite myself, I liked them, and genuinely did hope they had some fun.

"Aw, come on, Bells," Dulles said, waving an arm out at the apartment. "Won't you stay and have some fun with us? You could use some, don't you think?" he added.

"It's not really my idea of fun for him to show me off to his buddies so they can laugh about how I'd been forced into marriage with him, Dulles," I told him, hearing a hint of something in my voice that sounded just a little bit like sadness.

"Oh, come on, it's not like that," Dulles insisted, shaking his head.

"Isn't it?" I shot back, wincing at the bitterness in my voice, inwardly wondering if I was always going to feel like the butt of some joke among the Esposito Family because of how I came to be a part of it.

"The party isn't even about you," Dawson said, getting my attention, making me realize I hadn't even asked what the party was about. I guess I figured it was like a belated wedding thing, some way for Primo to show me off like he'd done on the way to the church and even when we went out to dinner.

"What is it about then?" I asked.

"Vissi," Dawson said, shrugging as he lined up several bottles of red wine.

They'd brought in several tables. From where, I had no idea. But there they were, scattered about. They were bar tables, meant for standing at, or to rest a drink or a small plate on, but also to encourage mingling, unlike normal tables with chairs.

"Vissi?" I asked.

"A cousin," Dawson supplied. "He just got back from Italy last night. He likes a good party. And since he's been away for a while, Primo decided to throw him something."

"Couldn't he have had an event at a bar or something?" I was nitpicking and I knew it. I even hated myself a little bit because of it.

"I get your distrust of my brother," Dulles said, shrugging. "But I think you're mistaken if you think he has any intentions of having anyone make fun of you. That's not who he is."

Damnit, I think a part of me actually believed that.

And I was angry about it.

"So, he's just a kidnapper and forced marriage arranger, not a guy who makes fun of women. That's such a relief," I said, making my way up the stairs.

To, yes, sulk.

That was exactly what it felt like I was doing as I heard Primo come home, turn on some music, and from the smells of things, start to cook.

That had been the real flaw in my plan.

I hadn't eaten dinner. I guess I figured the coffee and my candy drawer were going to cut it. And maybe they would have—I'd had many such dinners over the years—if the smells of food didn't waft their way up to the loft and under the door. Taunting me. They were taunting me, I tell you.

Before long, my stomach was not just grumbling but twisting and aching so bad that I actually curled up on my side to try to ease the pangs.

It was no use.

I'd gotten a damn taste of Primo's cooking.

And now my body wanted more.

It was sheer pride that kept me up in my room as the sounds of people grew louder and louder beneath me.

But at a certain point around almost nine at night, even my pride was bowing down before the hunger. Leaving me climbing out of bed and walking to the bathroom, taking a look at myself in the mirror.

I wasn't party-ready.

I still had traces of my makeup on, but I was wearing simple black bootcut jeans and a black and gray striped knot-front blouse.

A dress would have been more suitable for a dinner party sort of situation. But I wasn't about to get dressed to draw even more attention to myself.

In fact, my plan was to try to sneak down, grab a plate, then sneak right back up without Primo noticing.

Was it a flawed plan from the beginning? Of course. But I figured it was worth a try. And since I didn't know if they were the 'cut things off by ten' or 'party until dawn' sort of people, I didn't want to risk being starving all night.

Taking a steadying breath, I peeked out the door.

Not seeing Primo anywhere facing me, I rushed down the stairs, trying to avoid drawing attention to myself. It wasn't a huge crowd. Maybe twenty people or so, all in all. But I was a clear outsider and curious gazes slid in my direction.

Primo ran a relatively young organization, I realized.

When you thought of the mafia, you tended to think about what TV shows you'd seen with mostly middle-aged men with round bellies and nagging wives at home. But Primo turned that stereotype on its head. Because if these were his capos, there didn't seem to be anyone over thirty-five. And, somehow, pretty much all of them were attractive.

I ducked my head, not wanting to make eye contact with anyone and invite their conversation. I just wanted food. Then to get back to the relative safety of the bedroom.

"And who are you?" a voice asked, making me pull to a stop, my stomach dropping.

I barely managed to suppress the grumble that grew inside me as my head lifted.

And there was another of those stupidly attractive guys.

Tall, fit, dark-haired, tan-skinned man, with a nice, sharp jawline, tattoos that snaked up his neck and covered his hands, black hair, and stormy blue eyes.

"Nobody," I said, trying to scoot past him, but he sidestepped right in front of me.

"Oh, come on now. You don't look like a nobody to me."

"Strange, because that's exactly what I am," I said, feinting to the left so I could rush past his right.

"Hey, Primo," the man called, making me realize I was walking right toward him as this random guy rushed past me to confront my... husband. "I'm gonna need you to introduce me to this pretty lady over here," he demanded.

I didn't even think Primo had seen me.

But suddenly his arm flew out, grabbing me around the waist, and pulling me into his side, then holding me there.

"I'm not dressed for this," I hissed in a whisper to him so no one else could hear. But Primo went right ahead and ignored me.

"Vissi," he said, addressing the man who'd been chasing me as well as the couple standing there already, "Anthony, Claudia, this is Isabella, my wife," he added.

I watched as the couple nodded and gave me warm smiles, clearly already having heard the news.

But Vissi, whoever he was, clearly was out of the loop. I swear he was gape-mouthed as if Primo just told him I was an alien who'd landed my spaceship on his roof and then ensnared him with my special sci-fi vagina.

"*What?*" Vissi asked, shaking his head.

"Nice meeting you, Isabella," Claudia said as her husband turned her to walk away, sensing that Vissi and Primo needed a private moment.

"Yeah, I think I will give you two a moment as well," I said, trying to step away, but it only made Primo hold me tighter, leaving me crushed against him.

His other hand reached for my wrist drawing it up to show Vissi my rings.

"My wife," Primo said as Vissi's gaze slid to my finger, looking no less confused by the evidence of our marriage situated there.

"Who are you?" he asked, tone accusing as his stormy blue eyes met mine again.

"Isabella... Costa," I added.

"Esposito. Isabella Esposito," Primo insisted, his fingers digging into my hip a bit, and the gesture felt possessive once again.

"Yeah, I think he got that part," I said, rolling my eyes. "That wasn't what he was asking."

"You married a fucking Costa?" Vissi asked, tone implying we were practically harbingers of viral plague. "And *you* married an Esposito?" he asked.

"We're not exactly *Romeo & Juliet* here. I didn't have a choice in the matter," I said, chin jerking up.

"You didn't... what?" he asked, looking up at Primo.

"Vissi has been in Italy for a long time. He doesn't know the things that have been going on with our Families."

"Oh, like you kidnapping Alessa and me?"

"Alessa Morelli? The fuck has been going on since I left?"

"Alessa's brother turned out to be the one who killed Due. It was Commission approved. And, as it turned out, deserved. But the marriage was a way to put an end to the distrust and fighting between us and the Costas, Morellis, and D'Onofrios."

"What about the Lombardis?" Vissi asked. "They're on board with this?"

"Who knows what those crazy fucks think about anything," Primo said, catching my attention.

"How crazy does someone have to be for your psychotic ass to call them that?" I grumbled, getting a surprised laugh out of Vissi. And it looked like an almost undetectable lip twitch from Primo. If I hadn't been so close, I would have missed it.

"Crazy. You're going to stay the fuck away from them," Primo told me, tone serious.

"Are all the Costa women as pretty as you?" Vissi asked, clearly the playboy type.

"No. They're all hideously unattractive, covered in warts, buck-toothed, with glandular conditions and terrible hygiene."

"Aw, come on, sweetheart, you don't want to introduce me to your sisters or cousins?"

"I wouldn't let another one of you touch another one of us with a ten-foot pole," I told him.

"Oh, we're not all as bad as the boss man here," Vissi insisted.

"No, you're right. Dawson and Dulles aren't so bad," I said, getting a charming smile out of Vissi.

"How long have you two been married?"

"Forever," I grumbled at the same time Primo told him about three days.

"Well, happy nuptials," Vissi declared, pressing a hand to his heart. "Even though I am quite put out that you didn't have me as the best man. I expect to be the kids' godfather when the time comes."

"Don't hold your breath on that one," I said, pretending not to notice the way Primo's gaze looked down at me with that damn brow raised again.

I knew the deal I made.

I wasn't going to go back on it.

Not because of him per se, but because I'd always wanted to be a mother. And this was now going to be my only way.

The Woman with the Ring

I figured when I was mentally and emotionally ready, I would track my fertility for a while, get damn near blackout drunk, and let him get the job done.

Not romantic, no, but that was the only way it was going to happen.

And I was just going to completely ignore the strange little flutter between my thighs at the idea of him above me, inside me.

That was just my tiredness and hunger signals getting misdirected or something.

That was the only logical explanation.

"I just came down for food," I admitted. "I haven't eaten," I added. "I just want to grab a plate and go back upstairs before anyone else makes fun of me."

"No one will make fun of you," Primo said, voice fierce.

"My entire existence here is you making fun of me," I reminded him.

Something about my words must have caught him off-guard because his arm loosened just enough for me to be able to slip away. And slip I did. Then I rushed to the kitchen, scooped various things onto a plate without really paying attention to what I was doing, then made my way across the space with my head down, not even caring that I looked like a coward. It wasn't like I was going to have a great reputation with any of these people to begin with.

I'd just gotten back to the room to sit on the bed when there was a tap at the door. And there was Vissi.

"I wasn't making fun of you," he told me, coming in with a bottle of water. "I want to make that clear. I was caught off-guard. Primo is my best friend. He didn't share shit about this with me."

"You should have better friends," I said, accepting the bottle when he handed it to me.

He retreated back to the door which he opened, then stood in the doorway of. "He seems worse at first than he is."

"He was willing to force a woman to marry him to end conflict instead of coming to a business agreement."

"I'm not saying the man isn't part neanderthal," Vissi said, getting a small laugh out of me. "I'm saying he didn't do this to make fun of you or to embarrass or shame you in any way. That's not who he is. For whatever reason, he truly believed this was the best solution to the situation. I understand that you might not believe yet that he is a good man, but he is."

"Good men don't kidnap women. Period. There's no way around that."

"Okay," Vissi said, taking a deep breath, then sighing it out. "I get it. I just wanted to throw my two cents in. I really do hope you can come to find some sort of happiness in this new life. It's not just Dawson and Dulles who aren't bad."

With that, he was gone, and I was left alone to mull over what he'd said.

I mean, from the outside, I imagined the Esposito Family viewed the Costas in a similar way that we viewed them. When each side wanted different things or operated in different ways, it was easy to villainize them. Especially their leaders.

Which meant it was possible that Primo wasn't the awful person that I'd been told he was. Clearly, his Family and friends loved and respected him.

I mean, I had witnessed the man nearly beat a stranger to death over a relatively small indiscretion.

And then there was the whole kidnapping and forced marriage thing.

He wasn't a *good* guy.

But perhaps he wasn't an altogether bad man, either.

"And he can cook," I mumbled to myself as I stuffed my face with a mix of finger foods he'd made. Bruschetta, stuffed mushrooms, antipasto skewers, and stuffed Prosciutto cups. "He can't be all bad if he can cook." I mean, I couldn't think of a single movie villain who could make food better than my mother.

After dinner, not sure what else to do with myself, I took myself into the bathroom for another long, lingering soak in the bathtub I'd struck up a pretty serious relationship with already.

Below me, the sounds of the party lowered and lowered until I was sure no one was left.

Except my husband who made his way upstairs a couple minutes later, going into the bedroom. I figured he would stop there.

But then the bathroom door opened.

"Hey, I'm in here," I called, arm slapping over my chest.

"I see that," Primo said, pulling off his cufflinks, then his watch, his belt.

"What are you doing?" I asked, pretending it was pure worry that had my mouth going so dry as he slipped out of his jacket then yanked his shirt out of his pants.

"What does it look like I'm doing?" he asked, making short work of the buttons, then whipping off his shirt.

"You can wait your turn," I told him.

"It's been a long day, Isabella," he told me as his hands went to his fly.

It was alright.

Really, it was no big deal.

I'd seen the man disrobe before.

Why he felt the need to do it right in front of me was completely beyond me, but it wasn't a big deal.

Except the weird thrumming of my pulse said it was maybe a little bit of a big deal.

Primo's slacks fell to his feet, leaving him in another pair of black boxer briefs, but this time giving me the view of them from the back.

I was not the kind of woman who was into a man's ass. It had never been my thing. I liked arms and hands and chests and backs, but not asses.

That said, Primo's ass?

It was a good one, okay.

High, firm, rounded, a testament to the time he must have spent in the gym, even though I hadn't seen him get up early to do so yet before he got showered and dressed for his day.

I figured he was going to go ahead and floss and brush, so he could get to sleep.

I did not expect for him to hook his fingers into those boxer briefs and start pulling them down.

I wanted to call it panic that flooded my system right then, even if a little voice in the back of my head knew better.

"Primo, get out," I demanded.

"There is one full bathroom in this apartment, Isabella. And you're in it," he told me as the boxer briefs fell to the floor, giving me a view of that perfect ass of his without the material covering it.

"Then leave, and I will get out of it," I said.

"No," he shot back.

And then he turned.

I repeat... the man turned.

And I got a full side view of his naked body.

I want to say I didn't look. If anyone ever asked, I would tell them I didn't. But I did. I absolutely did.

There were all the firm lines I'd become acquainted with when he'd undressed before. But there was one part of him I hadn't seen. Felt, when I woke up on top of him? Yes. But never seen.

Even not hard, though, he was impressive in size.

And I became very aware of the hollow space inside me, and the way he would fill it perfectly.

What?

No.

Damnit.

My gaze lowered as Primo made his way into the shower stall, turning on the water at full blast, then walking into the spray before it even got a chance to warm up.

What kind of animal did that?

Then, well, I had nothing to do. I couldn't get away from him. Not without him getting a good eyeful of me since my towel would require me to stand up to reach for it. So I just had to stay there.

What can I say?

My curiosity got the better of me right then.

And my head raised just a bit; my gaze lifted.

Then there he was.

In all of his naked glory.

He stood under the spray, one hand resting on the wall, letting the water cascade down his neck and body. Delicate white soap bubbles drifted down over his skin—neck, shoulders, back, stomach, ass, and legs.

But none of that really held my attention at all.

Because something else was demanding it.

Namely, the fact that his cock had hardened while he stood there, stretching out, impossibly long and thick, just begging for release.

I wasn't exactly surprised by the throbbing between my thighs right then. It was a normal, healthy response from the body of a woman looking at a man's naked body. It had nothing to do with him personally.

What did shock me, though, was the fact that with a long-suffering-sounding sigh, Primo's other arm raised, and his hand closed around his hard length.

I could hear my own breath catching in surprise, and stayed statue-still for a long moment, worried he'd heard too, that he maybe looked over, that he knew I'd seen.

It wasn't like he was hiding what he was doing. I was in clear view of the shower. But I didn't want him to know that I'd been watching. It would undermine my insistence that I wanted nothing at all to do with him.

There was just no reasoning with a biological reaction, though.

It rarely made any sort of sense.

It was why I had lusted so hard after my bad boy high school boyfriend who treated me like shit, but then had only tepid feelings for the guy I'd dated afterward who treated me like gold, no matter how much I wanted to want him. You just couldn't argue with your biology.

And some cavewoman part of me responded to the man in the room across from me.

It made sense if you thought about it. He was, objectively, a practically perfect male specimen. He was tall, wide-shouldered, fit, with classically handsome features, a rough, masculine demeanor, and, you know… the great cock.

I told myself I wasn't going to risk looking again.

But the sound of his breath hissing out had heat igniting through my system, making my skin feel flushed and overly sensitive. The throbbing got worse and worse until I didn't seem to have any sort of control as my eyes looked up from under my lashes.

His muscles were tense, taut, as he worked his fist up and down his long length.

His other hand balled into a fist on the wall as his breathing got more and more ragged.

The Woman with the Ring

I pressed my thighs more tightly together, trying to calm the chaos between—the throbbing, insistent ache that my body was begging me to ease.

My breath felt caught, making my chest tight as I watched Primo take himself closer and closer, getting nearer and nearer to that edge.

Then pushing himself right over.

His fist slammed against the tile, as a low, almost ragged groan escaped him as he came.

My gaze slid away then, knowing he would be less distracted and more likely to catch me watching, even just under my lashes.

Even with my head down, though, the insistent aching between my legs didn't ease. If anything, it seemed to get even more insistent, making me realize that once he was gone, I was going to need to do something about it if I wanted to be able to fall asleep.

The water cut off a minute later, and I swear I was so hyper-aware of everything at that moment that I could hear him toweling off before making his way in my direction.

Toward the closets, not me.

Except, no, he wasn't making his way to the closets.

He was walking toward me, then stopping.

I could feel his gaze on me and I swear my skin felt heated everywhere his eyes roamed.

I knew I needed to tell him to fuck off, to get away from me, but I couldn't seem to get the thoughts to my mouth. And I wasn't even sure that I meant them.

I mean, of course I meant them on a logical level, just not on that primal, animalistic one that had my sex throbbing along with my heartbeat as he towered over me for a moment.

And then his hand was reaching out, his finger snagging my chin, forcing it up so he could look at my face. I didn't have to see myself to know what he saw when he looked at me right then. I could feel the flush to my cheeks and the heaviness to my eyelids.

"You like to watch, huh, baby?" he asked, voice smooth and deep, a sound that washed over me.

My lips parted, and some sound did come out, the beginning of an objection, surely. But it didn't quite escape me.

Primo's thumb moved out, stroking along my lower lip for a second before he released me.

"I like to touch more," he told me.

And just like that, his arm was plunging under the water, and his big hand was sliding between my thighs, stroking up my slick and aching cleft.

I knew I needed to push him away, that this kind of thing was only going to complicate things, make it harder for me to set much-needed boundaries.

But my body wasn't listening.

My thighs parted for him, resting against the cold sides of the tub as his finger started to stroke up my sex, teasing around the edge of my clit, but not quite touching it.

"Did you see how hard you made me?" he asked, the pad of his finger dipping down with his words, doing a quick pass over my clit, but moving right away even as my breath caught at the hint of pleasure.

"Do you know how difficult it's been," he started, doing light strokes over my clit, "to wake up to you draped over me in the morning?" he asked as my breathing got faster and more shallow. "How I have to keep my hands to myself when what I want to do is tear off your panties and slip inside you," he told me. "Like this," he added as two of his fingers thrust inside me, making a surprised moan escape me. My muscles clenched around him, making a low groan escape him. "One day, you're going to squeeze my cock like this," he told me just before his fingers started to thrust.

It wasn't slow or sweet or explorative.

He fucked me with his fingers until my hips were writhing against his touch, until my whimpers became loud moans, until my hand slid down, pressing his palm against my cleft, engaging my clit with his motions.

His fingers got rougher and more demanding as I got closer and closer, my walls tightening around him as he pushed me toward that edge that, with one more little push, would send me free-falling into oblivion.

"Nope," he said, his fingers slipping out of me. "If you want to come, Isabella, you're going to come around my cock," he told me, shooting me a devilish smirk as he pulled his hand out of the water, then made his way back toward the bedroom.

Alone, the embarrassment had a weak, pathetic whimper escaping me as my hands rose, covering my face, not sure how the hell I was ever going to be able to face the man again after that.

It would have been bad enough if I'd had an orgasm. But it was somehow much worse that he'd denied me it.

"Damnit damnit damnit," I grumbled to myself, opening the drain, and sitting there until the tub emptied completely while calling myself any number of things, but all of them having to do with being a complete freaking idiot.

Cold and frustrated, I toweled off. Then took a really long time to lotion, brush and braid my hair, do my skin routine, then finally get dressed for bed.

Long enough had passed that I figured there was no way the man could possibly still be awake. I cracked the door and listened, hearing the steady, deep breathing that said I was right.

Then I scurried right the hell out of there and down the stairs to curl up on the couch instead.

Remnants of the party were all around. The tables were all set up. The bottles of liquor, both full and empty, were still on the makeshift bar they'd set up. The glasses were lined up beside the sink and the dishes were in it, but I figured they would stay that way until Primo's housekeeper showed up to deal with it.

The housekeeper that sucked his dick the day of our wedding.

I had no right to feel as pissy about that as I did as I snatched my jacket off the rack to use as a makeshift blanket.

I tried to tell myself it was just a matter of tact. How the hell was I, the wife, supposed to exist in the same space as her, the housekeeper, and sucker of my husband's cock? It created a weird dynamic. I wasn't looking forward to navigating it.

Maybe I'd find some excuse to get out of the house the next day before she showed up. I would have someone on my guard shift. They could take me somewhere.

The idea of more shopping made me a little sick, but this was the city. There was never a shortage of places to go or things to do. I could, I don't know, take a class or join the gym, something that would give me a reason to leave the house more often so I didn't start going stir crazy since it didn't look like Primo was going to want me to work. And, quite frankly, why should I? He was the one who forced me into this whole mess. He could be the one to finance having a wife.

Decision made, I flicked on the TV to drown out the voices in my head, then curled up and went to sleep.

But what did I do?

I dreamed of him, of course.

The sweaty kind of dream, too.

Because my body needed more of that.

Right before we got to the really hot part of the dream, though, I felt hands grabbing me, leaving me to wake up with a gasp to find myself being lifted up into Primo's arms yet again.

"Stubborn ass," he mumbled as he cradled me to his chest.

"Put me down, Primo," I demanded, voice sharp.

"No."

"Put. Me. Down," I demanded, emphasizing each word with a jolt of my body, hoping he'd get annoyed and put me onto my own feet again. But, nope. This was Primo we were talking about. In his giant arms, I might as well have been a flailing toddler.

"You sleep in my bed. We've been over this," he told me, walking toward the stairs. "I don't give a fuck if your ego is bruised, you sleep next to me."

"My ego is not bruised," I grumbled, leaning as far away from his chest as I could get with how hard he was holding onto me, even if a small part of me wanted to lean in and take a deep breath of the body wash that smelled just like his cologne that was clinging to his skin.

"Fine. Then you're in a pissy-ass mood because I wouldn't let you come. Whatever way you want to put it."

"Don't flatter yourself, Primo. I don't need *you* to help me come," I told him, bitterness slipping into my words. "I've managed just fine without you in the past," I added as we went up the stairs. "By myself... and not."

"Don't," he snapped, stopping in his tracks and giving my body a little shake. "Do not talk about other men you've been with to me."

"Primo, if you wanted a starry-eyed virgin who would mistakenly believe your cock is the best one in the whole wide world, you chose wrong," I told him, enjoying the way anger had a muscle in his jaw ticking. Maybe it wasn't smart to poke a bear like him, but I took a little bit of comfort in knowing I could get a rise out of him, that he wasn't the only one who wielded a little power in this relationship.

"I bet you would be singing a different tune if I ripped off your panties and started to fuck you."

"Yeah, that's not going to happen," I said, shooting him a saccharine smile.

"I bet if I slipped my fingers into your cunt right now, you'd be dripping for me."

"Feel free to imagine any sort of absurd situations you want, Primo. But if there is one thing I am sure about right now, it is the only way you are going to fuck me is if I am practically passed-out drunk. I want absolutely *nothing* to do with you physically," I told him, tone seething. It was a nasty enough sound that he looked taken aback by it.

Good.

I hoped he was sweating.

I hoped he was wondering how the hell he was going to get an heir if his wife wanted nothing to do with his hands on her ever again.

"We'll see about that," Primo said, dropping me down onto the bed, then going around to climb into his side.

We each turned our backs on each other.

And as I lay there not sleeping, I wondered if this was going to be how our marriage would always be.

Anger and resentment and trying to one-up the other one in a battle of wills and biting comments.

It was going to be a long life if that was the case.

But I couldn't see any way around it.

Because I was pretty sure I hated him then more than I did when he'd been threatening to murder my family in front of me if I didn't agree to marry him.

I didn't think there was a way to come back from this.

9

Primo

Living with Isabella taught me that if I ever needed someone with ice in their veins to do a job for me, I probably should source out to a woman.

That first morning after the shower and tub thing, I woke up without her sprawled over me. Which seemed weird since she'd done that involuntarily in the past. It wasn't until she got up out of the bed and I ran back upstairs to grab my watch that I realized she'd kept herself on her side of the bed by placing a line of books between us, so she would roll into them, wake up, and get herself back on her side of the bed.

I probably should have let the woman come.

I'd miscalculated when I thought it would only make her want me more.

It was my mistake, forgetting for even a moment that a huge part of her was determined to despise me because of the circumstances of our marriage. When I caught her in a soft moment, I should have been taking full advantage of it, not fucking around with her. That was the only way I was going to eventually soften her to the idea of actually being a wife in a real way, not the front we put on for others while she hated me in private.

It was going to take time.

The problem was that I wasn't exactly a patient man.

I had to keep reminding myself that this was for life, so if she needed to waste a week or two giving me the cold shoulder, I could deal.

Even if my balls felt ready to burst. Especially now knowing that even if her head didn't want to be in on it, her body absolutely responded to me. I would have been better off not knowing that yet.

It was just after seven on a Friday night a week after the bath situation. I'd planned on getting home and inviting her out to dinner. A peace offering, of sorts, since I'd been just as stubborn as she had since then, refusing to be the one to break the silence first. I figured that if we got out of the apartment together, maybe she would loosen up a bit, hold a conversation with me, and we could move forward.

I walked into the scents of cooking in my apartment.

Moving in, I could see Isabella in the kitchen, busy at work.

She was never fully casual, but this was as close as she got, wearing dark wash bootcut jeans and a simple lightweight camel-colored sweater. Her silky hair was pulled into a loose braid down her back, likely to keep it out of her face while she cooked.

I didn't know what she was making.

But I did know one thing.

She wasn't going to make enough for me.

She never did.

It was actually impressive that she managed to fight against what had to be a lifetime of Italian-mom-training to be a good future hostess, someone who always made more than enough for everyone around her.

But I had to give her credit, she sure as fuck managed.

Every single morning, I would walk down to her making just enough breakfast for herself. I wasn't typically home early enough to catch her making dinner, but there were never any leftovers in the fridge for me, either.

Interestingly enough, though, she did apparently cook for Dulles and Dawson when they were pulling guard shifts. I knew because they'd raved about my wife's cooking skills and I'd needed to hastily change the subject to avoid having to admit that she despised me so much that she would rather let me starve than feed me.

Sighing, I took off my jacket, laying it over the back of the couch, then pulling off my cufflinks, and put them down on the coffee table. Rolling up my sleeves, I made my way into the kitchen, seeing the pasta in the pot and the fresh herbs and cheeses spread across the counter.

Lasagne.

The woman was making some sort of lasagne.

And it sounded fucking amazing.

But there was no way I was going to start making my own at that hour.

So I grabbed some frozen filo dough, loaded it up with feta, olive oil, mozzarella, basil, and parsley, and threw my makeshift pizza into the oven. The entire time, Isabella danced around me like I didn't exist. I may as well have been a damn ghost in my own kitchen the way she completely ignored my presence. Even when I tried to get in her way, or stick my hand in the same container of cut spices she was reaching into, she managed to move around me and snatch her hand back before there could be any proof that I was actually there.

I had to find a way to get on her good side.

Because while it was originally funny and maybe even a little cute that she could act like I didn't exist in my own fucking home, it was getting old fast.

A week was long enough.

The problem was, I had no idea what I could do to make shit right.

I lucked out the next day, though.

I'd just been making my way down to grab some coffee and head out when Terzo rushed into the apartment, eyes telling.

"We have a situation," he said," he said, glancing over at Isabella who was sitting at the dining room table with her coffee and writing down what was likely a grocery list since we were getting low on everything.

"Okay," I agreed, skipping the coffee, and following him, keeping my mouth shut until we were in the elevator. "Where are we going?"

"The alley," he said, making my brows pinch. "You need to see it for yourself," he said, shaking his head at me.

Interest piqued, I followed him down to the ground floor, and out into the alley.

Where I found Vissi holding the leather-jacket-clad arm of a woman.

"I swear to fucking God if you don't let go of my arm, I am going to cut each one of your fingers off with a really dull set of scissors," she growled at Vissi, staring at him with daggers in her eyes.

Fierce enough that I was sure she was actually capable.

She had different coloring than Isabella, looking more like their brother Emilio with her medium-brown shoulder-length hair, and the blue eyes that came from their mother's side of the family.

But there was no mistaking the soft, feminine face shape, the deep-set eyes, and the plump lips.

"Mirabella," I greeted her, watching as her head whipped over, brows lifted, surprised that I knew who she was. As if the family resemblance wasn't almost painfully obvious.

"Mira," she corrected, chin lifting in a move that was so much like her sister that I felt my lips twitching.

"Mira," I said, nodding. "You know you're not supposed to be here."

"Why? Why am I not supposed to be here? Because you're doing awful shit to my sister, and don't want the Families to know? Is that why?"

"As I told your brother and Lorenzo, Isabella won't come to harm from my Family or me."

"Yeah, right, because I am just supposed to take the word of a fucking psychopath, right? 'Oh, no harm will come to her. Except, you know, the whole kidnapping and forced marriage thing,' you fucking lunatic."

"I'm not seeing the family resemblance to your sweet wife," Vissi said, shaking his head as Mira glowered at him.

"Only because you have yet to piss Isabella off," I said, snorting.

"So you admit it. You're pissing her off."

"I piss her off by existing, Mira," I said, shrugging. "But I don't put my hands on her."

"Just keep her trapped in a tower like fucking *Rapunzel*. Totally normal thing to do to your supposed wife."

"She is free to move around."

"With babysitters," Mira snapped.

"With guards. For her own safety," I corrected.

"Oh, so she *is* free to come and see me then, right? Great. Send her down."

"I can't do that."

"Right. Because she's not your wife. She's your fucking prisoner."

"As I told your brother, once Isabella settles into her life here, she will be able to be in contact with all of you again."

"Oh, when she is so brainwashed by your stupid face and your big-dick-energy that she will forget that she is here against her will, you mean?"

"My stupid face," I repeated, lips twitching.

"Would you prefer me calling it 'punchable?' Because it is that too."

"Don't you know better than to threaten a boss?" Terzo growled.

"Oh, please. And what do you think you're going to do to me?" she asked, eyes rolling. "One hair on my head goes out of place while I am here and my brother will sic Brio on you so fast that you won't be able to reach for your gun before he's plucking each of your teeth out with a set of pliers."

She wasn't exactly wrong about that.

She might have called me a psycho, but the title for that absolutely went to Brio, who was a member of the Costa Family. I'd never seen anyone who enjoyed blood and pain and death as much as he did.

"Mira, you have my word that Isabella will see you again in the near future."

"That near future is now," Mira declared, gaze holding mine.

I'd known lifelong mobsters, professional hitmen, who wouldn't dare to speak to me or look at me the way she was right then.

You had to admire her balls.

"And if I have bruises, you fuckface," she said, looking over at Vissi again after she tried to pull her arm loose, "I am going to find out where you live, let myself in, and pour hot grease all over your twig and berries," she told him, and there was something a bit chilling in her eyes as she gave him the threat, something that made me think she was completely capable of doing exactly that.

Vissi seemed to pick up on it too because his grip loosened ever so slightly.

"Let me see my fucking sister, you monster."

She said that with a smile, too.

I didn't know dick about Mirabella Costa, but it seemed like I needed to have some of the guys look into her. I guess I'd figured that Emilio's sisters had been raised at an arm's length from the Family business, so they would all be softer and sweeter. But Mira had a toughness about her that said she brushed shoulders with bosses and capos, and managed to hold her own around them, too.

I wasn't intimidated.

We both knew she didn't have a leg to stand on, that her sister and the Families had all agreed to this plan. Whether she liked it or not.

The reason I wasn't immediately telling Vissi to drag her back out of my borough had nothing to do with her.

And everything to do with the fact that I had a woman a couple of floors off who might stop giving me the silent treatment if I let her sister visit.

"Tell you what," I said. "If Isabella agrees, you can visit for a bit," I said, ignoring Terzo's gaze on my profile. "But you will have the visit here," I told her.

"Fine. Whatever. I just need to see her," Mira said, shrugging.

"Give me five, then lead her up," I told Vissi, then turned, and made my way back upstairs.

"Dulles, do you think we can take a trip to... oh," she said, her smile falling as her gaze landed on me.

"I have a proposition for you," I said, watching as her cold gaze cut to me. Her brow rose slowly when I didn't immediately go on. "I'm willing to let you have something you're probably really desperate for right now if you stop acting like I'm a ghost in my own fucking home."

"I am not desperate for a fucking orgasm, Primo," she growled. Growled. The woman growled at me.

"I wasn't talking about your pussy, though I am always up for that," I said, watching in amusement as her eyes turned to slits.

"What were you talking about then?" she asked, crossing her arms.

It was not even eight in the morning and this woman was ready to fight.

I liked that about her.

"Agree to stop dancing around me," I demanded, hearing the elevator.

"Only if what you have to offer is good enough," she said, chin raising.

"Oh, it's good enough. But you take the deal now. No more silent treatment shit. You got a problem with me, you say it."

"When it comes to you, Primo, I always have a problem with you," she said. If looks could kill, I would be full of bullets right then.

"You tell him!" Mira's voice called from behind me, and I got to watch as Isabella's eyes got huge.

"Is that..." she said, voice sounding like it was quivering, making me feel shittier than I had in a long time. That was pure desperation in her gaze right then.

"It is," I said, nodding. "I need you to agree first," I reminded her, seeing her eyes getting glassy.

"I agree. I agree. Just let me see my sister," she demanded as a tear slipped down her cheek. "Please," she added, sniffling.

I wasn't a gentle man.

But I had an almost overwhelming urge to go to her, to wipe the tears from her cheeks, to pull her into my arms, and assure her that it was going to be okay.

Only, I couldn't do any of that.

So I took a step back and nodded toward Vissi who released Mira's arm.

And she bolted into the space, ramming me hard with her arm as she passed, then throwing herself into her sister's arms.

"This was the right move," Vissi said, coming up next to me. "In case you needed someone to tell you that, this was the right move. This is what a man with the right intentions would do. The Costas will see that. It will ease the tensions."

He was right.

But I didn't give a shit about the Costas right that moment.

Because my gaze was fixed on my wife. Who was bawling in the arms of her sister, her entire body racking with the sobs that escaped her.

I'd never really felt small in my life.

But I felt fucking infinitesimal right then.

"And in case you can't see it for yourself, it will help the tensions between you and the missus."

I could hope.

10

Isabella

Primo was not the sort of man who went back on his word.

Which was what made him letting my sister visit all the more shocking.

I was half-sure I was hearing voices when Mira called to me from the elevator.

But then there she was.

And I just... I shattered.

I was actually embarrassed after the tears dried and my sister and I made our way to the kitchen just how hard I'd cried on her.

"I guess I've been bottling up more than I realized," I admitted as I went to the coffee machine since no one I knew liked caffeine quite as much as my sister.

I had to admit to myself at least that ever since the tub incident and the wedge it had put between Primo and me, the loneliness had really started to creep in. Sure, I had Dawson and Dulles who were steadily becoming more like friends than just guards. But I felt like I needed to be really careful what I said around them since their loyalty would always be to their brother, to their Family.

I didn't really ever recognize just how much I'd come to rely on my family for emotional regulation until I couldn't just pick up a phone and call them or drop over and see them.

Without them, I felt so incredibly, bone-deep alone.

"It's no wonder with that fucking monster you married," Mira said, dropping down on the stool at the island, tapping her short nails on the counter. Energy, she always had a lot of it. Likely from all the aforementioned caffeine.

"I'm okay," I told her, passing her the cup of coffee and some sugar. "Really. Crazy emotional display aside, I'm okay," I insisted, reaching across the island to give her hand a squeeze. "He's... he's kept his word."

"And you?" she asked, gaze guarded. "Have you kept your word? Has he made you..."

"No," I said, fast, too fast. She was likely immediately suspicious, but the response had nothing to do with anything I could ever tell her. "No. He hasn't made me do anything really. Aside from sleeping in the same bed which he claims is for safety reasons in case there was ever a, I don't know, drive-by or something."

"There are a lot of windows here," she said, nodding at them. "They have some sort of block on them, though. You can't see in. Even with night vision."

"You've been watching the apartment with night vision?"

"No. This was the first time I got into this area of The Bronx. His little guards are everywhere. And we look a lot alike. There was no way they wouldn't know who I was and that I didn't belong. But the kid that is usually watching the street was being hassled by the cops, so I was able to sneak in. Then got caught by that stupidly good looking asshole."

"Which one? They are all infuriatingly attractive."

"Viggi? Vicci? I don't know. Something ridiculous like that."

"Vissi," I supplied. "He's really not so bad."

"If I have bruises on my arm, I have to pay him a visit."

"You did not threaten them," I grumbled, eyes closing, looking for a little patience.

"Only to cut off his fingers and potentially pour hot grease over his nether regions."

"Oh, is that all?" I asked, deadpan, getting a smile out of her.

"You do seem... okay," she said. "Aside from the crying."

"I missed you. I miss everyone," I admitted. "I think I was just overwhelmed."

"Honestly, I'm kind of shocked he let me see you. I just figured I might catch sight of you, or you might hear me, and know we love you and are impatiently waiting for you to be able to contact us."

"I think you caught him in a relatively good mood," I told her.

"If that was a good mood, then I really am worried about you."

"Don't be," I demanded, topping off my cool coffee. "Really, don't. I'm okay. I mean I miss you guys so much I can barely breathe at times. But they're not hurting me or being super restrictive or anything. It's just..."

"Lonely," Mira piped in.

"Yeah."

"You'd think you would appreciate the break from the relentless texts from everyone and Mom's calls telling you that she gave your number to her hairdresser's son. Who is gay, mind you. It was the first thing he told me when he called out of familial obligation."

"Well, at least she can say one of her kids is married now," I said, shaking my head.

"Hey, she's not happy about it, Bells. She wanted you to settle down, but not like this."

"You know, it could be worse. I mean, I don't know how to put this. But like… I could have ended up married to someone I loved and who I thought loved me, then found out he was disrespecting me by screwing everything that walked while I was home raising his kids."

"I mean, but Primo…"

"Is actually surprisingly a traditionalist about marriage. He doesn't believe in cheating."

"Even if you aren't sleeping with him?" Mira asked, dubious.

"Even then, he claims."

"Interesting. But are you going to?" she asked.

"Sleep with him?" I clarified.

"Yeah."

"Some day, I am going to have to," I told her. "I want kids."

"I mean, I can think of worse guys to share a bed with. Plus, that man has the most BDE I've ever seen."

"BDE?"

"Big-dick-energy," Mira told me.

"Oh, ah, yeah, I guess." I mean, he totally had a big dick, but I didn't want to tell her how I knew that. "How is everyone?" I asked, wanting to steer the conversation away from Primo and our future sex life. "Emilio?" I asked, wincing.

"Emilio is treating the whole situation like it is his fault," Mira told me. "He's been in a bit of a dark place lately, to be honest."

It was hard to picture Emilio in a dark place. He was usually the lightest of all of us, never taking life—or even work—too seriously. I guess the older brother in a large family had to learn to adopt an easy-going demeanor to survive the chaos his younger siblings brought along with them.

"It's not his fault. Tell him I said that. I will tell him when I get to see him too, but you tell him now."

"I will, but you know how the Costa men are."

Stubborn.

Our other brother, Anthony, had relentlessly chased a spot in the Family at only eighteen years old when Lorenzo took over for his father after his death. Despite all of us begging him to take some time, to live his life, maybe to go to college for that experience. He was dead-set on a life in the Family. And that was exactly what he got.

"And Mom?"

"Mom is flip-flopping between forced optimism and low moods. I think she will feel better when she hears I got to speak to you, and can confirm that you aren't being abused in any way. The thing I don't get is, if you are being treated okay, why aren't you allowed to contact us?"

"Well, you know the famous Costa men's stubbornness?"

"Yeah."

"Well, imagine that ten-fold for the Esposito men." Mira made a disgusted sound that had me smiling. "Exactly. I guess he's worried that I might try to stage a plan to run. But I agreed to this. And even if it takes some adjustment, I am happy to be able to be a part of ending all the feuding between the families."

"I should have thought of sneaking you in a cell phone. I honestly didn't think I would get to see you face-to-face or I would have thought of it."

"Maybe if we can prove that you're not trying to steal me, or hatch some plan to overthrow the treaty, Primo will be more open to you visiting on occasion. Maybe even bringing Mom. Emilio and the others will likely be a hard sell, but I'm sure we will get there eventually."

"So I have to play by the rules," Mira grumbled.

"I know. It's hard for you," I agreed, smiling. "But for now, yeah."

"I'm not apologizing for threatening that asshole, though."

"I don't think anyone expects you to. For all their flaws, the Esposito men don't seem wholly opposed to loud-mouthed and opinionated women. If anything, Primo gets pissy if I don't mouth off to him. He really hates the silent treatment. Though, I had to agree to stop doing that if I want to see you."

"Small sacrifice. So what was the wedding like?"

"Rushed," I told her. "But he had a dress and shoes and flowers," I said, waving over toward the dining room table.

"And they're still looking that good?" she asked, dubious, making my gaze shoot over to realize, no, of course not. He must have had them replaced. And seeing as he didn't strike me as a man who wanted fresh flowers in the home for himself—least of all my favorite kind of flower—he'd clearly done so for me.

That was kind of thoughtful, right?

Even if he didn't bring them personally, he'd thought to tell someone else to. Even when I was giving him the silent treatment.

"And a ring?" Mira asked.

Unlike me, she'd never been marriage-crazy. In fact, she scoffed at the whole institution and broke our mother's heart by declaring she was *never* going to get married.

"Yeah," I said, holding out my hand.

"You know I'm not a jewelry kind of girl, but this is pretty amazing."

It was, actually. I found myself looking down at it often, running my finger over the stones in anxious moments.

"Your nails are a wreck, though."

"I've been putting it off. I've dragged Dulles and Dawson to so many stores already. I was giving them a break from the girly shit."

"Those are the brothers, right?"

"Twins. But a different mom from Primo, Due, and Terzo. I haven't really figured out more than that."

"What with the whole not speaking to your husband thing," Mira said, nodding.

"Yeah."

"I'm starting to think you got a kind of sweet deal, all in all," Mira said. "You get to live in this fancy-ass apartment, spend all his money, not work, and you don't even have to fuck him?"

"Well, I will eventually," I reminded her. "He does want an heir."

"Okay, well, don't hate me, but would it really be a hardship to fuck him? He's almost annoyingly attractive."

"I don't know. Maybe the dynamic will improve, and I'll feel differently over time. It's all new," I added.

"Yeah. And you're young. There's time. I just hope that you get some more freedom soon. Sunday dinner has felt so weird without you there."

"And by that you mean Mom is trying to force you to learn to cook finally since I am not there to help out."

"Listen, it was *your* job as the first daughter to learn all that shit. Now you have abandoned us, and I'm learning all sorts of crap about sauces and pasta shapes that I never really ever wanted to know."

"Hey, it would be nice to be able to feed yourself once in a while," I told her, knowing she was a chronic order-in or take-out woman. I'd never seen someone with more menus than she had. The only items in her fridge were sauces to go along with whatever she'd ordered in, soda, and some ice cream in the freezer. That was my sister. And I was a little sad that I didn't get to be around to watch our mom boss her around the kitchen while she got more and more frazzled by the second.

How many things like that had I missed? And would continue to miss? How long would it be before Primo allowed me to have my family in my life again?

I imagined however long he had in mind would only be lengthened by my resistance to my circumstances.

Maybe it was time for me to at least try to play the part I'd agreed to take.

Maybe if I was kinder and more accommodating, he would ease up with the restrictions, and this would feel more like a partnership than a prison I was stuck in.

I wouldn't claim it would be easy. The more time went on, the more resentful I was feeling about parts of the arrangement. But if I could just work past that, play the part for a while, then maybe I would be able to negotiate for the things I wanted more of in my life.

Like my family.

"Listen, I'm okay with not knowing how to create the family meatballs. That's why I have Mom and you. Hey, do you think you're going to be dragging Primo to Sunday dinners in the future?"

"Oh, God. I hadn't even thought about that," I admitted.

But, of course, I would have to, wouldn't I? They were my family. And he was, for all intents and purposes, my husband. It would be inappropriate for me to say he couldn't go with me.

"What?" Mira asked when a strange, choked laugh bubbled up and burst out of me.

"It's just... can you imagine Primo sitting across from Emilio and Anthony?" I asked, somehow able to picture it in vivid detail.

"The scowling," Mira said, smiling over the rim of her coffee cup.

"Right?" I agreed.

"So, are you going to give me a tour of the house, or what?" Mira asked, waving around.

With that, I gave her a tour, and we ended up back in the living room on the couch, talking about her and our family and *the Family*.

Until she got a call.

"It's Emilio," she said, showing me the screen. "Do you want to talk to him?"

I did.

God, I did.

But would talking to him be stepping over a line? Would it set me backward, make Primo less likely to allow Mira to visit?

"No one is going to know," she said, handing me the phone then jumping up to make sure no one was around eavesdropping. "Go ahead."

What was that phrase I'd heard my brothers toss around all the time as kids? Something about it being better to ask for forgiveness than permission.

With that, I swiped my finger across the screen before the call could end.

"Emilio?" I said, voice small.

"Bells?" Milo asked, sounding choked.

"Yeah, it's me," I said, feeling the sting of tears in my eyes again, not realizing how much I needed to hear his voice.

"Did you run away? Where are you? I will come get you."

"No. No. I didn't. I'm... I'm at my new... home," I told him, wincing at how forced the words sounded. "Mira showed up here today, threatening to break things and pour grease on other things. You know her," I added, lips twitching a little as she shot me small eyes from across the room.

"Primo let her see you?" Emilio asked, dubious.

"I know. I was surprised too. I think... I think he's trying, Emilio."

"Trying to do what?"

"Not be a complete asshole," I said, shrugging.

"It's too fucking late for that," Milo snapped.

I'd never considered my brother an angry person. That was all Mira's department. Emilio was always laid back and kind of carefree. Sure, he managed to do work for the Costa Family, but he wasn't an overachiever or someone who did a lot of the dirty work.

It was weird to hear him angry.

Not just angry.

Enraged.

"I agreed to this, Milo," I reminded him. "And, really, it's been okay. It's like being roommates most of the time. He's not around much."

"Roommates," Emilio scoffed. "Roommates would be able to leave."

"I can leave," I told him. "The day after the wedding, I went on an all-day shopping spree. I just can't leave the area yet. And he has guards with me. But him letting Mira come up and see me today was a step in the right direction."

Emilio was silent to that, knowing he couldn't argue, but so dead-set on hating Primo that he didn't want to claim anything he did was okay.

"I miss you," I told him, feeling my heart squeeze.

"I miss you too," he told me. "And I'm sorry. I'm so fucking sorry."

"It's not your fault. You need to stop blaming yourself." From the side of me, Mira stiffened and gave me the wrap-it-up gesture, making me think the elevator had started. "Listen, Emilio, I have to go. But I love you. And I will talk to you as soon as I can, okay? And I'm okay. You don't need to worry about me, okay? I'm fine."

With that, I hung up and handed Mira her phone to tuck away just as the elevator doors chimed as they opened.

"Alright, Sunshine," Vissi said, addressing my sister who shot him a glowering look at the pet name that in no way described her personality in the least, "let's get you on your way."

"Sunshine?" Mira griped, crossing her arms over her chest.

"Yep. Pretty, but will burn the fuck out of you," Vissi said, getting a lip twitch out of Mira who was determined not to be charmed by him. Which wasn't easy. Because Vissi was very charming.

"I just got here," Mira insisted.

"Actually, you've been here a couple hours. Long enough to fill her head with all sorts of ways to murder her husband in his sleep, no doubt."

"If you recall, I didn't say I'd murder you. Just maim you pretty horribly," Mira said, shrugging, but she seemed to sense that she didn't want to push them. So she made her way toward me and gave me a hug that felt like it would break my bones, promising to come back soon, then following Vissi out.

And me, well, I went to the grocery store with Dulles who snuck two king-sized candy bars into the cart, then I made my way back to the warehouse to start dinner.

This time, for the two of us.

11

Isabella

The tangy scents of red sauce, garlic, onions, and peppers filled the kitchen by the time Primo came waltzing in around six-thirty that night.

"I guess I made the right decision," he said by way of greeting when he glanced over to see that I'd set the dining room table for two for the first time.

I forced myself to pause, to take a deep breath, trying not to bristle at his words. Because, after all, it wasn't *his* decision to tell me who I could or who I could not see. But I was trying to play the long-game here.

My tongue felt slimy when I looked over at him, held his gaze, and forced the words that felt so wrong to say. "Thank you for letting me see Mira," I said, not sure if my tone came out as sharp as it seemed to my own ears.

In what was probably a good move for keeping the peace, Primo didn't tell me I was welcome. Instead, he shrugged and shot me a smirk. "She was, ah, determined."

"Was Vissi still intact after the elevator ride down?" I asked. "He called her 'Sunshine' when he came back to pick her up."

"Can't imagine that went over well," he said, coming up to the kitchen island, watching me with those dark, unreadable eyes of his.

"It did not," I said, shaking my head.

"How come Mira isn't in the Family?" Primo asked, coming around the island to grab a cup of coffee while I fiddled with the garlic bread.

"I don't think it was, you know, an option."

"Because she's a woman," Primo concluded, leaning against the counter, watching me as I went to the stove to stir the pasta.

"Yeah. I mean, I guess. Lorenzo Costa hasn't been in power for that long. And before him, his father was, you know…"

"A waste of flesh?" Primo supplied, making my brows pinch.

"If you hated him so much, why were you so resistant to Lorenzo taking over?"

"My resistance wasn't to the man himself, but his policies that clearly favored the Costa, Morelli, and D'Onofrio Families while leaving the Espositos and Lombardis with shitty deals."

"Why couldn't you have just explained that?" I asked.

"I did. Many times. In detail. But Lorenzo is a stubborn fucking ass. Must be a Costa trait," he added, eyes bright.

"Right. Because you are *so* flexible," I shot back, rolling my eyes.

The Woman with the Ring

"It's not something I'm known for, no," he agreed. "But I'm working on it," he added, looking at me.

"Will I be able to see Mira again?" I asked, glancing over at him, not realizing how close he was as I stirred the sauce.

That strange, heated sensation spreading through my system, it had to be from the steaming pots. It was the only thing that made sense.

"That depends," Primo said, voice low, smooth.

"On?" I asked.

Why the hell did I sound so breathless?

"Did she lend you some sort of device to kill me with?" he asked, lips twitching.

"Don't be silly," I said, reaching for the giant knife I'd been using to cut up the vegetables and making a show of wiping off the side with my fingertip. "I'm sure if I wanted a weapon to use against you, I wouldn't need any help finding it."

And that?

That did something that almost seemed impossible.

It got a low, deep chuckle out of him.

"You realize you just threatened a boss, right?" he asked, putting down his coffee cup.

"What are you going to do? Send me into the ocean with cement stilettos?" I asked, smirking over at him.

"Careful with that sass, lamb," he said, voice getting rough.

Why did that sound send a shiver through my insides?

"Lamb," I scoffed, even if a little part of me did sort of appreciate the nickname. A lifetime of 'babe' had me enjoying anything with a little more originality. Even if he'd first said it in a pretty terrible way.

"You can scoff all you want, Isabella," he said, leaning a little closer. "But you've got a shit poker face. You like it when I call you that."

"You're ridiculous," I declared, but made sure my focus was on the food and not on him.

"Try saying that again," he demanded, grabbing my wrist, forcing the spoon out of it, then pulling it down, and reaching with his other hand to force my chin up and over to look at him. "To my face this time," he added, voice hardly more than a dark whisper.

My chin jerked up a little higher.

"You're ridiculous," I told him, keeping eye contact even when something in his gaze told me I should look away.

"You know there are *bosses* in this world who would never say something like that to me."

"Maybe you should have married one of them then," I said, watching as he tried to keep his lip from twitching at those words.

I was sure for one breath-stealing moment that he was going to kiss me.

But then, just as suddenly as he'd grabbed me, he released me.

"What are you making?" he asked, motioning around.

"Sausage, peppers, and onions on pasta with garlic bread and a salad."

"Is everything done?" he asked, making me gesture around to my three active prep stations. "Put me to work then," he demanded, pulling off his cufflinks then rolling up his sleeves.

I put him on the salad so I could focus on my task. It was a simple thing. But my gaze kept slipping to him as he chopped the lettuce, radicchio, tomatoes, onions, Pepperoncini peppers, and olives. I told myself it was to make sure he wasn't screwing anything up. But I hardly even noticed what he was putting in the bowl because my gaze was focused almost exclusively on the man's hands and forearms, watching at the way his muscles and tendons flexed.

I did not—absolutely did not—think about how those hands and arms would look when they were doing another, very distinctive motion between my thighs.

Ugh.

What the hell was wrong with me?

"Baby?" Primo called, making my gaze shoot up.

"Huh?"

"Called you three times," Primo told me, lips curved upward a bit at one side.

"Oh, sorry. I was, ah, worrying about your fingers," I told him, trying to make it sound the least bit convincing.

"How so?"

"You know... because you chop so fast," I lied.

"Are you sure you were worrying about my fingers, and not thinking about my fingers inside your pussy again?" he asked, making my sex clench hard at the memory.

"Why... why would I want to think about that?" I asked, turning toward the stove as I said it so he couldn't see what I was thinking.

It wasn't until I'd dumped the pasta into the strainer that I realized he'd abandoned his post making his salad, and had crossed the space to come up behind me.

"Because, lamb," he said, his front pressing into my back as his hands grabbed the counter on either side of my body, trapping me in, "you might have put on a good act afterward, but I know you've been thinking about me making you come every day since then."

"No, I..." I started, but lost my sentence as Primo leaned down further, his face in my neck, his warm breath on my skin.

"No?" he asked, and I could feel his lips on me as he spoke.

That time, the shiver wasn't just inside.

My whole body trembled.

Which made one of those low, sexy chuckles move through Primo again.

"Primo, I have to finish dinner," I told him, hearing the breathlessness in my own voice, knowing there was no way he missed it.

"Fuck dinner," he said as his hand slid off the counter and across my lower stomach.

In one move, he flicked open the fly of my pants and plunged his hand inside, his fingers stroking up my cleft.

"Already wet for me, hm, baby?" he asked, voice a smooth sound that washed over me, making me helpless but to lean back into him as his thumb found my clit. "Good, hm?" his voice rumbled as my head fell back onto his chest and a low, throaty whimper escaped me. "More?" he asked as two of his fingers drifted downward to tap at the entrance to my body.

"Yes," I moaned as my hips wiggled against his touch, demanding more.

And just like that, his fingers slid inside me as a little growling sound vibrated through Primo's chest as my walls tightened around him, pulled him in.

His fingers were slow and gentle at first, teasing me, driving me crazy, hinting at fulfillment, but making it clear he was going to drag it out first.

"I bet you're thinking about my cock in—"

I was barely cognizant of the beeping sound. A part of me was so far gone that I thought it was possibly the sausage in the oven. In which case, I was willing to let them stay in and dry out if I got relief from the clawing need for release growing inside me.

But I knew the moment I felt Primo stiffen and slip his fingers not only out of my pussy but my pants as a whole that it wasn't the oven.

Which left... the elevator.

"I'm sorry to break it to you, Izzy, but they didn't have the dessert... oh, hey, Primo," Dulles said, sounding surprised to see his brother there. "Am I interrupting something?" he asked, making Primo move away from me.

"No, I was telling my wife that she's supposed to save some of the pasta water to put inside the sauce," Primo said, making me stiffen as I turned, not knowing if my cheeks were flushed, but figuring Dulles would blame anger or the heat in the kitchen if they were.

"And I was just about to tell him that I already put the pasta water in the sauce. Honestly," I mumbled to myself, a little riled even though I was aware that Primo was just trying to create a cover, "like I haven't been making sauce since I was in elementary school," I said, moving the strained pasta into the pot. "Thinking I need cooking advice," I grumbled, wiping the drips of water from the colander off the counter.

"The bakery didn't have the Pear Almond Cake," Dulles said, looking uncomfortable, thinking he was interrupting yet more tension between his brother and me. "But I got Lemon Ricotta Cake with Almonds instead. Figured it was better than nothing," he added, shrugging. "Smells good in here," he told me, making my lips quirk up.

Because if there was one thing I knew about Italian men it was that they were always hungry.

"Do you want to stay for dinner, Dulles?" I asked, watching Primo's brow raise. Like he wasn't happy I hadn't consulted him. But in all the households I knew, the wives never asked the husbands if they could invite a hungry family member to share a table for dinner. That was just what you did. You offered food. It was our way of showing love.

"I haven't eaten," Dulles admitted.

"Then it's settled. You'll stay. Your brother will set you a place," I added, watching as Primo's lips twitched.

"Oh, I will, will I?" he asked.

"You will," I said, nodding, getting a snorting laugh from him.

And then this man, a mafia don, hopped to and set a place at the table for his brother.

I was still kind of riding that high, mingled with the one from all the praise I'd gotten for my dinner, when Dulles eventually headed out.

"Come get ready for bed," Primo demanded as I washed what felt like the fiftieth pot from dinner. But his words, and the insinuation beneath them, made my belly shiver in anticipation.

"I can't go to bed with a full sink," I admitted. "I won't be able to sleep," I told him.

"Alright," Primo said, shrugging, and heading up toward the bedroom.

I made my way up twenty minutes later, going into the bathroom to find him already standing there, shaping up the scruff on his face.

It felt weird to go through my evening routine in the same bathroom as someone else. Even when I'd partially lived with men in the past, we'd always just taken turns in the bathroom. Probably because New York bathrooms were usually barely big enough for one person to move around, let alone two.

But with a bathroom nearly as big as my old living room, I figured there was no reason to waste time twiddling my thumbs when I could have gotten started on my skincare.

I was on step two—my vitamin c serum—when we heard it.

A crash.

Glass breaking.

Below us somewhere, but it was impossible to tell how far below, if it was in our apartment or one of the lower floors where Primo's work operation took place.

My gaze shot to Primo's whose jaw went tight as he immediately dropped the razor, reaching instead for his gun that he had hanging in the holster along with his jacket on a hook behind the door.

"Here," he said, grabbing it, and coming back to me.

"No. You need it," I said, shaking my head.

I couldn't claim to be super comfortable with guns. Sure, I'd been around them my whole life, but I'd always been really thankful that I hadn't ever needed to use one myself.

"Isabella, you need to take this. Go into the closet. And if anyone comes in that isn't me, you shoot them, got it?" he asked, voice firm, commanding.

"I..."

"Do you know how to use it?"

"Y...yes," I said, nodding a little frantically, the adrenaline making my insides feel shaky.

"Good. Get in the closet. Use it if you need to. And, baby, if someone gets in here past me, you need to, okay?"

"Okay," I agreed.

"Closet," he demanded, voice a little softer than usual, picking up on my panic. "Now, lamb," he added, tone firmer. Because he knew he needed to get down there, had to see what was going on.

"Okay," I agreed, walking on numb legs into the closet, hearing him already closing the bathroom door, then rummaging around in the bedroom, likely getting another gun since he'd given me his own.

I didn't, as I probably should have, find myself going into my side of the closet to sit amongst the things that belonged to me.

No.

For reasons I didn't really understand, I turned into Primo's closet, walking along the lines of suits, and climbing in the small space between his shoe cabinet and the wall, the long legs of his pants falling in front of me like a curtain.

It smelled like him in there, like the spicy cologne and body wash he used. I found myself taking deep breaths, breathing him in, somehow finding that the scent eased the frantic slamming of my heartbeat in my chest.

Time slowed down when you were scared.

It was one of nature's cruel jokes, I guess.

It dragged out the suspense and the uncertainty, giving your body a chance to really get worked up.

And mine did.

See, I'd lived a relatively safe life, considering my connection to the Costa Family.

Sure, there were issues with other organizations or even in-fighting at times. But the women and children had always been relatively insulated from it all. Especially when we moved out to live our own lives.

I was suddenly kicking myself for spending the last week being pissy and distant when I really should have been spending it trying to get to know more about the Esposito Family now that I was a part of it.

My brother and cousins had always considered the Espositos and Lombardis some of the most volatile of the Five Families. If there were going to be bouts of violence, chances were that it involved one of those two Families more so than the other three.

And instead of getting to know what those threats might be, how often they could be expected to take place, and what the risks were to me now that I was married to the boss, I'd been shopping and moping and avoiding my husband.

Smart.

Really smart.

And now there might very well be a serious threat, and I was sitting in a closet like it was any sort of protection against an invader bent on hurting the Esposito Family. Maybe even using me to do so.

I mean, sure, I had a gun.

And I was terrified enough to use it.

But even if I did, even if I killed one guy who showed up to hurt me, what were the chances that I could get away?

I mean, like Primo said, if anyone showed up other than him, I needed to shoot my way out. Well, if they got past Primo, that meant he was dead or taken. As were his guards. So even if I killed the one guy who came looking for me, there would be others.

A low whimper escaped me.

I hated myself for it, but I couldn't seem to keep it in, either.

See, I'd been scared when I'd been taken, when hands grabbed me off the street and shoved me in a van to some unknown fate. I'd been scared of the prospect of being married to a man like Primo.

But those fears paled in comparison to the fear that was gripping my system as I sat in that closet with my mind running away with me.

If something happened to Primo and his guys, even if I managed to get away from the infiltrators, I was all alone in a borough that I knew nothing about, with no friends or family nearby, no cell phone, and no cash or cards since

Primo's brothers usually carried those around until—they claimed—my new one with my name came in the mail.

I mean, sure, I could try to find someone to help me. But I didn't have a lot of faith in that idea seeing as this neighborhood had witnessed my initial kidnapping and had done nothing to stop it.

And, yes, the tried and true method is to run to the police station. But I had no idea where that was. I had a vague memory of passing it while running errands with Dawson and Dulles, but I couldn't retrace the streets in my head.

If I survived this, I was going to demand to have a map and to have the guys show me around the area until I could commit some important places to memory.

I placed the gun down on the floor right at my side, drying my sweaty palms on my shirt before reaching for it again.

It felt like it was taking entirely too much time to investigate a little crashing noise.

But then, I heard a horrific sound.

Gunshots.

The steady pop-pop-pop followed by an eerie silence.

And then not a few moments later, footsteps.

Coming up the stairs.

My stomach twisted into a painful knot as my breath seemed to shake through my chest as I pulled my legs in tighter and tighter to my chest, terrified of being seen.

If it was Primo, he would be calling for me, right? So I didn't accidentally shoot him when he came in?

Shit.

Shit shit shit.

The footsteps came up the stairs at a jog, then moved through the bedroom.

I was pretty sure my entire body was shaking violently at that point before I heard the opening and closing of cabinets.

Cabinets?

Were they looking for something?

What the hell would Primo keep in the bathroom cabinets?

Well, I guess, it was a place most people wouldn't look, right? Like a children's bedroom. Or in the pet supplies. No one stores valuables there.

Except, maybe Primo did. And maybe he had some kind of leak in the organization, and someone else found out about it.

If they were in the bathroom, though, it meant that Primo was either dead or incapacitated.

And we were going to go ahead and pretend that the thought of that didn't make my stomach twist painfully, hard enough that my free hand moved there, pressing against my belly like I could rub away the ache.

I didn't have time to analyze that right that moment, though. If something had happened to Primo and his brothers and his men, that was out of my hands.

What was in my hands, though, was my own life.

And I was going to do whatever it took to make it out of this situation.

If that meant using the Costa name to garner some fear in Primo's enemies, or if it meant shooting my way out.

Whatever it took.

I'd been through just enough shit beyond my will. I would be damned if I endured anything else.

Decision made, I rose up slowly, silently, and made my way across the floor of the walk-in.

Taking a slow, deep breath that burned through my chest, I raised my arm, aimed the gun, and stepped into the doorway of the bathroom.

To find freaking *Primo* standing there, flicking on the water.

My gaze slid to those hands, watching as the blood swirled off of them and into the drain, getting diluted to a pink before it slid down the drain.

My head snapped up again.

He must have seen a movement in the mirror, or simply sensed me there, because his head turned toward me, eyes dark, intense.

"Good girl, lamb," he said, nodding. "You do what you gotta do," he added, looking back down at his hands as he scrubbed at the blood.

"You were just going to let me sit in that closet sick to my stomach that I was going to be raped and murdered while you *washed your hands*?" I hissed, lowering the gun to my side, realizing I was somehow shaking harder than I'd been in the closet when I was scared for my life.

Primo ignored that as he left the water on, but brought his hands to his shirt, flicking the buttons open.

I felt an involuntary spasm of anticipation before he was shrugging off his shirt, tossing it to the side, and I realized what was more pressing than telling me I was safe.

The gaping hole in his side.

"Oh, my God," I gasped, momentarily frozen as I stared at the bullet hole on his hip just above the waistband of his pants. *"OhmyGod,"* I hissed, my gaze shooting up to his face, finding his gaze on me.

"It's fine, lamb. Go on and get to bed."

"It's *fine*?" I said, waving a hand toward his body. "A gaping hole in your body is *fine*? You need to go to the hospital."

"Hospitals mean questions. Which I can't answer right now."

"Why not? Someone tried to break into your home."

"My home, Isabella, where we pack meat with drugs and ship them across the country. Committing federal crimes," he reminded me.

"But... but... don't you have, I don't know, doctors?" I asked, putting the gun down, feeling a little queasy as my gaze slid down to the wound again. "Or like vets or something that you blackmail into helping you?"

"Been watching too many mobster movies, baby," he said, shaking his head."

"How are you so calm right now? You have a hole in your body, Primo."

"It's not the first time I've been shot," he told me, shrugging it off as though past experience with pain meant he couldn't possibly be in pain currently.

"It still hurts," I insisted.

"Worried about me, lamb?" he asked with a devilish smirk toying at his lips.

"More worried than you were about me," I grumbled to myself, forgetting that Primo had the hearing of a dog.

"I took a bullet protecting you tonight, Isabella," he told me, voice low.

"You took a bullet to protect yourself, your Family, and your drug empire," I shot back, chin jerking up.

I guess whatever control he had over himself to stay so calm snapped at that moment, because he stormed across the space between us, paying absolutely no mind to the hole in his torso that had to be killing him, coming right up to me, and grabbing the back of my neck hard, yanking me almost up against him by it.

"Make no mistake," he growled in a voice that had no right to be sexy when it was so clearly pissed at me, but there was no way to deny it, either, "I protect what is mine."

"I'm not your fucking poss—"

I didn't get to finish that sentence.

Because I suddenly found myself yanked firmly against him as his lips crashed down on mine. Hard, borderline punishing. His lips bruised into mine as his fingers crushed into my skull.

And what did I do?

Did I bring up my hands between us, push against his chest, or even take a cheap shot and push around his injury to get him to release me?

No.

No, I did not do that.

My stupid, traitorous body sang at the contact.

A damn shudder moved through me at the feel of my soft curves crushing against his firm lines.

A low whimper escaped me, a sound that had Primo's hand softening on the back of my neck, fingertips massaging the bruises he'd no doubt left with the rough contact.

His lips softened a bit as well, but only a bit, going from punishing to passionate as he bent my head backward, lips slanting over mine again and again until my whole body flooded with desire, hummed with the need for more of it.

Primo's teeth nipped my lower lip, tugging, demanding entrance. With no choice, I granted him it, and his tongue slipped inside to claim mine.

Claimed.

That was exactly how I felt at that moment.

Like every bit of my desire, like every inch of my body, belonged to him.

My arm lifted, one hand drifting up his forearm, arm, and shoulder before sliding behind his neck, holding on as his lips slanted over mine and his hand left the back of my neck, slipping down my spine, then sinking into my ass, his grip firm and possessive, sending a jolt of desire between my thighs.

A moan moved through me as my back arched, pressing my breasts more firmly against him, a move that had a growl ripping through Primo's chest as he turned us and walked me backward until my legs slammed into the bathroom counter.

His greedy hands roamed up my stomach, grabbing my breasts through my shirt. Feeling the peaks of my breasts pebbling at his touch, he rolled them between his thumb and forefingers until I was whimpering and arching into his hands.

On an impatient growl, his hands left me, going down to my pants and panties, and pulling them down my legs.

I won't even pretend I hesitated in stepping out of them.

His lips broke from mine long enough for him to lean down, grabbing the backs of my knees, and lifting me off my feet, dropping my ass down on the cold bathroom counter.

I could barely even adjust to the new position before his hand was slipping between my thighs, sliding up my cleft, then working my clit with just the right amount of pressure.

Without even being aware of telling it to do so, my free hand moved down the center of his chest and abdomen, feeling the muscles twitch under the contact as I blazed a path downward.

My fingers impatiently worked his button and zipper free before slipping inside, running my palm over his hard cock straining against the material of his boxer briefs.

A rumbling noise moved through Primo's chest at the contact, making his fingers abandon my clit and thrust inside me again.

My mouth broke from his on a low moan as I leaned back, placing my arms on the counter behind me, angling up to look at him.

His dark eyes were heated, molten, and heavy-lidded with his own desire.

Inside me, his fingers hooked and stroked against my top wall, engaging my G-spot with expert precision.

At the sound of my needy whimper, a ghost of a smile tugged at the corners of his mouth. He gave me a little encouraging nod when my hand started to move up toward the waistband of his boxer briefs. I hesitated for the barest of seconds, and got to watch as an impatient muscle ticked in his jaw. Encouraged by his slipping self-control, my hand slid inside to close around his velvety soft, straining cock.

A shudder moved through me as my hand didn't quite close around him, realizing just how perfectly full he would fill me.

"Thinking about me in your tight pussy, lamb?" Primo asked, his voice a smooth sound that slithered across my nerve endings, making another involuntary tremble move through me. "Like this?" he asked, thrusting in and out of me. Slowly at first, then faster and faster as my walls tightened around his fingers. "Tell me," he demanded as his fingers started to twist inside me as he continued to thrust.

My finger swiped over the head of his cock, feeling the wetness there.

"Yes," I whimpered, taking a slow, deep breath as he drove me closer and closer to that edge.

"No, Isabella," he rumbled, his hand turning so his palm pressed against my clit as he continued to fuck me with his fingers. "Tell me," he demanded. When I looked up at him with uncertain eyes, his head tipped to the side, watching me as another finger slipped inside me, filling me a little more. "Tell me you want me to fuck your tight pussy," he demanded as he moved his fingers in circles inside me.

"I... I want you to fuck me," I told him. There was no denying it. There was time to think about what that meant, what the repercussions of this would be, some other time. Right then, I needed him inside me with the same sort of urgency that I needed my next breath.

"Good girl," he murmured, grabbing my chin with his fingers, pulling my head up higher as his head lowered down, his lips sealing over mine again as he started thrusting again.

My hand moved up and down his cock, driving him up with me, wanting him as far gone as I was.

It wasn't long before he was yanking his mouth away as his hand pushed mine away and off of him.

His hand went there instead as his fingers slid out of me. He urged my thigh upward as he pressed closer to me.

His cock stroked up and down my cleft several times, tapping the head against my throbbing clit, making a needy moan escape me.

The sound seemed to be his undoing.

His cock slipped down and slammed inside me, one hard, deep thrust, filling me completely, stretching me with just a pinch of discomfort.

"Fuck," Primo hissed, his fingers sinking into my hip as he froze inside me, buried impossibly deep.

He was looking for some sort of control.

But at that moment, I didn't want him to have that.

I wanted him as desperate for release as I felt.

My hips started moving in impatient circles, making me acutely aware of each thick inch of him.

Primo's head pulled back, watching me with those heavy-lidded eyes. I got to watch as his eyes closed a bit each time my hips rolled and my walls tightened around him.

"Primo, please," I whimpered, needing him to move, needing release from the aching desire inside. "Please," I begged again.

That seemed to break through.

Because he went from being completely still to fucking me in the span of a single breath.

There was nothing slow or sweet about it.

He fucked me.

Hard.

Fast.

Deep.

Taking every inch of me with each thrust.

My arms went up, wrapping around his shoulders, holding on as he fucked me harder and harder, the sounds of my moans, his groans and curses, and our bodies slamming together filled my ears.

"Don't stop," I cried, feeling pushed right toward that edge, and dying to be shoved over, to freewill into the orgasm. "Please don't stop," I pleaded as my face pressed into his chest.

"Come for me, lamb," he demanded, voice tight. "Come," he urged even as my walls started to spasm, even as the pleasure got a tight grip on my system.

I was pretty sure it was his name I cried out over and over as the first waves crashed through me, the intensity of which I wasn't even aware existed before.

"Fuck, Isabella," Primo groaned, thrusting through my orgasm, dragging it out, making it last, before finally slamming deep, his whole body jerking hard as he came.

The Woman with the Ring

I couldn't tell you how long I clung to him as the unexpected aftershocks racked my system, but by the time my brain seemed to kick back in.

Everything seemed to come at me at once.

I slept with Primo. Which absolutely would have an impact on our dynamic. I couldn't claim I didn't want him anymore. I couldn't keep throwing this forced marriage in his face if I clearly enjoyed being with him.

Second, I'd just let him fuck me without any protection. *Without protection.* I'd always been insanely careful about things like that. I took my Pill. I used condoms. Always. I'd literally never let someone have that level of intimacy with me before. Not only was that a huge deal to me, but I'd also, you know, been ripped from my life. Which meant I didn't have my Pills.

Oh, God.

Oh, *God*.

But even as those thoughts were crossing my mind, so was another one.

Primo was shot.

He was shot, and I could feel the hot, sticky blood from his wound moving down my side.

My hands pressed into his chest and pushed him backward.

"You're bleeding," I told him, feeling a little frazzled and overwhelmed and a little bit, well, horrified.

"And you're dripping with my come," he said, making my whole body jolt at his words.

"You're an asshole," I snapped, shoving him back a step so I could slip off the counter.

"Yeah, but you're the one who wants to fuck me," he agreed as I did a penguin waddle toward the shower. Thankfully, Primo was busy getting his cock back in his boxer briefs and pants, so he wasn't looking.

Reaching in, I turned the shower on full tilt before ripping off my shirt, and moving inside. Looking down, I could see his blood spread all over my stomach, hip, and thigh. I looked like a freaking crime scene.

I went right to scrubbing at the blood with the soap until all traces of it were off me before I even let my gaze slip back toward the rest of the bathroom.

And there was Primo, bent forward, looking down at his wound. One hand was placed over the top of it, stretching the skin taut, while the other hand reached for a long tweezer, and started to dig inside his wound.

My stomach roiled at the image, making my gaze slip away.

But even with my gaze averted, the image stayed in my mind, making me need to take slow, deep breaths, trying to fight back the bile that rose up my throat.

I was vaguely aware a moment later of a slight tinging sound, like the bullet dropping into the sink.

Which only managed to make another wave of nausea move through my system.

Not even a moment later, though, the shower door was opening, and I was all-too-aware of Primo moving into the space. Granted, it wasn't a normal shower; eight people probably could have stood in it comfortably. But I swear it felt like he was sucking up all the air as soon as he moved inside.

Or maybe that was just because I was starting to feel a little woozy from the whole fishing a bullet out of his own body thing.

"Is it the blood?" Primo asked a moment later, tone curious. To my surprise, there didn't seem to be even a hint of mocking even though I was pretty sure my entire face was green at that moment.

Swallowing hard, I told him, "It's the… the tweezers… and the… ugh," I grumbled, pressing a hand to my mouth, practically tasting the bile.

"Go," Primo said, tone surprisingly soft, at least for him. "Go to bed," he added.

"You have a hole in your stomach."

"I will have Vissi stitch it," Primo told me.

"Oh, God," I grumbled, not even bothering to turn off the shower head I was standing under as I rushed out of the enclosure.

I grabbed a towel and went into my walk-in closet for a moment, trying to get myself together. As soon as I was sure I could move around without getting sick, I slipped into some pajamas, and rushed through the bathroom to throw myself under the covers in the bed.

Normally, that would be my chance to overthink having sex with Primo, but it wasn't long before I heard Vissi come up and go into the bathroom. Where I knew he was going to take a needle and thread to Primo's skin without, you know, numbing agents or anything.

The thought of that kept me occupied with my nausea until, eventually, I passed out from all the events of the day.

12

Primo

My side hurt like a motherfucker.

Only an idiot decided to fuck their wife while they had a bullet wedged in their body and a gaping, bleeding hole around it.

That said, it was worth it.

Fuck, was it worth it.

And, hey, the pain helped me stay focused when every fiber of my being wanted to slam deep and come inside her within minutes of feeling her tight walls grabbing my cock.

I hadn't anticipated that all playing out when I made my way up the stairs to deal with the bullet wedged in my side. It wasn't the first time, and it probably wouldn't be the last, so fishing out a bullet wasn't the big deal it might have been for most people.

But then she'd come out of that closet, terrified, but ready to fight her way out of a bad situation if necessary, and I'd never really been more sure about my choice as I'd been at that moment.

Until a couple minutes later, of course, when she was begging for me to fuck her, when she was taking me inside her, when she was milking my orgasm from me with her own.

I'd fucked her raw.

I never did that shit.

Ever.

First, because you never wanted to catch anything. Second, I didn't want any unintentional babies. If I was going to have one, I wanted it to be right. With my wife.

And, I guess, that was why I hadn't paused to find a condom.

Because Isabella was my wife, even if she hadn't exactly been thrilled about that fact.

And, fuck, I thought sex was good before, but being able to come inside my woman? Yeah, that shit was next-level. It was such an intense feeling that anytime it even flashed across my mind afterward, I felt myself starting to get hard again.

So I had to stop letting my mind go there.

Because there was shit to be done.

Like getting the fucking wound stitched up which was every bit as unpleasant as it sounded. And then I had to get back down to my men to have a meeting.

I wasn't an idiot.

It wasn't just some neighborhood moron who got brave and tried to steal from me. Quite frankly, no one was that fucking stupid around here.

The problem was, I'd been acting out of a protective instinct, knowing Isabella was sitting in the closet terrified, instead of using my head, and making sure the fucker stayed alive for me to get answers out of.

I'd nearly severed his head from his fucking body with the knife I'd grabbed along with my gun. If it weren't for my brothers, I probably would have done it.

I wouldn't try to claim that I was the most even-tempered of men, but I wasn't typically someone who acted out with fits of uncontrolled violence, either. For me, violence was a tactic and it needed to be used, but carefully and wisely to bring about the result I wanted.

But this was the second time I'd raged out and acted like a lunatic.

And, it had to be said, both times were because of Isabella.

When the fucker touched her in the restaurant.

And when someone threatened her safety in her own home.

I couldn't say for certain where that overwhelming response came from. It wasn't like I was passionately in love with the woman. I didn't really even believe in that shit. But she was mine. And no one touched, threatened, or hurt what was mine.

"She's going to be pissed," Dulles told me early the next morning. None of us had actually gotten any sleep. We'd been up late checking the security cameras and trying to figure out who the shithead was that had tried to get into the building. Then, of course, I'd had to call all of my men individually to tell them shit was going down again. And as soon as the city started to wake up, I had to go down and have a chat with some of the people in the neighborhood.

The problem was, we'd all hit dead-end after dead-end.

We were no closer to figuring out who the bastard was or who he worked for than we were right after I'd killed him.

The Woman with the Ring

So I'd needed to come up with a new plan to make sure Isabella stayed safe while we figured it all out.

Dulles was right; she was going to be pissed.

"She doesn't usually sleep this late," Dawson added, frowning.

"Primo said she was sick after she saw him pull the bullet out of himself," Terzo said, shrugging.

I'd never actually seen someone look green before, but she sure as fuck had in that shower when I'd walked in.

"Yeah, said it wasn't the blood, just the whole digging the bullet out thing," I said, going over to make her a cup of coffee when I finally heard her moving around upstairs. I figured maybe a small kind gesture might soften the blow of what I had to tell her.

She came down a few minutes later with her hair piled on top of her head and fresh-faced, but dressed in blue skinny jeans and a heavy red sweater.

And fuck if she wasn't as beautiful right then as she'd been in her wedding dress. Or when she took time to get herself all dolled up.

"Oh, hey," she said, looking surprised to see my brothers and Vissi hanging around all at once. "Are you guys up early, or am I late?" she asked, accepting the coffee from me, but being careful not to let our fingers brush or our gazes meet.

"You're late," Terzo said, always surly. "We have to get moving," he added, looking at me. "Get it over with," he demanded, making his way toward the door.

No one spoke to me that way. Not even Terzo. But I was going to go ahead and blame it on the fact that he hadn't gotten any sleep. And since it was only our brothers and Vissi, who was practically a brother, around, I didn't have to worry about what anyone thought about it. We were all allowed to have a shit day here and there.

"Get what over with?" Isabella asked, but was looking at Dawson and Dulles as she did so.

Oh, this really wasn't going to go over well if she'd already decided she wasn't happy with me.

Oh, well.

It had to be done.

Whether she liked it or not.

"Giving you some news you're not going to like," Dulles said, getting up and whacking Dawson across the chest. The two of them started making their way toward the door.

"Chickenshits," Vissi mumbled under his breath, shooting me a smirk.

"What news am I not going to like?" Isabella asked, stiffening.

"We don't know who tried to break in here last night," I told her. "Well, we know who did, but we don't know who sent him."

"Oh, okay," she said, frowning. "That's it?" she asked, sensing that it wasn't.

"No, that's not it," I said, placing my mug down on the counter, internally bracing for her anger. "Until we figure out who it was and neutralize the threat, you are going to be confined to the loft."

"I... *what?*" she snapped, eyes flickering into fires in a blink.

"You heard me," I said, nodding. "It's not safe."

"It's not safe," she repeated. I might not have known everything about a woman's anger, but I did know that when they started repeating everything you said with absolute murder in their eyes, that shit was about to hit the fan.

"Are you allowed to leave?" she asked, chin arching up.

"Oh, shit. Okay. I'm just gonna..." Vissi said, pointing toward the door, then rushing off in that direction.

"Of course I can leave."

"Of course you can leave," Isabella parroted, raising her mug, and taking a slow sip. "And why is that, Primo?"

"Because I have business to conduct."

"Right. And I'm just the captive little housewife, right? Fucking asshole," she snapped, slamming her mug down on the island hard enough that I was surprised it didn't shatter. "You can't keep me a prisoner here," she said, waving around the loft.

"It's hardly a third-world jail cell, lamb."

"That's not the point!" she snapped.

"What is the point then?"

"That I'm fucking stuck here as it is," she said, wrapping her arms around herself. "In this place I don't know, around these people I don't know, not allowed to see or talk to my loved ones whenever I want. And now you're telling me you're going to narrow my world even more?"

"It's for your own safety."

"Yet you get to walk out there with a target on your head," she snapped, waving toward the windows.

"I'm going to go out there and find who this is, so I can deal with them, and your world can expand again."

"But until then, I'm your little captive, right? Can't go anywhere. Can't get the hell away from you."

"Seems I remember you liking being close to me," I said, watching as her eyes widened before she averted her gaze. "In fact," I started, taking steps toward her, knowing she was too damn stubborn to retreat, "I think you like me so close that I'm inside you," I reminded her, seeing the way her breathing went fast and shallow. She could pretend all she wanted that she didn't like me, that she didn't want me, but her body would betray her every single time.

"No," she said in a choked whisper.

"No?" I repeated. "So that wasn't your dripping wet pussy squeezing my cock last night?" I asked. "That wasn't you begging me to fuck you?" I went on. "Those weren't your thighs my come was dripping down either?"

She struggled for a moment, battling the desire growing in her body. In the end, though, her indignation over not being allowed to leave the apartment won out, and her head raised, her eyes shooting daggers at me.

"I hope you enjoyed that. Because it is never going to happen again," she told me, turning on her heel, and storming away.

I wanted to tell her that it absolutely was going to happen again. And often. In different locations. From different angles. I was going to learn every inch of her body, was going to find all her little hotspots, so I could use them to torture her with her need for release.

But it would only piss her off more to say it.

I could let her stew in her anger for a while.

I imagined she would be all the hotter for me if she was angry with me.

I was going to see for myself eventually.

But first, I had to figure out who was coming for my Family this week.

Then show them exactly why all the rumors about me being a ruthless monster were true.

13

Isabella

"What a joke," I grumbled, watching as Primo walked up the steps of the church across the street, going in for Sunday service like a good little observer of the Bible.

We were going on day six of me not being allowed to leave the apartment.

I never truly understood the concept of "cabin fever" before. But I was becoming intimately acquainted with it then.

See, I'd never truly been in the house for more than maybe two days in a row except that one time I had the flu, and my fever was so bad that I was delirious, so I wasn't even aware of the passing of time.

Life made it impossible not to leave the house.

In my old life, I had to work. I had errands. I had a demanding family who wanted to see me frequently.

But I didn't have to work anymore. The groceries were delivered by Primo's brothers. And I wasn't allowed to see my family.

So there was no reason I had to leave the building.

Except, of course, the fact that I was going absolutely insane.

That seemed dramatic. I mean, wasn't six days at home with absolutely no responsibilities the dream for most people? And here I was, annoyed about it. But the difference was, this hadn't been a choice I'd made. It was something that was forced on me because of some ridiculous notion Primo got in his head about me not being safe, even if I never went anywhere without his brothers as bodyguards.

Meanwhile, his carefree ass got to go to church with the rest of the neighborhood, putting on the mask of "one of the good guys" while he kept the wife he'd acquired through force locked up in the building across the street.

Yeah, he was a real prince, that one.

Luckily for me, he'd been busy the past week. Doing what, I had no idea. But it didn't matter. All that mattered was he wasn't around pestering me, saying things he had no business saying to my body that hadn't exactly gotten the memo that I decided to be right back to hating him.

Oh, and to add to the column of good things, the day he told me I was now a prisoner in a fancy jail, I'd also managed to get my period. I guess the rough sex had brought it on early. And thank God because I'd woken up still sick to my stomach that morning and all I could hear was my mom's voice in my head as she said she knew it the next morning that she was pregnant with each of us because she was immediately nauseated in the mornings.

But, yeah, that was one crisis averted and over with. Though a part of me was wondering if maybe it wouldn't have been good to actually be pregnant from that bathroom session because then it would be over with. Primo would have his heir. And I would never have to let him touch me again.

Plus, you know, I'd get to be a mom. Which was something I'd always wanted. Even if I did have to share the baby with Primo.

At least it would give my floundering life a little purpose now that I had no job and no family to fill my days.

Oh, well.

It was an opportunity lost, regardless.

Aunt Flo had come and gone, so there was no baby in my immediate future.

Which meant that I would have to sleep with Primo again in the future.

My stupid body thrilled at the idea, making me let out a whimper as I bumped my forehead against the wall beside the windows to the street.

Not only was I going stir crazy in the apartment, but I felt like a freaking wild animal in heat. I'd always figured I had an average enough sex drive. But all of a sudden, I literally couldn't think about anything else.

I tried to convince myself it was because I had nothing else going on. I couldn't fool myself completely, though. And the hard truth was, despite how I felt about him on a personal level, my stupid body craved Primo. Especially now that I'd gotten a taste of what he had to offer sexually.

"Ahem," a voice said, making me jolt and turn.

Because it wasn't one of Primo's brothers.

No.

It was a female voice.

"Sorry, didn't mean to startle you," she said, giving me a tight smile as I took in the woman standing in the living room.

She was pretty. Tall, lithe, with blonde hair and blue eyes, and wearing a long-sleeved button-up shirt and a skirt.

"I'm Cassidy," she said, as if that meant something to me. At my blank look, she added, "The housekeeper."

Oh.

Okay.

Yeah, I knew she showed up on occasion. But in the past, it always seemed to happen when I was out with Primo's brothers.

Now that I was in lockdown for who knew how long, I guess I would run into her on occasion. Which felt really awkward. Who wanted to stand around while someone else cleaned their house?

"Oh, right," I said, nodding, starting to smile before some other thoughts started to form.

Like what kind of housekeeper came to work in a skirt?

The kind that wanted to fuck your husband, that's who.

I already knew from Primo himself that this Cassidy woman sucked him off whenever he wanted a release. Clearly, though, she wanted it to be more than just time on her knees.

He was a *married man.*

It didn't matter that it was a sham of a marriage. It didn't matter that I wasn't a willing participant in it. What mattered was it was an undeniable fact that Primo was my husband. And this bitch still thought she would put any part of her body on his.

I didn't like to think of women in derogatory terms.

And the vast majority of the time, if your man cheated, the woman he cheated with likely had no idea that you even existed. So you couldn't even be angry with her.

Every once in a while, though, there was a case where the woman knew. And just didn't care. Didn't have enough respect not to put her hands on someone who belonged to someone else.

And that was, well, a bitch.

Because no one deserved to be cheated on.

Not even me with my bullshit marriage.

"Well," I said, waving around as I went to grab my cup of coffee, "don't let me get in your way. Oh, and the cabinets could use to be cleaned out and scrubbed."

Was my tone set pretty firmly at Ice-Queen-Level? Yes. Yes, absolutely. Judging by the spark of anger I saw in her pretty blue eyes, she wasn't happy about me being there. Or about me making demands on her. In my own goddamn house. Where she was supposed to be working. And not on her knees or her back.

Before I could get any more irritated, I took myself upstairs to get myself dressed. A part of me wondered why the hell I bothered to get out of my pajamas at all, let alone put on makeup, and especially slipping heels on my feet. It wasn't looking like I would be able to go anywhere for a good, long while. Maybe it was silly, but taking time to put myself together gave my days at least a little structure. If I got myself dressed for the day, then I had to get myself undressed later, taking off my makeup, getting into new pajamas. It would be too easy to fall into depression if I didn't put a little effort in.

I went ahead and admitted to myself that I'd chosen a skintight wine-red sweater dress that dipped a little low in the bodice even if the skirt skimmed the middle of my calves simply because I wanted to look good in front of the woman who was okay with being a homewrecker.

I also slipped on the expensive gold earrings I'd bought on Primo's dollar. I spritzed on my perfume, and even strapped on some heels.

By the time I'd finished, I could hear Primo's voice on the floor below.

Reaching up, I mussed my hair, took one more look at my outfit, then made my way out of the bedroom, then down the stairs.

From the top landing, I could see Primo sitting on the couch in the living room. And despite all the cookware being all over the island in the kitchen, suggesting she hadn't finished with the cabinets, where was Cassidy? Bending forward over the coffee table "dusting it off." Which, last time I'd dusted it, didn't require quite as much jiggling as she was doing.

I tried to tell myself that it wasn't jealousy or possessiveness that was gripping my system right then, but righteous indignation at being disrespected in my own home.

I had to put up with a lot of shit from Primo.

But I would be damned if I put up with it from anyone else.

Primo's gaze lifted at the sound of my heels on the steps. Even from across the room, I could see—hell, I could *feel*— his gaze moving over me, a slow and thorough once-over that only made its way back to my face when I made it to the bottom landing.

It was then that Cassidy went ahead and straightened as to not to so blatantly attempt to entice my husband right in front of me.

"Oh, you're home," I said, forcing a fake smile as I made my way across the living room, watching as Primo's brows drew together in confusion since I'd done nothing but snarl and scowl at him since he'd told me about my new prison sentence. "I'm so disappointed I couldn't come, but I understand you're trying to keep me safe," I said, walking right up to him, and dropping my ass into his lap.

"The fuck is this?" Primo whispered, but his arm immediately went around me, wrapping around my back with his hand settling at the very low part of my stomach as I leaned my side into his chest.

"Did you miss me?" I asked, tone full-on coquettish as I ran my fingers up and down his tie as I actually fluttered my lashes at him.

I won't lie. I got more pleasure than I probably should have at the confusion on Primo's face. What can I say? I had to get my kicks somewhere. And shocking a mafia boss was surprisingly entertaining.

I glanced back over Primo's shoulder like I was noticing the mess in the kitchen for the first time, then rested my head on Primo's shoulder as I looked over at Cassidy.

"Was there a problem with the cabinets, Candy?" I asked, deliberately screwing up her name. Because girls like her hated to be forgettable.

"Oh, ah, no. I was letting them dry," she claimed, looking uncomfortable. "But, ah, they should be dry now," she said, turning and rushing off.

It was right about then that Primo seemed to register what was going on.

An amused smile tugged at his lips.

"Jealous, baby?" he asked, brow quirking up.

"I thought we covered this," I told him, tone icy again. "I better not have something to be jealous about. Or you won't have to worry about *outside* threats on your life," I told him as I sat up, but didn't move off his lap because I really wanted to drive it home to Cassidy that Primo was mine and mine alone, even if I didn't want him that way. Or, more accurately, I didn't want to want him that way.

"Gave you my word on that," he told me, voice firm.

"And yet I walk out to her shaking her tits at you," I said, chin jerking up.

"I think I like possessiveness on you, lamb," he said, eyes bright.

"I'm not possessive of you," I scoffed. "I don't like anyone thinking they can disrespect me like that in my own home."

In the kitchen, Cassidy was slamming around as she put all the pots and pans back before I could hear her running the sink to, I imagine, load the dishwasher.

"Didn't think about it like that," Primo admitted, nodding. "She'll be gone tomorrow."

A part of me wanted to insist that he didn't have to do that. I didn't exactly like the idea of being the reason someone lost a job they were probably relying on. But then again, you shouldn't get to keep a job when you were being inappropriate either.

So I went ahead and decided to be okay with it.

"Good," I said, nodding. "What are you doing?" I asked as Primo's fingers started to slide up the skirt of my dress up over my calves.

"Got all dressed up for me, hm?" he asked, and I tried to pretend my belly wasn't fluttering as I felt his fingertips tracing the side of my knee, then my thigh, as he continued to move the material upward.

"Absolutely not," I said, hoping my voice didn't sound as breathless as I felt.

"No one else here to see you," he told me, voice a low, smooth sound that I swear felt like it washed over me even as his fingertips grazed my inner thigh.

I should have been telling him to stop.

But those words refused to move from my brain to my lips.

"I dress for myself, not for you," I insisted, trying to hold onto a small shred of pride even as my damn traitorous thighs spread a little for his explorative fingers.

"Oh, that's right," he said, eyes molten. "You *un*dress for me," he said.

And I would have objected, jumped up, gotten the hell away from him for that.

But the second he said it, his fingers were pressing against my panties.

Suddenly, not even my pride mattered anymore as his thumb sought and found the bud of my clit through the barely-there material, and started working it in slow, practiced circles.

"You..." I started, sucking in a deep breath at the sensation.

"I, what?"

"Can't," I choked out.

"Seems like I can, lamb," he said, pressing a little more firmly. "And it seems like you like it," he added, lips close to my ear. "Your pussy is already dripping for me, and I've barely touched you," he went on.

I wanted to deny it.

But it was true.

Whether it was logical or not, my body was aching for his touch, was throbbing with the need for release. And his fingers hadn't even slipped under my panties yet.

Even as I thought that, though, his hand shifted up and dipped under the material. A soft gasp escaped me as he traced between my lips, circling around, but refusing to touch my clit.

His gaze was fixed on me the whole time, dark and penetrative, heavy-lidded with his own growing desire.

"Shh," he murmured when he thrust two fingers suddenly inside me and a choked whimper escaped me.

His other hand moved up, pressing my head down on his shoulder, and holding me tight against him so my lips were on his neck, muffling the sounds as his fingers started to fuck me.

"Haven't been able to stop thinking about this pussy in a week," he told me as my hips started to rock against his thrusts. "Been waking up every morning fucking aching to be inside you again," he went on.

They weren't love words.

Not by a long shot.

But my damn heart still managed to start fluttering in my chest at them.

"You've been missing my cock too." It wasn't a question. And a part of me wanted to object, but I knew it wouldn't come out even halfway truthful since I knew he was right. "You moan out my name when you're sleeping," he added, making a flush break out across my face, neck, and chest at the idea. "Took more self-control than I thought I even had not to press you back and wake you up with the cock you were begging for," he added, thrusting a little faster with his fingers.

Feeling his cock pressing against me, I shifted my legs out of the way so my hand could slip down and massage the head of him through his pants.

Primo's sharp indrawn breath was all the encouragement I needed as my hand moved up, working his button and zipper free, then reaching inside to wrap around his bare cock, finding him heavy and straining for more contact.

And at that moment, I didn't care about keeping up pretenses, about not letting him know how desperate I was for him, despite my better judgement.

So I stroked him to the rhythm that his fingers were fucking me.

"I need to fuck you," Primo growled as his fingers twisted inside me, stroking against my top wall, the sensation making my whole body jolt.

"We can't," I said, still vaguely aware of Cassidy loading the dishwasher not too far from us.

I should have been horrified at the idea of being caught doing something so intimate with someone. But a petty little part of me almost wanted her to look, wanted her to see Primo finger-fucking me, see me stroking him, see all the things she would never get to experience with him.

"The fuck we can't," Primo responded, voice tight as my thumb traced the head of his cock.

"Not until she..." I started to say, breaking off on a muffled whimper as his fingers started to tap against my G-spot.

"Cassidy, wrap it up and head out," Primo called, and I was sure he could feel the smile on the lips I had pressed into his neck. My palm tightened around his cock even as my walls tightened around his fingers, something that made a growl move through him. "Actually, just head out now," he called, tone dismissive.

There was an angry slamming in the kitchen along with no small amount of huffing and mumbling under her breath before I heard her moving toward the door, then slamming it hard for good measure.

The second she was gone, Primo was pulling his fingers out of me, then grabbing me with both hands, adjusting me up onto his lap before yanking up the skirt of my dress, and ripping off my panties in an impatient and primal move that had my belly fluttering.

"Ride me," he demanded, fisting his cock and rubbing it roughly up and down between my lips, tapping against my clit, then holding it at the entrance to my body. "Fucking ride me, Isabella," he growled, bucking upward even as I sank down on him, too far gone to even care about the consequences, just needing to feel him fill me, stretch me.

A low, long moan escaped me as my hips dropped down on his lap, taking a moment to feel him.

On an impatient grumble, Primo's hands moved out, grabbing the already low neckline of my dress, and yanking it down, then pulling it down my arms for good measure, only leaving me dressed in the midsection. His hands went behind my back, working the clasps of my bra free, then pulling it off, and tossing it impatiently to the floor.

He sucked in a slow, deep breath that made his chest shake as his gaze landed on my chest that somehow felt heavier and heavier under his inspection.

I expected for his hands to reach out, to squeeze and tease.

But his arm closed around my back instead, holding my weight as he leaned me backward so he could lean in and suck one of my nipples into his mouth.

A surprised gasp escaped me as I arched up into his lips that were sucking hard for a moment before his teeth started to nip.

His free hand moved up, closing over my other breast, tracing my nipple, then rolling it between his thumb and forefinger.

Impatient, needing relief from the clawing ache between my thighs, my hips started to rock against him. It was a small, barely-there movement, but his cock was positioned just right to stroke against my top wall, engaging my G-spot as my hips moved against him.

A groan moved through Primo, vibrating against my nipple before he was releasing it, going across my chest to continue the torment.

"Primo," I whimpered as the frustration at the lack of movement grew by the second. "Primo, please," I said, hands grabbing his shoulders, pushing until he moved to sit back against the cushions. "I need..." I started.

"This?" he asked, starting to piston his hips up into me.

Fast.

God, so fast.

"Yes, that," I moaned, rolling my hips in circles as he continued to fuck me, driving me up toward that cliff faster than seemed possible. "I'm..." I started, voice catching on a groan.

"Come," he demanded. "Come for me," he continued. "I need to feel you squeeze my cock."

His hips thrust.

Mine rolled.

And I just freaking shattered apart, a moan interrupted by the fact that it suddenly seemed impossible to draw in a breath as the waves crashed through my system again and again, dragged out as Primo kept thrusting through it.

"You feel so fucking good," Primo growled as I fell forward into him, clinging to him as the last few hard spasms moved through me. "I'm not done, lamb," he said, voice sounding something like a warning as his hands grabbed me and tossed me across the couch.

He grabbed my ankles, yanking my legs upward to rest against his chest, pinning them against him with his forearm as he surged inside me again.

Hard.

That was how he fucked me then.

Not fast and frantic.

Hard and controlled, taking every last inch of me with each powerful thrust.

His free hand moved down, pressing hard on my lower stomach, making me feel him even more intensely inside me as he fucked me.

"You gonna come again for me?" he asked, voice rough.

"I... can't..." I claimed, even as I felt the need growing again.

"You can. You will," he added as his hand left my belly to press between my thighs, engaging my clit as he kept fucking me.

He proved me wrong.

Not only could I, but I could hard, and way, way too fast.

I should have needed more recovery time. I always had in the past. But Primo was proving me wrong about a lot of things I previously believed about myself.

"Still not done," he informed me as I finally came back down from the second soul-shattering orgasm.

"Primo, please," I whimpered, feeling unusually overwhelmed and fragile right then. "I can't... it's too much," I added, trying to suck in slow, deep breaths, trying to pull myself back together.

"Shh," he said, reaching for me, pulling me up as he dropped down onto his ass, pulling me over him, but with my back against his chest, straddling his legs backward. "Stop overthinking it," he demanded as he grabbed his cock and started rubbing it against my clit, side to side, over and over. "Just feel it," he added as his cock slid down and pressed inside me.

Slowly.

God, so slowly.

I felt every last inch of him against my overly sensitive walls, a sensation that was almost pain, but not quite.

Primo's arm anchored around the center of my chest, holding me against him as his other hand grabbed my chin, pulling, turning me just enough for his lips to seal over mine.

And there was none of that hard, possessiveness that I'd thought was what some primal part of me had been attracted to in him.

No.

If anything, this kiss was slow and deep and lingering.

It was the kiss of a lover, not someone you were just fucking for release.

Realizing that, getting lost in the sensations of it, a warmth bloomed across my chest before spreading outward until it enveloped me like a warm hug.

"Mmm," Primo rumbled against my lips as my walls started to tighten around him again. His lips ripped from mine, his eyes molten. "Tell me who this pussy belongs to," he demanded, voice soft as my hips rocked ever so slightly against him. "Tell me," he demanded when the word didn't come because some part of me still wanted to deny it.

But, hell, he'd already proved it twice.

"You," I said, the sound barely even a whisper.

"That's right," he agreed. "This is my fucking pussy," he added as he knifed up, turning me, bending me over the arm of the couch, and fucking me from behind.

Hard *and* fast this time, and there was nothing I could do but take it, but feel my body driven upward yet again even if my brain tried to convince it that it wasn't possible.

His hand moved between my thighs, stroking my aching clit with his thumb for a long moment before moving away.

His palm slapped down on my ass on one side as the hand that had just been between my thighs slipped across my cheek, his thumb pressing against my ass, then slipping inside.

A growl vibrated through him as an unexpected moan escaped me at the sensation.

His other hand left my ass, slipping into the hair at the nape of my neck instead, curling, then yanking until I had no choice but to arch my head back against his hold to ease the pain shooting across my scalp.

"This is my ass too," he said, rocking his thumb inside me. "Say it," he demanded, voice rough as his hand yanked on my hair.

"It's yours too," I said, sure at that moment that I wouldn't deny him anything as the need for release had a death grip on my system.

"No, lamb, say it. Say your ass is mine," he growled, thrusting harder and faster.

"My ass is yours," I told him, too close to oblivion to give a shit about what I was even saying.

"You're going to let me fuck you here," he told me, wiggling his thumb again.

There was no use denying that I wanted it.

"Yes."

Another of those far too sexy growls moved through him.

"Good girl," he praised, and then he was done talking as he focused on fucking me.

Hard.

Fast.

Deep.

Unrelenting.

Not giving my body a second for my orgasm to retreat.

"Come, fucking come for me," Primo hissed, voice tight, close himself. "Squeeze my cock," he demanded as the orgasm slammed through my system, leaving me crying out his name. "Fuck, yeah, baby," he hissed, thrusting faster and faster. "Milk my come from me," he added as he slammed deep, his body jolting hard as he came. "Fuck," he hissed. "Oh, fuck, baby," he growled as he folded forward over me, his face burying in my neck as his body contracted hard two more times before he went still.

We stayed that way for what felt like forever, both of us trying to catch our breaths, and my body racked with aftershocks that made it impossible to deny how intense that had been.

And, honestly, for that whole recovery period, not a single freaking thought managed to cross my foggy mind.

As soon as I managed to pull in a proper breath and my body stopped shaking, though, one very prominent thought penetrated.

I'd just fucked Primo again.

Without freaking protection.

What the hell was wrong with me?

Against my back, a chuckle moved through Primo as, I guess, my body stiffened.

"Regretting me already, lamb?" he asked, moving backward and sliding out of me.

"Always," I claimed, even if I knew it was a lie. I mean, yes, objectively, fucking him was just stupid on so many levels. And fucking him without protection was completely mental. But my body, well, it didn't have any regrets.

"Maybe you should tell your pussy to stop being so greedy for my cock then," he said as I yanked up my bodice and pulled down my skirt before turning to face him, my thighs squeezed together to remind me how careless I'd been yet again.

"You're such an asshole," I hissed. "You can fool all your neighborhood fans into thinking you're the good, church-going guy. But you can't fool me. You're a man who forces a woman into marriage then locks her in a gilded cage."

"That may all be true, lamb," he said, zipping his pants, then stalking over to me, moving so close that I had to crane my neck up to keep eye contact. "But you're the one who wants to fuck her warden."

With that, and nothing more, he walked right out of the apartment.

Leaving me to clean up *myself* and then the mess that Cassidy had left.

Which was good.

Because I needed something to distract me from the running internal monologue that listed all the various ways I'd screwed up over the past hour or so.

Making Primo think I was being possessive of him? Check.

Letting him think I dressed up for him? Check.

Letting him fuck me again? That was a giant check.

Without protection? Yep, check again.

"Ugh," I grumbled, tapping my forehead into the cupboard.

What the hell was wrong with me?

How could I dislike a man so much, but not be able to control my body around him?

And every time I let him fuck me, I gave him more power.

He wasn't taking it from me.

I was freaking willingly giving it to him.

Like an idiot.

Well, it wasn't going to happen again, that was for damn sure.

14

Primo

My work always came with risks.

I knew that.

My men knew that.

We took those risks willingly. And, after time, without much thought. Sure, we were careful. We had multiple steps of security in place. But avoiding all threats had never been a constant worry of mine.

Until Isabella.

I was consumed with it, day and night. It was a gnawing sensation in my gut, knowing that my world now put more than my men and me at risk. She was relying completely on me for her safety.

I guess a part of me had imagined that since she came from a mafia Family, she would have gotten used to the possible threats as well. But she'd been terrified hiding in my closet, making it abundantly clear to me that the Costa Family had a lot less upheaval than mine had always known.

That made her even more vulnerable.

Which was why I'd refused to let up on her so-called "imprisonment" even after one week rolled into another without any new attempts on me or my organization.

Even if she hated me more for it with each passing day.

Though, to be fair, she also hated me because, instead of trying to deescalate the situation after we'd fucked again, and she was having conflicting feelings about it, I'd doubled down and made shit worse, turning what could have been a turning point for us, steps forward toward a real relationship, into a fight and ten steps backward for us.

She was back to avoiding me, refusing to make food for me even if she was cooking for herself, and stubbornly falling asleep on the couch, making me carry her back to bed every night. While she hissed and scratched and demanded I put her down.

"It's not fair, that's all I'm saying," Dawson griped as he made himself a cup of coffee.

See, Isabella had let her resentment spread outward, getting pissed not only at me, but at all my brothers and guards who she saw in complicit as her "imprisonment."

So she wouldn't talk to them anymore.

And, which was what was upsetting Dawson right then, she wouldn't cook for them anymore either.

I didn't really care that much about Dawson's problems, but I was starting to get some real concerns over the way Isabella was isolating herself even more.

I knew a surefire way to lift her mood was to let her sister visit again. But I also knew that if I let Mira come over, I would be in a world of shit with the Costas when they got wind of Isabella being in lockdown.

It was a lose-lose for me.

So even though it would have been good for my wife—and an increasing part of me was constantly preoccupied with what would make her life better—I had to hold myself back.

"Is she really not going to come out of her room?" Dulles asked, glancing up toward the master bedroom.

It was almost eleven. My brothers had shown up around six, before Isabella had even gotten a chance to come down for her morning coffee.

She had to be dying for it. And starving too.

But she was too damn stubborn to willingly walk around by my brothers or me.

"She's really not," I said, walking over to the coffee machine and making her a cup.

Maybe she hated me, but the feeling wasn't mutual. And while I did firmly believe I was doing what was best for her, I didn't like that she was so unhappy.

Women, I figured, appreciated small gestures.

Even when they were being fucking stubborn asses.

So I was going to bring her some coffee since we were still waiting for Vissi and Terzo to show up, so we could discuss some possible threats.

"I'll be right back," I said, motioning with the cup.

To that, I got nods as I made my way upstairs, surprised when I didn't find her in the bed.

Curious, I moved through the cracked door to the bathroom.

And promptly froze.

Because there she was in the shower, half-bent forward, her face in her hands, sobbing.

Sobbing.

I wasn't a gentle man.

I wasn't soft when it came to emotions.

I'd never been moved by the sight of a woman's tears before.

But something about the sight of her right then, crying in the shower to muffle the sounds, yeah, that shit got through to me.

I didn't even stop to undress, just placed the mug on the counter, then moved into the shower enclosure, grabbing the back of her neck, and pulling her against my chest before she could register that I was even there.

She stiffened immediately, not wanting to accept comfort from someone who was the cause of all her tears, but I wrapped my other arm around her back, keeping her crushed to me as she put up a bit of a fight before just melting into me, burying her face in my chest, and letting out a choked sob.

"I'm sorry you're so unhappy," I murmured, arm tightening around her as my other hand massaged the back of her neck. "That was never my intention," I added. Hearing her snort, I couldn't help but feel my lips twitch. Even crying into my chest, she found it in her to be annoyed with me. "It wasn't. I've tried to give you a good life here, Isabella. There are just some situations that are out of my control. And I can't put you at risk."

"Heaven forbid your little white flag gets killed and voids your peace treaty," she grumbled, sniffling hard, trying to pull herself together.

"It's not that."

"Of course it is that."

"Isabella, it's not," I insisted, my hand moving from the back of her neck to her chin, yanking it up so she had to look at me. "You're my wife."

"It's a sham marriage," she insisted through a quivering lower lip. Her eyelids were swollen, and the whites of her eyes bright red. Like she'd been crying for a long time before I happened upon her.

"It's not," I insisted.

"Bullshit. You're not a real husband."

"Not a real husband," I repeated as I pressed her back against the wall, holding my hand on her shoulder, keeping her in place. "Do I not provide for you like a husband should? Do I not give you a home and food and anything you want to buy? Do I not protect you?" I asked, feeling my anger start to bubble up at the defiant look on her face, knowing she was going to say something snarky, something that was going to set me off, then set her off, and it was going to blow up in our faces.

Yet again.

"Do I not please you like a husband should?" I added, my voice dropping low and suggestive, watching as the surprise, then the rush of heat filled her eyes.

"You don't—" she started, cutting off when I suddenly dropped down on my knees in front of her, grabbing her knee, yanking it up, and pinning it to the wall as my tongue traced up her cleft, feeling the way her thighs shook at the unexpected contact.

My head angled up, eyes watching her as my tongue moved out to trace over her clit. I watched as she tried to erect those walls she wanted to keep between us, but then also as they promptly tumbled as she took a slow, deep breath that ended on a little mewling noise as my tongue continued to work her clit.

Knowing she wasn't going to try to push me away, I ducked my head and focused, licking and sucking her clit until her hands slammed down only my head, holding me tightly against her as her hips rocked impatiently.

I pressed two fingers inside her tight, hot, dripping pussy, trying to keep the focus on her, not what it would feel like to be buried inside her once again.

She was quick, though. Just a moment after her thighs started to shake and her walls tightened around my fingers, the orgasm was slamming through her system, leaving her crying out for me.

I couldn't be the good, selfless guy right then.

Hell, I could barely get my cock out of my pants in my desperation to feel her around me again.

Her eyes opened as a gasp escaped her, surprise and pleasure fighting for dominance on her face.

"If you tell me you don't like how my cock feels right now," I said, jerking my hips upward into her, "I will stop," I said. Even if it would kill me, and it almost felt like it might.

"I... I..." she started, breath fast and erratic as soft little sounds escaped her.

"You can't, can you?" I asked, jerking up into her just a little harder. "You fucking love how this feels, don't you?" I asked, my hand going around her throat, not cutting off any air, just holding there.

"I..."

"Say it," I demanded.

"Yes," she said as her fingernails sank into my shoulder as she held on.

"No, lamb," I said, shaking my head. "Tell me you love my cock in your pussy."

A whimpering sound escaped her. "I love your cock inside me," she admitted, as if there was any way she could deny it as her hips started to drop down on each of my upward thrusts.

"I know," I said, nodding. "Why do you keep denying yourself this?" I asked. "Your pussy aches thinking about me, admit it."

She was too far gone to even try to think of her walls, of her guards, of her pride.

"Yes."

"So stop denying yourself what you really want," I said as my other hand moved between us, working her clit, driving her up harder and faster, knowing this wasn't going to be an all-day thing because my walls were screaming with their need for release. It had been too long. I needed the feel of her too fucking much. I'd been miserable without being able to touch her.

"You can have my cock anytime you want it, lamb," I told her. "In your pussy. In your ass," I said, knowing we would get there one day, that she wanted it as much as I did. But I finished with a darker desire of mine, one I wasn't even sure she would ever give me. "In your mouth," I added, watching as a flicker of heat crossed her eyes at the thought, giving me hope.

Maybe someday.

If we could find a middle ground.

If we could stop making each other miserable.

But this wasn't that day.

And her pussy was crushing my cock, hinting at her release just seconds before it crashed through her system, milking mine from me at the same time, leaving us both spent and panting afterward.

"Told you I please you like a husband should," I told her after, watching as her heavy lids flickered open.

"It's not enough, Primo," she said, voice small, sad, and a lot more vulnerable than she was usually willing to give me. "It's not enough."

"What would be enough, lamb? What do you want from me?"

"Christmas," she said, her eyes glassing up again. "I want Christmas."

"You can have Christmas. You can have anything you want for Christmas."

"I want to see my family," she said, and it was all starting to make sense even as another couple of tears slipped down her face. "You're stealing Christmas from me. It's not fair. I just want one fucking day. And you are too much of a monster even to give me that."

"Isabella, you didn't even ask."

"You won't give me that. You would never let me go. You're such a—"

"No," I cut her off, shaking my head. "No. We're not having a Goddamn argument when I'm still fucking inside you," I said, feeling no small bit of pleasure when her pussy tightened around me at the words. "You can have it. One day," I said, shrugging. "But I have to come."

"What? No. You hate my family. My family *hates* you."

"I don't hate your family. And your family doesn't know me."

"You can't go."

"It's with me or not at all, lamb. Are you going to ruin your own Christmas just because you're being stubborn?"

"I hate you," she hissed.

"Baby, that gets less and less convincing each time you say it," I told her with a smirk as I slid out of her and moved away.

"You have a day to decide," I told her, getting out of the shower and going to get changed before heading down to talk to my brothers.

I went ahead and set up the security plan for taking her to her family's house.

Because Isabella was stubborn. But there was no way she was going to say no. She wanted to go too much.

And I wanted it for her.

Even if the whole thing sounded like a nightmare.

It was only one day.

If it all went off without any major upset, it could even prove to be the turning point for us I'd been waiting for.

15

Isabella

I'd sort of resigned myself to my first Christmas without my family in my entire life. Which was such a depressing thought that I went ahead and told myself that I wasn't going to celebrate at all.

No decor or gifts. No endless cookie baking. No singing carols. And certainly no curling up on the couch with hot chocolate and watching cheesy, made-for-TV romantic Christmas movies.

I was just going to have a full-on boycott.

Which, admittedly, was almost as depressing as missing the holiday with my family.

And that was how I found myself in the shower, crying my heart out for something that was wholly out of my control.

I expected to be left alone because, as a whole, Primo had been giving me the space I clearly wanted. Probably because if he bothered me, I was quick to pick a fight. The only time he forced himself into my space was when I fell asleep on the couch and he came down and carried me to bed. Which, apparently, he viewed as a safety issue. And, admittedly, I kind of got that.

If someone broke in, I much preferred they shot Primo instead of me.

I never expected him to reach for me in one of my lowest moments. And instead of teasing me or telling me I was being dramatic, he just held me, just let me have my feelings. Then he offered me a solution to them.

Was I thrilled at the idea of bringing him home to meet my family? God, no. But if it was the only option, I wasn't going to turn him down either.

Did I think it was going to be an absolute nightmare? Yeah, probably. But it was out of the apartment. And it was with my family. I would take a nightmare with my family over bliss in my gilded cage any day.

So with very little notice, I tripped into overdrive. I ran Dawson, Dulles, Vissi, and even Terzo ragged running my errands, grabbing gifts and supplies, and even some decor for the loft because I was suddenly feeling the spirit.

I spent endless hours putting up the giant tree, getting the ornaments just right, wrapping presents for my family, baking, and listening to my Christmas carols.

I didn't watch my cheesy movies, though.

I guess my heart just couldn't take it, watching all those couples get their romantic happily-ever-afters, knowing for sure now that I was never going to get the chance myself.

But still, by the time Christmas Eve rolled around and it was nearly time to head to my mom's house, I was feeling pretty filled with the holiday spirit.

"Can you keep an eye on my baked ziti?" I asked, and it took Primo a moment to realize I'd been addressing him.

Yeah, that was how infrequently I spoke directly to him.

At his drawn-together brows, I said, "I need to get changed." I waved down at my leggings and tee that I'd been cooking and baking in. "But I don't want to burn the baked ziti. Can you keep an eye on it for me?"

I might have found it difficult to let myself admit that Primo had some positive traits. His cooking skills were one of them. I never trusted anyone with my food, but I knew he would take it out at exactly the right time.

Dawson and Dulles had been taking the packages out to the car.

They weren't coming along.

Apparently, the brothers all had a tradition of getting Chinese food on Christmas Eve, and got together on Christmas Day for a meal. So my family traditions weren't screwing with theirs.

I shouldn't have cared.

But I knew what it was like to have your traditions stripped away. I didn't want to be a part of doing that to anyone else.

Christmas Eve dinner at my mom's house was a big to-do. I'd needed to order a new dress for it because my mom expected us to dress for the occasion. Luckily, I didn't need to advise Primo on it since the man lived in suits.

It was pretty messed up that a man's everyday attire could also be considered his fancy clothes when women had to buy new clothes and slip into uncomfortable outfits to be deemed appropriately dressed.

That said, I was actually kind of excited to get dressed up.

First, just because getting out of the apartment was reason alone to put some extra care into my appearance. And, of course, I wanted to look nice just because it was expected.

But more so than any of that, a part of me wanted to project to my family that everything was okay, that I was okay. I didn't want them to worry about me.

That was also why I'd decided not to tell them about all the problems in my "marriage." I wasn't going to tell them about how we fought or the fact that he kept me inside the apartment, not even allowed to breathe in some damn fresh air.

It would serve no purpose to tell them all that.

So I was just going to avoid the topics when it was possible, or brush over it if I couldn't.

I pulled my hair from the clip I'd put it in when it had still been damp so it got a little wave to it, put on some mascara and a bright red lip, then slipped into my dress.

It was a red velvet dress that hugged my frame. It had a scalloped bodice and while it was floor-length, there was a slit halfway up one thigh.

Normally, my mother would hate it.

You have to leave something to a man's imagination.

But something told me that she wouldn't object so much if I was already, whether anyone liked it or not, married.

Married women could get away with a lot more than single women who she saw as constantly looking for their future husbands, and therefore should model their behavior accordingly.

Finally, I slipped into my heels, spritzed on some perfume, and made my way down toward the first floor.

"That's one hell of a dress, lamb," Primo said, his hungry eyes roaming over me.

My body heated at his gaze, at the hunger in it, but I banked it all right back down.

"Thanks. Is the ziti ready? We need to get going," I added, going to grab my coat.

"Ready, wrapped up, and on its way to the car," Primo said, nodding.

"Why aren't we going then?" I asked, impatient to be on our way, knowing it was a good forty-minute drive from Primo's place to my mom's. And that was on a good day, without holiday traffic.

"You're forgetting something," Primo said, making me instinctively pat myself down. Like I might have in my old life. Before I remembered I had no cell phone and no credit cards to check for.

My gaze slipped back to Primo's just in time to find him reaching into his breast pocket, producing a small black jewelry box with a red bow on top.

"What's this?" I asked, feeling my stomach twisting at the idea of him buying me a Christmas present. Especially because I hadn't gotten him anything.

"Open it," he demanded instead of answering, holding onto the bottom of the box, as he held it out to me to pop the top up.

So I did.

And found a gorgeous set of earrings inside. Tear-shaped, lever-back gold earrings encrusted with diamonds. That had likely cost a small fortune.

"That's too much," I said, even if it was taking a lot more self-control than I expected not to rip them out of their little padded prison and shove into my ear holes.

"It's not," he insisted. "Put them on so we can go."

I didn't need to be told twice.

So I did that.

And I even murmured a little thank you to him for them because, even if I was determined to dislike the man, it had been an unexpectedly nice gesture.

With that, we were shuffling out into the car with an actual black-out glass partition to keep us hidden from whichever driver and guard or guards we had taking us from the Bronx and back to my mom's brownstone in Manhattan.

We sat in silence the whole time, but I could feel his gaze on my hands when I would find myself easing some of my anxiety by rolling my engagement ring around on my finger.

"Looks busy," Primo said as our driver double-parked so we could climb out.

"It always is," I agreed, excitement bubbling up in my system, mixed with no small amount of anxiety at the consequences of bringing Primo Esposito, the man who'd tricked me into marriage with him, into a Costa home for a holiday.

But there wasn't a lot of time to consider that as Primo took the bags and even the baked ziti, somehow managing to do it all with one hand as his other hand moved out, pressing into my lower back for some added stability as I walked up the rock-salted path that wasn't doing a whole hell of a lot for the ice that had formed there.

"It's going to be fine," Primo said as I stood in front of the door, hearing the sounds of my loved ones inside— happy, carefree—too uncertain to raise my hand and open the door. A part of me was irrationally worried that my presence might damper their holiday spirit. "What are you worried about?" he asked when I stood there immobilized by my own fears.

"That I'm going to ruin Christmas," I admitted, looking over at him.

"Ruin it?" Primo repeated, brows pinching. "Your family loves and misses you, Isabella."

"But my presence is only going to remind them that I'm not around anymore."

"Baby, the lack of your presence would have left a hole," he told me, shrugging. "They might not have openly said so, but everyone would have felt it. You're anxious for no reason."

Was Primo a soft and sweet on-the-spot therapist? No, not at all. But did he manage to get the job done? He sure did.

Taking a deep breath, I reached for the knob.

"Good girl," Primo murmured, and damn it if my belly didn't flip-flop a little at his words.

There wasn't time to analyze my reaction to what he'd said, though, because as soon as the door pushed open, and everyone gathered in the living room at the front of the house saw me, it was chaos.

There was a second of stunned silence. And a few worried glances at the man towering over me.

But the shock was quickly replaced with shrieks as Mira bounded toward me in her ballet flats and wearing a dress I knew she hated, but put on because our mother would have had a fit if she didn't.

"Oh my God! I can't believe you're here! Why didn't you tell anyone?" she asked as my mother ran over, tears already ruining her carefully-applied makeup as her arms went around me, wrapping me up tighter than ever before.

"Oh, my girl. My girl. I've missed you so much."

"I've missed you too, Mom," I assured her, blinking hard at my own tears.

It was the women who greeted me first. And their love had been immediate and easy.

But it was the men I was most nervous about.

In particular, Emilio and Anthony. Even if Anthony was the baby of the family, he had managed to get himself on the books with the Costa Family. And as such, he would hate Primo not only because he'd forced me into marriage, but just on principle because of the animosity between the Families that went back for years.

They were standing off near the center staircase, both in matching black suits. Emilio was leaner in build, and wearing one of his trademarked obnoxious belt buckles—and I couldn't help but wonder if my mother had yet realized that it was mistletoe printed on it, or what he was insinuating there. Anthony was younger, but more widely built, looking like the football player he'd been in high school since he'd lucked out to attend a school that actually offered it.

I was vaguely aware of my female family members taking the ziti and bags from Primo and offering him friendly enough greetings, but my focus was on my brothers.

"It's going to be fine," Primo said again, pressing his hand into my lower back and actually pushing me forward when my feet refused to carry me on their own.

"Hey." That was all I could manage to squeak out as Primo forced me forward until I was standing directly in front of my brothers. "Ah, Merry Christmas," I added, feeling my heart sinking.

It must have been on my face, too, because suddenly, of all people, Primo came to my rescue.

"You're seriously going to let her stand here and feel like her brothers don't give a shit about her anymore just because you don't like the situation? The fuck kind of family is this?"

"I don't know who the fuck you think—" Emilio started, the rage inside him something I'd never really seen before, something I didn't like seeing there. He'd always been the laid-back member of the Costa Family, the easy-going guy who still managed to get work done.

"I'm the man who won't stand by and watch his wife get disrespected. Not even by her own brothers," Primo cut him off, voice low and chilling.

So, yeah, we weren't exactly off to a great start.

"Your wife," Anthony scoffed.

"Yes, my wife," Primo said, voice firm.

"Primo," I said, pressing a hand into his stomach, something that had his gaze snapping to me since I usually tried not to deliberately touch him.

Seeming to sense the plea in my face or in my voice, his jaw loosened. "How about I get you a glass of wine?" he offered.

"Yes," I said, nodding, giving him my silent gratitude. "That would be great."

"I'll be right back," he said, giving my hip a squeeze, then walking off.

"I hoped you'd be happy to see me," I said as soon as Primo was gone, but I noticed that Emilio's gaze followed Primo until he heard me speak.

I hadn't been trying to hide the vulnerability in my voice. I was upset. And I wasn't accustomed to hiding that around my family. That wasn't how we operated. We gave one another pure authenticity, even when it was raw and ugly.

"Oh, Bells," Emilio said, anger falling, getting replaced almost immediately with sadness. "Of course I'm happy to see you," he said, already reaching for me. "Are you okay?" he asked, holding me tightly against him. "Mira said you were okay. But I couldn't believe it without seeing it myself."

"I'm okay," I told him. "I've just missed you all so much," I said, reaching my other arm out to pull Anthony into the hug. He wasn't usually one for allowing me to be affectionate with him. But he let me have my way this time.

"Missed you too," he admitted, giving me a squeeze before they both pulled away.

"If you're looking for bruises," I started, seeing the way Emilio's gaze was checking my arms, "you can stop. He doesn't hit me. He would never."

"Never," Anthony scoffed.

"Never," I confirmed.

"His old man used to beat the shit out of his mom," Emilio said.

"Which is why he wouldn't put his hands on me," I insisted. I didn't know everything about the Esposito children, but I knew that Primo and Terzo had loved their mom. And, clearly, hated his dad since you couldn't go a month without hearing the story of how Primo killed his father with his dinner knife at the table, then wiped it off, and sat back down to finish eating.

I imagined more than a small bit of that hatred came from how his father had treated his mom. And, let's face it, if his father had been a wife-beater, then it was almost guaranteed that the kids got knocked around too.

A little part of me ached for that boy Primo had been once upon a time. Big enough to know it was wrong, that his mom was crying and begging for it to stop, but too small to stand up to his big, mean father.

It must have been easy to grow up to be cold and ruthless when you had such a monster for a father. And softness in that household would have likely been beaten out of his children.

Though I had to admit, while Primo absolutely was cold and ruthless—along with being an arrogant asshole at times—he must have had a little of his mom in him.

I guess visiting with my family and having to say aloud that Primo wasn't a terrible man was making it so that I had to admit to myself the same thing. And I'd been trying so hard not to do that, not to find positive traits about him because I was so determined to dislike and resent him on principle rather than on merit.

"I swear to you, Emilio," I said, nodding. "This might not have been the future I wanted for myself, but he's not a monster. When he realized I was upset about not seeing you guys for Christmas, he immediately set up a plan for us to come."

"You're talking like the man loves you," Anthony said, looking disgusted at the idea.

"He has very traditional ideas about marriage. It's important to him. He seems to want to do it right."

"That's not what I wanted for you," Emilio insisted, voice sad.

"A 'real' marriage could have been miserable too. All those potentially hurt feelings because a man might not have taken the vows so seriously. Is this a fairy tale? No. But it's not..."

"Better?" Primo asked, moving in at my side, and handing me my glass of wine. Which I went ahead and took a hefty sip of. "Is that a no?" he asked, frowning down at me.

"It's a 'family is complicated' and 'my brothers are stubborn assholes' kind of thing," I clarified.

"Well, they are Costas," he said, and a laugh bubbled up and burst out of me.

"I'm not that bad," I insisted, knowing it was a lie.

"Lamb, fucking skyscrapers bend and budge more than you do."

That actually got a chuckle out of both of my brothers, and I couldn't help but think that was a step in the right direction.

Right then was when a new, recently arrived set of relatives barged in and wanted to see and talk to me.

Eventually, I was tugged to and fro so much that I'd lost sight of Primo. Then I'd been dragged off to the kitchen to help out because my mother didn't care if I'd been kidnapped and held hostage by pirates at sea for years, she expected the girls to pitch in when dinner was being prepared.

"Go tell your husband and you two get your seats up by me," my mother demanded when the food was being put on the platters to bring into the dining room.

My husband.

That was still going to take some getting used to.

"Okay," I agreed before moving back into the front of the house, looking around, and ready to head outside to see if some of my family members had taken him outside for a fistfight or something, when I caught sight of a big, dark, beautiful man.

Sitting on the floor.

Reading a copy of *The Night Before Christmas* to a round-faced toddler.

When I tell you my ovaries exploded... I mean it.

I guess I'd always viewed being a mother and having a child with Primo as almost two separate things in my mind. Because I'd been so hellbent on not associating anything positive with him, I guess.

But, of course, we would be parenting together.

And I would walk in on a scene just like the one in front of me.

But maybe the toddler he was sitting beside would look a little more like him, or a little more like me.

I wanted that.

God, I wanted that.

I knew I was going to love motherhood, that I was going to put everything I had into being a good mother. And Primo, I had to admit, was going to be a good father. Yes, he was cold and hard. But he was strong and loyal and had what it took to overcome his nature at times when someone in his family needed him to be softer, be warmer.

He had what it would take to be a good dad.

Even as the thought formed in my head, Primo finished the story, his gaze lifting, and landing right on me.

I swear there was something in his eyes then, something that said his mind was on the same sort of thing, that he was picturing a future where he could read to his own child, where he could create traditions and play Santa after the kid went to bed, then wake up far too early the next morning to watch the magic unfold.

I didn't stop to think as the toddler, now bored, got up and started tugging on the closest man's pants—my great uncle Marty. Which meant the poor kid was going to get the bumpiest horseback ride of his life—and just stalked right over toward Primo, reaching my hand out to him.

Primo's gaze slipped up to my hand, brows furrowed until his gaze landed on my ring. His ring. The ring that sealed this whole deal.

And then he was reaching up, taking my hand, getting to his feet, and letting me lead him away.

Sure, dinner was "starting." But that was a rather loose term in my family. There would be at least five kind calls over the course of fifteen minutes to get everyone to the table before my mom would get pissed and start ranting and raving about slaving away all day at a meal no one seemed interested in eating. She would then need to be comforted for a good ten more minutes. And then, finally, one of my aunts or my sister would pitch a holy fit, yelling, scolding, and demanding everyone get into the dining room to eat.

It was a ritual that took at least an hour. Which was why we'd long since started using warmers on the sidebars in the dining room, so all the food didn't get cold while it all went down.

Primo's fingers laced through mine as I led him toward the abandoned back staircase, then going up to the second floor, down the hall, and into a room I always visited a couple times a year. The room my mother had kept the exact same as when I'd moved out just shy of twenty years old.

Primo said nothing, just moved inside with me, watched me as I closed and locked the door, even though I knew no one would come upstairs. Because they never did. All the fun was in the chaos on the floor below.

"Lamb, what—" Primo started just a second before I pressed him back against the door, grabbed the back of his neck to pull him down, and sealed my lips to his.

There wasn't even a second of hesitation before his hand was going to the base of my skull, grabbing, holding onto me as he deepened the kiss, his lips crushing into mine. His other arm went around my lower back, pulling me tightly against his body.

Sure, there was still that little, defiant voice in the back of my head that told me I had to hate this man on principle, that I needed to make him suffer for all that he stole from me.

But that voice was suddenly drowned out by another, less bitter, one. One that understood that the best marriages were built on steady foundations of respect and determination to make it work. Even if I sometimes wanted to slap the smirk off the man's face, I had to admit he was someone worth respecting. If for nothing else, then because of his traditional beliefs. He was also determined to turn this sham of a marriage of ours into something that worked. Would it necessarily work the same way many other marriages worked? No. But that didn't mean it had to be awful and miserable all the time, that I had to work so hard to be unhappy.

Primo had, objectively, been good to me.

He gave me space when I needed it. He was there for me when I needed that as well, even if it wasn't something that came naturally to him. He protected me. He provided for me. He didn't ask or demand for me to change for him.

It wasn't a bad way to start a marriage.

And the chemistry, well, that sort of spoke for itself. I never needed to work so hard to pretend to not be attracted to someone as I did with Primo.

Primo's hands slid down my back, massaging over the curve of my ass, then gathering up my long skirt until it was stuck around my waist. His hands moved up, palming my ass before sinking in hard. Hard enough that he pulled me off of my feet by it, lifting me up, and waiting for my legs to wrap around his waist.

Which they did.

His teeth nipped my lower lip as he turned and walked toward my old bed, turning, and sitting down with me straddling him.

His hands were hungry then, moving over my bare ass cheeks, toying with the barely-there little strap of my thong, slipping up my sides, closing over the swells of my breasts, then yanking down my bodice, flicking off my bra, then cupping my exposed skin, and teasing over my nipples.

My body was a complete inferno even before Primo's lips were moving from mine, making a trail down my jaw, then my neck, the scratch of his stubble unexpectedly erotic.

I wanted him inside of me and the release as much as I wanted my next breath.

But not quite as much as I wanted to show him that things were different now. Or, at least, they were starting to be different.

And I could accomplish that by taking the lead, by giving as much as I had received in the past.

So before Primo could continue his kisses down my chest and toward my breasts, I was pushing back, then sliding off his long legs.

My gaze held his heavy-lidded one as I went down on my knees in front of him.

My hands landed at his knees and slid forward up his thighs, watching as the surprise and pleasure crossed his handsome features as my fingers worked his button and zipper free.

Reaching inside, I pulled out his thick, straining cock. Then, gaze holding his, I let my mouth fall open, my tongue teasing the edge of my lips. A literal open invitation.

"Fuck, lamb," he groaned, fisting his cock at the base and tracing my lower lip with the head. "Lick it," he demanded, holding it as my tongue moved out to trace over his head, tasting him, wetting him more as a surprising rush of pleasure filled my body. "Wider," he demanded as his free hand cupped my jaw, waiting for my lips to part more to accommodate his thickness.

"Good girl," he murmured as his cock started to slide into my waiting mouth. "Fuck," he hissed as my lips closed around him.

His hand slid from my jaw to gather up my hair and pin it behind my head as I started to suck him, slow and tentative at first, but gaining in speed and enthusiasm as I found the rhythm that worked for him, as his hisses for breath and his quiet groans spurred me on.

His other hand slid to the back of my neck after a moment, putting firm pressure until I started to take him deep. "Look at me," he demanded, and my eyes opened to find him watching me with the most intense eyes I'd ever seen. "More, baby," he groaned, putting more pressure on the back of my neck.

I didn't think I could take more.

I'd never done that before.

"You can," he assured me, voice soft, coaxing. "Take a breath and swallow," he added.

Figuring it was worth a try, I followed his instructions. And just as I swallowed, Primo bucked his hips up into my mouth. The head of his cock hit the back of my throat. "Don't fight it, lamb," he instructed, voice tight, clearly enjoying the sensation. "You feel so fucking good," he groaned, chest heaving with his erratic breaths. "Let me fuck your mouth," he went on. "You can tap out," he said, reaching for my hand and pressing it onto his thigh. "But let me fuck your mouth, baby."

I never thought I would allow a man to do that to me.

It had never sounded even remotely sexy.

But when Primo said it?

He almost made me believe I could enjoy it as well somehow.

So I gave him the smallest of nods that had him exhaling hard as his hand cupped my throat as the other gripped the back of my neck.

And then he fucked my mouth, his hips bucking up into my throat as his hands guided my head up and down on him.

Impossibly, even as the tears slipped down my cheeks and my saliva and his precum slipped down my chin, I could feel my walls tightening hard, somehow enjoying this savage sort of selflessness as Primo's breathing got even more ragged, as his groans became little hisses of pleasure.

I wasn't going to tap out.

Not when a man as powerful as he was utterly at my mercy, his pleasure was completely in my hands.

So the hand that he'd put on his thigh for tapping out slid between us, massaging his balls as he fucked my mouth faster and faster, getting closer and closer.

"Let me come down your throat, lamb," he hissed, making my sex clench hard, never really realizing before how hot a partner checking in on you could be, how asking for consent didn't have to be awkward and uncomfortable.

Mouth full, all I could managed was a "Mmmmm" sound that had him cursing as his hips bucked hard one last time, the head slamming against the back of my throat before I tasted his release a second before it slid down my throat.

"Fuck," Primo hissed, his whole body convulsing hard once, then twice.

And I never before felt quite as powerful as I did right then.

"Fuck, lamb," he said after sucking in a deep breath, pulling me backward gently by my hair. "Come here," he demanded, pulling again until his cock slid from my lips with a pop. His thumb stopped to trace my lower lip as I swear this man looked at me with actual reverence in his gaze before he was pulling me up onto his lap again, and sealing his lips over mine.

Long and deep.

Until my lips felt tingly.

He broke the contact first, pressing my face into his neck as his hand started to sift through my hair as the other held me pinned to his chest.

"I've wanted that for a long time," he admitted, voice low. "Never thought I was going to get it," he added, making my lips curve up into a smile.

"I wanted to," I admitted. "I liked that," I added, wincing a little at the admission, at the vulnerability behind it.

"I'm a lucky fucking man, then," he said, releasing me when I pushed.

"Did you make a mess of me?" I asked, wiping under my eyes, knowing how bad they'd been tearing.

"You're fucking beautiful," he countered, and my belly squeezed hard at the praise.

"Thank you," I said, gaze slipping from his, a little uncomfortable at how much his words meant, and not sure I was ready for him to see that. "But that's not what I meant.

"Your cheeks are a little red. It will fade," he added. "I can think of a way to kill the time," he went on, a dark promise in his eyes as my gaze lifted to his face again.

"You don't have to," I said, shaking my head. "That wasn't why I did it."

"I know. That's even more reason for me to want to. But, baby, I could eat your pussy for every fucking meal and not get tired of it," he told me as he suddenly lowered back on the bed. "Now be a good girl and ride my face," he demanded, grabbing the backs of my knees when I didn't move to do exactly that.

He yanked me into position.

And before I could even object, his fingers were pulling my panties to the side, and his tongue was tracing up my pussy to work my clit.

Then, well, I did what he wanted me to do.

I rode his face.

And I just barely remembered to bite my lip to keep from screaming as the orgasm slammed through me—shaking legs and all—a few moments later.

I collapsed down at the side of him, pulling myself together even as he tucked himself away, then slowly got off the bed, reaching down to yank my skirt back into place, then handing me my bra.

"I'll be right back," he said before going out into the hall.

I took the chance to strap my boobs back into my bra and get my dress in order and then attempt to tame my hair.

He came back then with a damp washcloth, coming toward me, reaching for my chin in one hand, then gently wiping at my cheeks and under my eyes with the other.

"Better?" I asked.

"I wouldn't say better, no. Better is me being able to see your mascara all over your cheeks from choking on my cock, lamb," he said, the words wicked, but his eyes were actually playful, as was the smile toying with his lips. "But this is more presentable for Christmas dinner."

"Oh, God," I groaned, slapping a hand to my forehead as I realized what we'd just done with my entire family one floor below us.

A chuckle, deep and sexy, moved through Primo.

"It's not funny," I grumbled.

"You getting so distracted by my cock and my tongue that you forgot all about Christmas dinner, lamb? Yeah, I'd say that's pretty fucking funny. Come on, let's get down there before anyone notices we're missing. They're getting quieter."

"Because we probably just missed all the yelling," I told him, accepting his hand when he offered it to me, then making our way downstairs where everyone was just filing into the dining room.

"Isabella, you are so flushed," one of my aunts said, making me stiffen.

"It is so hot in here," I complained, fanning myself.

"I told your mother we needed to crack a window, but no. Now her daughter is going to pass out," my aunt went on, already walking off to find something else to be mildly irritated about.

"Shut up," I snapped in a low hiss as I felt his gaze on me.

"I didn't say anything."

"Your eyes are being profane right now."

To that, a chuckle moved through him as he walked me to an empty seat and pulled out my chair for me, then pushed me in, a move that I saw Emilio watching from across the table.

When he took his seat, his hand went to my thigh, giving it a squeeze, then just sitting there as my mother finally got everyone quiet enough to give her annual, emotional speech, thanking more saints and angels than I realized even existed, before declaring it was finally time to eat.

And then this man who technically belonged to me, he did an unfathomable thing.

He told me to stay where I was.

And then *he* went to get *me* a plate.

I was pretty sure I stared at his back with bug eyes as he lined up with all the *women* who were making their *men* plates.

"That's a keeper," a great, great aunt told me from her position at the head of the table in her wheelchair, likely getting tended to by one of her daughters.

"He cooks too," I said, disbelief in my voice. "Don't ever tell him this, but he cooks better than me," I told her, shaking my head at myself.

"What a blessing," my aunt said, absentmindedly patting her wedding band, likely thinking of her husband she'd lost a decade before. "And don't you worry, dear," she said, leaning closer like we were sharing some great secret. "I won't tell him you said that about him."

"Talking about me, ladies?" Primo asked, making my aunt's eyes go comically wide at possibly being caught.

"Don't flatter yourself," I said, giving him a smile as he placed a heaping plate in front of me before putting his own down.

"One of your cousins elbowed me in the rib to get the last dinner roll," he said, shaking his head.

"Don't worry. In about... three-point-five minutes, my mother is going to pop up in her seat and gasp about forgetting the rolls in the oven. Then before she goes to take them out, she will scold all of us at large for not reminding her about them."

When about three minutes passed and my mother did exactly that, Primo's amused gaze slid to me.

"Told you," I said, nodding.

Dinner was what Christmas dinner always was.

As was the rest of the night.

Loud, over-the-top, funny, and amazing.

And I had to admit to myself that it was maybe even nicer to share the evening with someone else, someone who I would share laughs and smiles and eye rolls with.

"I told you, lamb," Primo said as we got on our coats and made our way onto the front path after about thirty whole minutes of goodbyes. "You didn't need to be nervous."

"I'm worried about Emilio," I admitted, linking my arm through Primo's because the ice had only gotten worse thanks to a freezing rain that had started sometime while we were inside.

"Why?" Primo asked, seeming genuinely interested as our car pulled up, and Primo pushed me in before sliding in beside me.

"He seems really unhappy," I told him, shrugging. "And that isn't how my brother is."

"This was all sprung on him," Primo said, shrugging. "He didn't get a chance to work through his thoughts on it. "Next time, it will be better."

"By next time, do you mean next Christmas?" I asked, heart sinking a little at the idea.

"I meant the next family function," he said, shrugging. "I imagine there are going to be many of them."

"You're going to let me go?"

"Let," he repeated, sighing at the word. "The current lockdown situation aside—and I'll remind you it is for your own safety—I don't want you to think of this as a prison anymore, like I'm the warden you need permission from to go places or have people over. That's not how I want this to be."

"Why the change of heart?" I asked, and for some reason, my own heart fluttered a little at the idea of his heart. But we were going to go ahead and just call that indigestion from all the food because anything else was just too much to consider right then.

To that, Primo sighed. "I, perhaps naively, thought that your connection to your family would keep you from making this marriage work. That was a miscalculation. I underestimated you," he said, giving my knee a squeeze.

"A man who admits when he's wrong," I said, pressing a hand dramatically to my chest. "Now I've seen everything."

The whole ride back to The Bronx was the same way. Light, conversational, missing all the anger and resentment that had been between us in the past.

It was a turning point, I could feel it.

Well, you know, if he didn't go and do something completely dickish again.

"What?" Primo asked when I let out a strange noise.

I half-turned in my seat to face him more, holding out a hand that had his brows furrowing. "Truce?" I asked.

The ghost of a smile on his lips was unexpectedly sweet.

"No, lamb," he said, reaching to cup my jaw. "I'd rather seal the deal this way," he said as his lips pressed down on mine.

Then he kissed me silly the rest of the way home, leaving me aching for more.

"Just gotta get inside," he said, reading the hunger in my eyes as he turned from me to push the door open, reaching inside to hold a hand out for me.

Which I took.

Happily.

Knowing in my soul that things had really changed for us that night.
And it was only going to get better from there.
But it was right then that the gunshots rang out.

16

Isabella

There was a split second of stunned inaction where Primo's wide-eyed gaze slipped to me.

But then he was yanking me down behind the opened door as he reached for his gun, looking out, listening, trying to figure out where the bullets were coming from even as his guards came running out from behind the building that was his business and our home.

Complete and utter shock overtook my whole system, wiping my mind blank, making my heartbeat pound, making my breathing go low and erratic.

I was frozen on the spot, feeling somehow both far too *in* the moment but also completely outside of the whole situation.

The gunshots rang out, some of them even from Primo's gun from his crouched position, but the sounds seemed to come from very far away, almost as if I was under water and the world was heavily distorted because of it.

That is until I felt hands grabbing me.

And my fight-or-flight instinct decided to go with fight.

So I clawed and shrieked, unable to think anything but that I needed to stay with Primo.

"Take her!" Primo yelled, making me realize the hands were friend, not foe.

"No," I cried, reaching out toward Primo as an arm went around my waist as another car pulled up to catty-corner the one we were ducked beside.

"Get her in the fucking safe room," he yelled at whoever had me.

"No! Primo!" I shrieked as I was pulled away.

His gaze slipped to mine for a minute, dark, intense, but more so than that, worried.

If Primo was worried, then I needed to be pee-myself scared.

"Fucking now, Vissi!" Primo growled.

And just like that, I was lifted off my feet as gunfire rang out. It wasn't until we were at the side of the building that I realized the shots had come from Primo and his men, that they were covering for Vissi and I as he got me out of the chaos.

"Put me down!" I hissed, fighting at his hands.

"I put you down, you run back out there like an idiot. Not only will Primo skin me alive, but your fucking hellion of a sister would come to feed my flesh back to me before killing me."

And with that, he dragged me into the building.

But not all the way up to the top floor to cower in the closet like I'd needed to do the last time we were attacked.

No.

He brought me into the meat-packing floor, and down the hall of freezers until we got to the second-to-last one.

"In," Vissi demanded after opening the door.

Inside was a freezer, technically. A walk-in like you'd see at any restaurant. With the thick metal walls.

But it was more than that, too.

There was a chair inside, wire racks filled with water and food, and what looked suspiciously like one of those compost toilet things in the corner.

Oh, and let's not forget the weapons.

Primo had called it a safe room.

And I guess it was.

But it was the last place I was going to feel safe.

Trapped in a small space... yet again.

"No. No, I can't. Take me upstairs," I said, trying to back away, only to feel my wrist snagged by Vissi.

"It's safe," he said. "The walls are reinforced with bullet-resistant material. It is temperature-controlled. There is food and water. And once you lock it from the inside, no one can get in. It's the safest place in the entire borough. And there is a camera feed right here," he said, dragging me inside to show me the screen beside the door. "Only unlock the door if you see Primo and he tells you it's safe, okay?"

"I can't. You can't put me in—" I started, yanking away, moving out of the freezer. Just as a bullet ripped through the glass of the building, lodging in the wall.

A small shriek escaped me as Vissi bent low, shoving a shoulder into my midsection, and tossing me over his shoulder.

"You need to stay, do you hear me? This is not good," he added, jaw tight. "Stay," he said, dropping me down onto my feet. "And lock this door when I leave, got it?"

Not sure if I was more scared of being trapped in the room, or being shot outside of it, I just gave him a nod as he walked out of the freezer, then closed the door.

It wasn't until he pounded on the door and said, "Lock it, Isabella," that I moved forward to press the red lock button, sealing myself into what had always been my biggest fear. Small spaces.

Except, maybe, it wasn't my biggest fear anymore.

Being claustrophobic paled in comparison to the idea of getting shot.

And that somehow paled in comparison to knowing these men that I knew and cared about—especially Primo—were out there in the street getting shot at.

What happened if something happened to them while I was trapped in the freezer?

No.

Nope.

I couldn't let my mind go there.

My stomach twisted hard at even entertaining it for a second.

Because Primo and I had just finally come to a truce, had decided to both be adults about the situation, go into our marriage as partners, and see what we could make out of it.

I had a sneaking suspicion that it could be something truly great if I finally gave it a chance to be.

A good, loyal husband who provided and cared in his own way, a kid or two that we could dote all our love on.

It wasn't exactly how I planned out my happily-ever-after, but I was starting to see that it could be a new version of that. An updated, mature version of it.

Shaking from my actual head to toe and not sure my legs would keep holding me, I moved back and dropped down on the chair, bringing my hands to my face, and taking slow, deep breaths.

I needed to stay calm.

It wasn't going to do anyone any good for me to work myself into a complete panic attack.

Trying to keep my calm under such an over-the-top scenario, though, proved harder than I could have anticipated as what felt like hours passed. There was a time stamp on the little TV screen beside the door, but I was too shaken to get up and check it. And, quite frankly, I wasn't sure I wanted to know how much time had passed without Primo coming to look for me.

That couldn't be good, right?

The freezer was completely insulated, the walls too thick to hear anything outside of, so I was stuck in there with nothing but my measured breaths to keep me company. And drive me, little by little, insane.

I almost breathed myself completely numb with all the extra oxygen when I saw a shadowy figure move into the camera feed.

My heart flew into my throat when it didn't come right over toward the door, look at the camera, and show me the face of the man I'd married through force, but was actively choosing to start a real relationship with.

Was it someone else?

Vissi? Dawson? Dulles? Terzo?

No.

No, it didn't fit this guy with his back to the camera.

It looked like Primo.

But if it was Primo, why wasn't he coming over to tell me it was safe to come out? Why wasn't he bringing me upstairs to make good on that promise he'd made earlier?

Why was I still in a box he knew I hated?

Taking another breath, I moved closer to the camera, watching it, wishing the room outside the freezer was just a little bit brighter.

The Woman with the Ring

But then the figured turned.

Turned.

And dropped to his knees.

And right before he brought his hands up to cover his face, I saw it was him.

Primo.

And something was really, really freaking wrong.

My hand slammed into the lock release.

I pushed hard against the door, then flew over toward Primo, dropping down in front of him. Both of my hands reached out, framing his neck.

"What's the matter? What happened?" I asked, feeling the grief just pouring off of him. "Vissi?" I asked, stomach clenching at the idea that the man who'd risked himself to get me safe might not have made it. "Dawson? Dulles?" I went on, heart crushing at the idea of the men who'd been so nice to me from the beginning no longer being around. "Terzo," I said, somehow knowing it even before the name left my lips. "Was it Terzo?" I asked, then watched as Primo's body folded more inward on itself. "Oh, Primo," I said, feeling the tears filling my eyes.

Did I have the same bond with Terzo as I had with Dawson and Dulles? No. But it was still Primo's brother.

My arms reached for my husband, pulling him against me, holding him as he tried to come to terms with the loss.

A while later, Vissi walked into the room, shoulders low, face defeated, a whole arm of his gray jacket bloody like he'd taken a bullet himself.

"We gotta get upstairs," he said, voice uncharacteristically hollow.

"Okay," I agreed, nodding at him, knowing that in this situation, it was my turn to take the lead, to be the strong one, to be there for my partner when he needed me.

I got to my feet, reaching down to pull Primo back onto his as well.

I wrapped an arm around his lower back, and pressed the other to his chest as I led him back toward the elevator.

Vissi gave me a nod, staying out of the car, and letting us ride up alone, knowing that Primo needed some time to grieve, to process, and not wanting to intrude.

I didn't know how to comfort someone who'd just lost a brother. That was so outside of my wheelhouse. But I did know that Terzo's blood was all over Primo's hands and shirt. I could at least help him with that.

So I led him through the apartment and up into the master bath, turning on the water in the shower, then moving back toward Primo, helping him out of his clothes as he just stood there, completely lost in his own grief. I wasn't even sure he even really registered my presence right then.

But that was okay.

It wasn't about me.

Once I had him undressed, I led him toward the shower, intending to go back and take off my own clothes first, but his hand refused to let me go, pulling me inside and under the spray of water with him.

My hands slid over his ribs, then wrapped around him as I moved into his chest. "I'm so sorry, Primo," I said, giving his big body a squeeze. "I don't know what else to say. Or what to do. So I'm just going to be here, okay?" I said, giving him another squeeze. "If you need anything, you can tell me. But for now, we can just do this," I added.

I don't know how long we stood there under the spray.

But I made sure the blood was gone before I finally cut off the water when we both started to sway a bit from standing so long.

I stripped out of my sopping clothes, then dried both of us off before leading him into the bed, getting him under the covers, then moving in beside him.

I couldn't even begin to fathom what his loss was like, how I would feel if something happened to Emilio or Anthony. But I did know that if something—God forbid—ever did, that I would want someone there with me, holding me, but expecting nothing from me.

So that was what I gave Primo.

I held him. I stroked his back. I ran my fingers through his hair.

Through it all, he seemed somewhere out of reach, his eyes a million miles away.

I planned to keep touching, stroking, hugging.

The problem was, it had been a long, crazy day and evening. And without any form of external stimulation, eventually, I passed out snuggled up to his chest.

Waking up alone was disorienting.

For a long moment, it felt like the whole night before had been a dream. One that started out amazing and lovely, but ended with bloodshed, fear, and grief so strong it shook a man as unshakable as Primo Esposito.

It wasn't until I stumbled out of bed and found Primo's bloodied clothes from the night before in the trash that I was sure it had all been real.

But if it was real, where the hell was Primo?

Mind on that, I rushed to throw on leggings and a tee, then flew out of the bedroom, rushing down the stairs so fast that I nearly face planted.

Then there he was, standing in the kitchen with a cup of coffee on the counter in front of him, and his phone in his hands, typing away.

"Primo?" I called, voice tentative, not sure how he'd gone from the broken man I'd held in the shower the night before back to his usual intimidating self, suit and all, within just a few short hours.

"Pack," he barked at me, the sound so sudden and firm that I actually jolted at it.

"I'm sorry?"

"Pack a bag, Isabella."

God, his voice was cold, chilling even.

I had no right to question his moods in the hours following such a world-shattering loss, but it still took me a second to take a deep breath so I acted out of compassion, not wounded pride.

"Are we going somewhere?" I asked.

"You are."

"Where am I going?" I asked, stomach swirling.

"To your brother's."

"What? No."

"It wasn't a request," Primo said in that same cold, flat tone.

"I'm not going to my brother's house. I belong here."

"You're going. Pack a bag, or wear your brother's clothes. Your choice."

"Primo, no. I need to be here." To help him come to terms with his loss in a less destructive way.

It showed just how far we'd come in such a short period of time. Because the woman I'd been a week or so ago wouldn't have asked a single question, wouldn't have even needed to pack a bag, would have just ran out the door and back to my family.

But I didn't want to do that.

I didn't want to leave Primo alone in his grief. Also, though, I just didn't want to leave. I'd gotten used to the idea of us giving it a real go. And now he wanted to take it away?

No.

It was too late for that.

"You're going. Walking on your own two feet, or thrown over my shoulder, but you're going."

"Primo," I tried again, voice soft, reaching for the hand he had resting on the counter, but he yanked it away and turned his back on me, going back to texting on his phone.

"You're going to have to drag me," I told him, moving up behind him. "I'm not going to willingly leave you right now," I informed him, pressing my face into his back, and letting my arms slip around him.

He let me do it.

For a couple long seconds before he yanked out of my hold.

"Suit yourself," he said, shrugging.

"Don't do this," I said, voice taking on a defeated edge.

"It's all but done."

"Primo," I sighed, grabbing his arm, forcing him around to face me. "Stop."

"Go get your shit," he said, barely sparing me a glance. "You're out of here."

I was a nice person, damnit.

I had compassion.

I would never yell at someone who just had a loved one murdered.

Well, I always *used* to be that way anyway.

There was no denying, though, that when my mouth opened again, I absolutely yelled.

"I've put up with a lot of shit from you. But being a complete fucking asshole to me when I'm trying to be nice to you because your loved one *died* is not going to be another of those things. Look at me, damnit," I snapped, shoving a hand into his chest to force his attention. "Your brother died," I said, lowering my voice.

"I'm very fucking aware of that, Isabella."

"You need to give yourself a chance to grieve."

"I don't need to be told what I need to do."

"Clearly, you do. This," I said, waving a hand at him and his perfectly put together appearance, "this isn't normal, Primo."

"It's not your problem."

"See this?" I said, waving my left hand at him. "This says it is my fucking problem, okay? You don't like it, too fucking bad. Build a time machine, go back, and don't kidnap and marry me. I don't know what to tell you. But I'm here now. You're not going to push me away."

"You're going."

"I'm not," I said, actually crossing my arms at him. "You're not pushing me away."

"I'm keeping you fucking *safe*," he yelled, whatever control he had over his emotions finally snapping. And as scary as Primo in anger-mode was, I preferred it over cold and locked-down Primo any damn day of the week. "I couldn't keep Terzo safe. I'm not fucking losing you too."

There it was.

I knew it was under there.

But I needed him to get open about it.

"Primo, you can't blame yourself for what happened to your brother," I told him, moving forward, pressing both hands against his chest.

"Of course I can," he said, voice low, a raw, ragged sound as his gaze slipped down to me. "Who the fuck else is to blame?" he added, his fingers sliding up my hip for a second before his hand fell again. "It's my job to keep everyone safe. I have to keep you safe, lamb," he said, eyes tortured.

"Okay, first of all—no, you are not to blame. The only person to blame is whoever was shooting at you. Secondly, you are one man, Primo. You can't protect everyone at one time. That's just not possible."

"He was my brother," Primo said, squeezing his eyes shut.

"I know. But you're not honoring him by pushing everyone else away."

"I'm not trying to push you away. I'm trying to protect you," he said, an arm slinging around my waist.

"You can keep me in here," I reminded him. "I'll even go into the stupid freezer room when you leave if you want. But don't make me go. I want to be here for you. I mean, I don't know what to do, or how to help. But I will figure it out and then do it."

A deep exhale escaped Primo as his arm tightened around me.

"You're doing it," he said, voice tight.

"Come on. Let's go back to bed," I said. Sure, I didn't personally know too much about grief, but I did know that most people took to bed during it.

"I can't. There's too much to do."

"Let someone else do it."

"They can't. I have to. I'm the boss. And I'm the next of kin," he added, making my heart crack for him.

Making funeral arrangements on Christmas morning.

"Are you leaving today?" I asked, knowing I had to accept his way of handling everything.

"No. I have to talk with my... with Dawson and Dulles. But downstairs."

"Okay. Have you eaten?" To that, I got a snort. "How about you go sit down, and I'll make you something, okay?" I offered.

I might not know how to comfort grief, but I did know that the women in my family always showed they cared with food. Which gave me something to do so I didn't feel completely useless.

"Okay," he agreed, pressing a kiss to the top of my head before walking off.

Grief made his steps slower, his shoulders more slumped. And when he sat, he dropped down, almost as if his legs wouldn't hold him anymore.

I could hear him on the phone as I cooked, and from the sound of things, it was with the funeral home.

Eventually, Vissi was the one to join me in the kitchen, looking just as wrecked and sleepless as Primo had. In the absence of Primo the night before, I imagined the weight of the family had landed on Vissi's shoulders since Terzo was gone.

"How is he?" he asked, accepting coffee when I passed it to him.

"It's Primo. He won't say exactly how he is. But he's... I think he's processing. Not repressing it, but dealing in his own way."

"There's a lot of death in our lives," Vissi said. "He's had a lot of men close to him die. But I think all of us always figured we would be exempt from that. Terzo took a bullet that was meant for Primo," Vissi explained. "Primo had bent down to grab a magazine he'd dropped at the exact second the bullet got Terzo, from an angle that said it likely would have hit Primo instead of his brother if he hadn't ducked down. So he's likely feeling guilty about that too."

"Was there... did anyone else..." I asked. I already knew Dawson and Dulles were okay. And Vissi, since he was right in front of me. And while I didn't know all the other men well, I did know some of them well enough to be a little sad if they were gone.

"Got one in critical, two more with gunshot wounds, but they're minor."

"Did you... do you know who it was?" I asked, knowing I wasn't supposed to ask questions like *Did you kill any of theirs? Will someone pay for this?*

To that, Vissi's jaw went tight.

"I'm sorry."

"Not as sorry as whoever this is when Primo gets his hands on them."

That was true.

"He tried to make me leave."

"You should leave," Vissi said, shaking his head. "This isn't over. No one wants you to be in danger."

"I'm not going anywhere. This is where I belong."

To that, Vissi's brow rose, and the ghost of a smile tugged at his lips.

"So, you're not a prisoner being kept by her warden anymore, hm?" he asked. "The boss man found his ride-or-die after all?"

"Well, I mean, I would really prefer not to die," I said, rolling my eyes. "But this is my place. I'm here. Through the good and the bad."

I didn't know then, though, just how bad it could still get.

17

Primo

I spent Christmas morning making funeral plans for my slain brother while looking at the tree Isabella had so painstakingly put up and decorated.

I'd wanted this morning to be something special for us. That was the plan after the evening with her family had gone so well.

We'd reached a turning point, and I wanted to keep taking strides in the right direction with her. I wanted to wake up early and make Christmas breakfast, knowing she was going to insist on making dinner. I wanted to sit with her on the couch and watch Christmas movies and discuss how nice it would be to maybe have a kid with us the following year.

I wanted happiness and new traditions.

And I got death and grief instead.

The night before was a bit of a blur in my mind.

The only truly clear moments were when the bullets first started to fly, and I knew that I needed to get Isabella safe, and hearing her scream for me as she was dragged away.

And then the moment I watched a bullet blow a hole open in my brother's head.

I'd known grief in my life. It started with uncles and cousins getting gunned down when I was barely a kid. Then my mother's death. Friends who became a part of the Family with me were long gone.

Death and grief and funerals were a normal part of my life.

But it was different with Terzo.

A brother.

And not a shithead like the other one who'd been killed.

Terzo was rough and cold, but he had been a good man. He'd been caring and loyal and hardworking. I'd naively thought I would always have him at my side.

This life was cruel and cutting and no one was guaranteed safety from it.

Except for Isabella.

She was off-limits.

No, this new generation of criminals didn't always respect the sanctity of family the way they had in the past. They kidnapped and raped and extorted to get what they wanted.

That said, I was going to send a very clear fucking message.

My wife—and my children someday—were off fucking limits.

Anyone who threatened them would call death a mercy by the time I was done with them.

I would have them gagging on their own blood, begging for me to put a bullet between their eyes and end their suffering.

But they'd find no goddamn sympathy from me.

When they did eventually die, slowly and in as much pain as the human body could endure, I would make it clear to anyone else who threatened what was mine that they could expect the same exact ending.

I failed to protect my brother.

I would not fail to protect my woman.

I'd gone right to her after. After the cops pried me off of Terzo's lifeless body to ask me inane questions about my business, about my enemies, as if I ever let the law handle my shit for me.

After all that was done, it was Isabella I turned to.

And it was Isabella who'd held me, who'd cleaned the blood off of me, who'd been there for me even when she hadn't been given a whole hell of a lot of reasons to give a shit about me and my pain.

It was Isabella who woke up in a panic, looking for me. And Isabella who stomped her foot and crossed her arms at the idea of me sending her away.

It was Isabella who made me breakfast while I told the funeral home which casket I needed for my brother, and what time worked best for the funeral.

It was also Isabella who curled up with me on the couch later, not making any demands on me, just sitting with me, resting her head on my chest, stroking her hand up and down my arm or my chest.

I didn't give a fuck how long it took or how much blood I had to spill, I would take out the entire syndicate that was coming for me and mine.

I would get and keep her safe.

"Primo," Vissi said, snapping me out of my swirling thoughts, bringing me back to the moment.
"What?"
"The neighborhood is scared," he said, shrugging.
The bullets had gone through a few windows. Luckily, the only casualties were a TV and a couch cushion. Both of which would be replaced as soon as the stores opened up again. Plus the owners got some extra cash for their worries.
"Yeah, I bet," I agreed, sighing.
As a whole my neighborhood was good. Loyal. They knew I took care of them, so they, in turn, turned their heads and minded their business about my dealings. That said, I never had a goddamn shootout in the streets like that before. I understood them being scared. For themselves, for their kids.
My mind was on the same things.
"And if the neighborhood gets antsy enough," Vissi reasoned, hating being the rational one, but I wasn't operating at my peak right then, "they are gonna start talking to the law."
"I know," I agreed. "The main problem last night was the scouts were home with their families." I'd been feeling altruistic. I figured that since I was taking Isabella home to see her family, I didn't need as many guards on the street as usual. That was my fuckup. It wouldn't happen again.
"And I think a lot of them know that. Since a lot of the scouts are from the neighborhood," Vissi said, shrugging. "And they did all come running to help when they heard the shots. It's just a mess. People are particularly upset because it's Christmas."
"We can use Christmas as an excuse to hand them all some cash," I said, shrugging.
I didn't live in the best area.
I'd chosen it on purpose.

First, because in bad areas, people tended to turn a blind eye to low-level criminal activity, so long as it didn't impact them.

There were also a lot of young adults hungry to make a living and a name for themselves. Which was why I'd managed to have as many scouts as I did from the jump.

I also kept the predatory crime out of the area. The vicious drug dealers, the abusive pimps, the gangs that might suck up their kids and spit them out into the prison industrial complex in a few short years, serving life sentences because there was no way out once you got in.

On top of that, they appreciated anyone who came in and gave back to the community. The church almost single-handedly stayed open thanks to my donations. The food pantry was full from my men dropping off supplies. I did toy drives every Christmas and baskets every Easter. I even set up a program to help keep the local kids fed during the summers when school was out, and the parents didn't have enough money to provide the meals the schools used to.

Was it asking too much to expect their silence for a wad of Christmas cash? Maybe. But if that cash came with a promise to handle the problem, and make sure it didn't keep happening, I was pretty sure neighborhood morale would improve.

"It would mean you have to go to church today, boss," Vissi said. "You sure you're up for that?"

Honestly, I wasn't.

I felt like shit.

But that church had been there for me in some of my lowest times growing up.

It would be good for me to go, to get an uplifting message.

On top of that, I never missed Christmas mass.

I was only disappointed that I couldn't bring Isabella with me.

But she needed to be home, where I could at least guarantee that no one could get to her. At least not without there being a fuckuva lot of shooting that would draw my attention anyway.

"Alright. Get the cards and the cash. And some extra hands. We don't have a lot of time."

With that, we set to work stuffing envelopes.

"Nope, doesn't look suspicious at all," Vissi said, shaking his head as we each picked up the giant bags we'd had to stash all the cards in.

I was leaving Dawson and Dulles with Isabella, then several other guards around the building, as well as the scouts who'd volunteered to miss Christmas morning with their families to help me make sure that the whole neighborhood stayed safe.

She was safer than Vissi and I were going to be.

But that was okay.

I'd rather have the guards on her, not me.

At least I knew that if I got taken out, someone would get her home safe to her people, and they would be able to keep her safe.

So, Vissi and I sat through mass. I said a prayer for my brother. And then we stood at the doors, handing out the cash as everyone left.

No gunshots. No nothing.

Everything was fine.

Or so I thought.

Until I rode the elevator up to my floor, expecting to excuse my brothers, then take Isabella upstairs with me. To get in bed. To talk. Or just sleep.

I just needed a break.

To process.

To sleep.

To get back on my game.

"Isabella?" I called as I walked into the living room.

I didn't immediately think anything of it. It was hard to hear if she was in the tub or the shower. She'd rushed downstairs to look for me first thing that morning, so she hadn't had time then to get ready.

But then shit started not to line up.

Like Dawson and Dulles were nowhere to be found, either. And it wasn't like there was a whole lot of space in the apartment for them to disappear into. I doubted they were both using the can at the same time.

What the fuck was going on?

"Isabella?" I called, something inside of me telling me to run.

So I did, tearing up the stairs to the second floor, bursting into the bedroom.

Finding nothing, I turned toward the bathroom, my stomach clenching hard as the hair on the back of my neck stood on end. I had no reason to think it yet, but a part of me knew something had gone down.

Taking a deep breath, I moved into the bathroom.

And there it was.

Proof of a struggle.

Isabella's clothes from earlier had been put into the hamper, but the pair of pants and sweater she must have set out for herself for after the shower were spread across the middle of the floor. Her makeup case had spilled all over the counter.

And there was blood on the floor.

There was fucking blood on the floor.

I wasn't even aware of the roar ripping through me at that moment, but it must have, because not a minute later, Vissi was running into the room, gun drawn.

"What happened?" Vissi asked.

"They're gone. They're all gone. And she was bleeding," I said, waving toward the floor.

"How the fuck could someone get in or out without any of the other guards seeing?" Vissi asked.

I didn't know either, but I tore down the stairs and down to the ground to ask just that.

"Who fucked up?" I yelled, slamming the guard there into the wall. "Did you run off to go get some cookies and milk or something? Who was not on their guard?" I screamed.

"Isabella is gone," Vissi said, translating my anger. "And so are Dawson and Dulles."

"Dawson and Dulles left not long after you went to mass," the guard, said, brows pinched, looking confused.

"The fuck do you..." I started, then released him as shit started to come to me.

"They said you texted them to check out a lead on the shooting, and to make sure no one went inside," the guard continued, but I was barely hearing him.

"No," Vissi said, shaking his head, mind going in the same direction as mine.

But yes.

Absolutely fucking yes.

The night of the break-in that had Isabella sitting in the closet shaking and me shot, Dawson and been right there, but not Dulles. He hadn't shown up until almost half an hour later. And the shooting the night before? Dawson hadn't been there until the shooting was over.

One was always around.

Creating an alibi for the other.

"Fuck," I growled, raking a hand through my hair. "Fuck!" I yelled.

I'd trusted her safety to them.

And they were the ones who were threatening everything we had.

"Primo, man, you need to cool down. You need to think."

"I need to find her, then rip their fucking throats out is what I need to do. And you can be with me or not, but you stay the fuck out of my way if you're not."

"I'm with you, man. Always." Vissi said.

After all this was done, Vissi would be the closest thing to family I would have left.

Vissi and Isabella.

If I could get to her before anything happened.

18

Isabella

What did one wear while preparing a low-fuss Christmas dinner for her grieving husband who just lost his brother?

It was a question that required a lot more thought than I could have realized. Because, obviously, I didn't want to dress up. But almost just as obviously, I didn't want to look completely frumpy either.

I'd settled on slacks and a simple green sweater.

I'd picked red first because it worked with my coloring better, but then I thought better of it, worrying that the red might remind Primo of blood. So green it was.

And I was going to go light on the makeup after my shower, just a little mascara and maybe some liner. I felt like maybe a hint of normal might be important in the grieving period. Especially if Primo wasn't going to grieve loud and hard like many of us would. If he wanted to stiff-upper-lip it most of the day, then give me some of the grief at night when we were alone, that was fine too.

I could play along.

Even if I personally thought it would be healthier for him to grieve like a normal person, not like a mafia boss.

I'd put on my underwear and the tank I was going to wear under the sweater on as I dried my hair, then started to pull out my makeup.

It was right then that I heard footsteps on the stairs.

It was too soon for mass to be over, so I knew better than to expect Primo.

Still, it felt a little weird that Dawson or Dulles would come upstairs without calling for me first. And I was reasonably sure no one had, unless the hair dryer had drowned it out.

I paused, reaching for my outfit, ready to quickly whip them on as I waited for Dawson or Dulles to knock on the closed bedroom door.

Because, surely, they would.

No one just barged into a woman's bedroom.

Their brother's wife's bedroom.

Except, of course, they did.

My stomach twisted hard as my heartbeat sped into overdrive, knowing from somewhere deep inside that something had just gone terribly wrong.

Or, rather, that it had been wrong since the beginning.

Because there Dawson and Dulles were, moving into the bathroom, gazes on me.

But these were not the same men who'd taken me shopping, who'd raved about my cooking, who had protected me—supposedly—with their lives.

I'd seen them as my allies even when I was viewing Primo as my enemy.

They'd been the bright spot in some of my darker days.

But these men who stood in front of me in the bathroom I hadn't invited them into didn't look like the same two I'd grown to like.

There was something cold and ugly in their eyes. And it was so intense that I was finding it hard to believe I'd never seen a hint of it before. How could they hide so much hatred? Why did they have it toward me to begin with?

My heartbeat hammered in my chest as I tried to remember to take slow, deep breaths. It wasn't going to help me to get so scared that I stopped thinking rationally.

"Hey, guys," I said, keeping my tone light. "Give a girl some warning, huh?" I said, rolling my eyes at them. "I'm not decent," I added.

"Decent enough," Dulles said.

"Like you better without any clothes on anyway," Dawson added, making my stomach drop at the implication.

And all I could think was *No*.

No, goddamnit.

I was finally starting to get used to this life. And, dare I say it, like it.

They were not going to rip it all away, turn it into something horrific.

"Come on, guys, give me a second," I said, wiggling my clothes like I wanted to get changed. When what I really wanted to do was run into the closet and find one of the guns I knew Primo had hidden on a shelf on his side.

"You won't need 'em," Dawson said, whacking Dulles in the chest in a silent demand.

"No!" I shrieked, flinging an arm out, knocking half of my makeup all over the counter.

I needed to get a weapon. I stood no chance against two men so much bigger than me if I didn't have something to defend myself with.

There wasn't anything close by.

The mirror.

But no way could I break it and get a piece of it to use as a knife before one of them grabbed me.

The toilet with a heavy tank was behind them.

And there was just... there was nothing else.

Panic gripped my system as my complete and utter helplessness became clear to me.

If they intended to take me somewhere, or simply rape and murder me right in my own bathroom, they would be able to do that, and I would have very little chance of stopping it.

Still, that didn't mean I was going to roll over and take it.

I tossed my clothes at Dulles as he approached me, giving me a distracted second to rush past him, intent on trying to get into the bedroom, then down into the house.

If I could just scream out a window or get downstairs, someone would help me.

I had to believe that.

Not all of Primo's men were bad.

Just these two.

The others would help me.

I just needed to get to them.

Rounding the tub, I grabbed a random bottle of bath bubbles and hurled them with all I had at Dulles who'd swatted the clothes away, and was barreling down on me.

"Fuck's sake. Enough of this," Dawson growled. And before I could even register what he was doing, his arm cocked back and sailed right at my face, colliding with the side of my mouth.

The pain was immediate, ricocheting through my whole jaw as my teeth knocked together. One too hard, it seemed, as blood started to fill my mouth even before I slammed down on my side.

Barely registering the impact, I pushed myself up, trying to scramble away, get into a less compromising position.

"No!" I shrieked as hands grabbed my ankles. Blood spilled out of my mouth and onto the floor.

"Hold her fucking still," Dulles demanded, voice tense.

Knees, and the full body weight of a man much larger than me, pressed down on my back, pinning me to the floor, stealing my breath so I couldn't even scream as Dawson grabbed my arm twisted, and pinned it to the floor.

I watched in horrified helplessness as Dulles's hand moved toward my arm with an open needle between his fingers.

A choked whimper escaped me as it stabbed into my vein.

There was a moment of complete disbelief before there was absolutely nothing else.

Consciousness came to me in a weird, dream-like state, making everything feel slow and fuzzy around the edges.

My stomach flip-flopped over itself, making me wonder if I was going to be sick as my arms flailed outward, only to be trapped in the small space I was confined in.

Confusion set in as I tried to access my memories, tried to make sense of where I was, and why I was in there.

My fingers moved out, tracing the material with what felt like a zipper from the top of my head down toward my feet.

A suitcase?

It felt like a suitcase.

No.

That didn't make any sense.

I mean, yes, my brother had once been a complete unfeeling asshole when we were teens and shoved me in one as a 'joke' because I was so small and slight, until he heard me screaming, then pulled me out and apologized profusely while begging me not to tell our mom.

But why was I in a suitcase now?

Even as the thought formed, I could feel the anxiety starting to form. It started as a pressure on my chest, then a strangling sensation around my throat. Following quickly behind that, my heartbeat started to pound so fast it felt like it was going to burst out of my chest.

My hands slammed as my feet kicked, all logic about finding the zipper tag completely abandoned in my panic.

Luckily enough—or unluckily enough, depending on how you were viewing the whole situation—all the fussing had someone coming over and starting to unzip it for me.

But that someone turned out to be a face my gut told me I didn't want to see, even though I had no real memory of why that would be.

Dawson.

A familiar face.

Someone who was there to save me, surely.

Save me from what, though?

God, what was wrong with my memory?

Everything felt weird and fuzzy and when I looked at Dawson for too long, my vision went weirdly double.

"Dawson?" I asked as I gulped in a deep breath, trying to think past the anxiety from my claustrophobia.

"Fucking shit never lasts long enough," Dulles grumbled from his position a dozen feet back from wherever I was.

Why couldn't I remember being put in the suitcase? Surely that was something someone who was terrified of small spaces would remember.

And why was I feeling so weird? Spacey and nauseous, and the double-vision thing that was making the nausea even worse. Like I was somehow in my body, but also outside of it.

That sounded a lot like...

Drugs.

Someone had drugged me?

But why?

And where was Primo?

"I don't..." I started, finding my brain moving like molasses. Each word seemed to get stuck before it could make it past my lips.

And, God, my face hurt.

Why did my face hurt?

Both on the inside and the out.

Had someone hit me? Had it knocked a tooth loose?

"Where's Primo?" I managed to ask, everything within me saying I needed him, that he would explain, that he would make it right, and would take care of me until I felt better.

"Oh, he'll be here shortly," Dulles said as he pulled a gun out of his waistband. "And we'll be ready for him."

It wasn't so much the words that got through to me, since my brain was just not processing like I needed it to. It was the look in Dulles's eyes when he said that. And when I looked over at Dawson, I saw the same dark, ugly look mirrored there.

"Lock him down tight, and make him watch us having fun with you," Dawson said, smirk full of evil promise.

But even as the words landed, as my sluggish brain registered them, and told me to run, to get away from the danger, I felt my wrist being snagged, and a handcuff tightening around it.

"I bet she'll scream," Dulles said, smiling as my stomach flipped over.

No.

This could not be happening.

Dawson and Dulles? They were the bad guys?

Even as my brain tried to reconcile that, little flashes started to come back to me. Not much. Just the sight of Dawson and Dulles in the master bathroom. Then a bottle of bath soap, and then, finally, a needle going into my arm.

They'd drugged and kidnapped me.

And, judging by the pain in my face, hit me too.

Why?

"Why?" I asked as Dawson dragged me over toward a metal support beam, yanking my free arm behind my back, then securing me around it with the cuffs.

"Why?" Dulles scoffed, shaking his head.

"Yes. Why? He's your brother," I insisted, anger growing. I liked anger. Anger would get me places that fear wouldn't. At least I hoped so, anyway.

"What? Just 'cause his father fucked our mom?" Dawson asked.

"As if she had any choice in the matter," Dulles added.

I didn't know much about this story. I knew the twins had a different mom who raised the boys away from Primo's dad for many years. I also knew she was dead. But that was all I knew. It didn't exactly seem like a topic anyone wanted to discuss.

"Who do you think killed our mom, huh?" Dawson asked.

"Not Primo," I said, sure of it. Yes, he was a ruthless bastard, but he had a moral code too.

"Nah, our old man," Dulles said, shaking his head. "Didn't like not knowing he had a couple more sons growing up without him. Took it out on our ma, then took us in with the others. Know what that house was like? Hell.

Pure fucking hell. Daily beatings and getting screamed at and made to feel like shit."

"I don't understand," I said, shaking my head. "Primo killed your father." For all those reasons, I was sure. By all accounts, the former boss of the Esposito Family had been an evil monster. No one, not even his own sons—least of all the son who'd killed him—mourned his death.

"Then became just like him," Dulles said, voice rough.

"No. Not like him."

"Cold, vicious, evil..." Dulles went on.

It sounded like they were describing themselves at that moment.

"For all his faults, he never drugged a woman and threatened to assault her," I insisted, proud of how strong my voice sounded, despite the circumstances.

"How the fuck do you know?" Dawson asked, making my stomach clench at the idea of the man I was beginning to think I might actually be falling for hurting another woman. "He put on a nice show with you. Protecting your honor and shit. Stupid fucking bitch forgetting he had you kidnapped and forced into marriage."

"She's got some Stockholm type shit," Dulles agreed, nodding. "Ever since he started fucking her. A little dick makes her lose her fucking mind," he added, shaking his head. "I wonder if a little more might make her get it back again," he said, jiggling his belt buckle around in what could only be considered a threat.

No.

Absolutely freaking not.

I was not going to be assaulted by my husband's mentally unstable half-brothers.

That was not going to be my fate.

I just had to think. I had to be smart. I had to bide my time.

I was sure that Primo would come looking for me.

I just had to keep these guys from touching me until then.

I had to keep them talking, explaining why they were doing what they were doing. People liked to talk about themselves. They seemed no different.

"When?" I asked, having to clear my throat to keep my tone calm. "When did you start hating him so much?" I asked, looking between the two of them.

"He was the oldest," Dulles said, eyes burning bright. "He could have protected us."

Even if Primo was the oldest, he'd been a victim of his father too. It was illogical to expect that Primo could have protected them back then. Which was probably why, as an adult, Primo pulled his brothers in close, creating a united front with them. He was trying to make up for all the times he couldn't protect them when they'd all been kids living in the house with a violent tyrant.

"But you've worked with him for years," I insisted, shaking my head.

"We worked against him for years," Dawson said, happy to share how they'd outsmarted a man who never looked at his brothers as perpetrators because he had such a firm belief in loyalty that he wouldn't have been able to fathom brothers who'd betrayed him. Especially when he clearly tried to do right by all his people.

"You've been stealing from him?" I asked, not quite willing to accept more than that.

"Stealing. Doing some carefully placed hits…" Dulles said.

"Can't forget getting Vissi chased out of the States," Dawson added.

"Did you… were you the ones who shot Terzo?"

"That fucking asshole," Dulles said, shaking his head.

Oh, God.

Poor Primo.

That was the dominant thought right then.

Not only did he have a brother murdered, but he never had the love and respect from these two that he'd always thought he had.

And, it seemed, he might very well lose me.

And his own life.

His grief leading up to that would be overwhelming.

"Have you been working alone?" I asked, knowing I needed to keep them talking even if each word they said made my stomach slosh around even more.

"At first. Then we found some friends," Dulles said, smirking. "They should be rounding up the rest of Primo's men soon."

The bile just kept rising up in my throat, making me sure I was going to be sick all over myself.

"I get that you want to hurt Primo. I mean... he's an asshole," I said, trying to endear myself to them even if I hated talking trash about Primo to these real assholes. "But why do you want to hurt me?" I asked.

"Please. You've been fucking him now. You're tainted too."

Tainted.

That was just lovely.

"Even if you think that, have you really thought this through?" I asked. "Have your friends? Because I'm not just a Esposito, remember?" I said, watching as they shared a look. And there was a hint of worry there.

But then Dulles declared. "Please, they wouldn't save you from Primo. They won't save you from us."

"The difference is I chose to be with Primo to end the war," I clarified. "It hadn't been a good choice, but it had been a choice. One that my Family would respect so long as no harm came to me. This? This is not the same. You hurt me, and they will come for you. I don't know if you've met this guy named Brio who is part of my Family," I went on, catching a look of real fear in their eyes. "But I heard he once kind of... you know... boiled a man to death. And that was over some kind of money thing, not something personal."

I could see their glee start to falter at that. Because anyone who knew anything about the New York City mafia knew that Brio was a warped psychopath who got literal joy out of finding new and interesting ways to make people suffer and die.

And he was part of *my* Family.

Even if I didn't personally have much of a connection to him, Brio would go to bat for me out of respect for my brothers.

Dulles gave Dawson a look, and then Dawson was reaching for his phone and heading off toward the far corner of the basement.

Good.

That was good.

I was biding my time.

Time for Primo to know what was going on.

And, hopefully, call in my Family as well, to show up in force and put an end to this once and for all.

I just needed to keep them distracted and second-guessing themselves.

Across the room, Dawson was having an animated, but hushed discussion, occasionally shooting his glance my way, which I noticed in my periphery since I was trying to keep an eye on Dulles who was pacing and raking his hands through his hair.

Losing control.

And that was not something that was going to work in my favor.

I needed them off balance, not out of their minds.

They were much more likely to panic and kill me if they were losing their grip.

"Dulles," I called, making him jerk and look over at me. "Was it all fake?" I asked, trying to make my voice small and vulnerable.

"Was all what fake?"

"I mean, we spent a lot of time together when I first... came to live with Primo. We went out. We shopped and got food together. I cooked for you. We shared stories. It felt really real to me," I told him, and there was a bit of genuine sadness in my voice then, because it had felt real. They had been the only decent part of my life those first few days of fear and uncertainty. "Was it all fake?"

To that, his shoulders slumped a little. "No," he admitted. "It wasn't all fake. I liked you," he admitted.

"I liked you too. You guys were all I had."

I saw those words penetrate, hit somewhere inside of him that was still human enough to feel.

"We were going to save you," Dulles admitted. "Deliver you back to your family. That was the plan. We don't like getting women involved in our business. But then," he said, jaw getting tight again, and I knew he was about to spiral, "but then you started fucking that sonofabitch. And you—"

He didn't get to finish that sentence.

Because the basement door was bursting inward, actually cracking off of its hinges, and flying several feet away.

And there he was.

The man I'd once seen as my enemy, as a punishment I'd have to endure.

But now?

The most welcome person in the world to me.

Not just because he was going to save me.

But just because that was how much things had changed for us.

I wanted to see him.

I wanted to go back home with him.

I wanted to grieve with him.

He looked like an avenging angel right then.

The look in his eyes was bone-chilling, and I couldn't help but be glad I wasn't on the receiving end of that kind of blind rage.

Men rushed in behind him, but it was Vissi who moved over toward me.

"Close your eyes, honey," he demanded, using his body to shield me as the screams started. "Trust me, you need to close your eyes," he added when I didn't immediately comply.

I didn't doubt he was right.

That the image of torture would be something that would live in my brain rent-free until the end of time, no matter how much these men would have deserved it.

Before the message could even relay from my brain to my eyes, though, I was helpless but to watch as Primo pulled out a knife and jabbed it into the throat of his brother. Not into the carotid where he would die almost instantly. No. Into his actual windpipe.

Even as I forced my eyes closed, the sounds coming from Dulles were something that I knew would haunt me. The gasping was followed by the sound of him choking on his own blood even as there were other noises from Primo that implied he continued to do... something to his brother until, eventually, I heard the slam of his body hitting the ground.

"No. No, Primo. We can talk about this," Dawson insisted from where, I imagined, he'd been incapacitated by Primo's other men.

"You came into my fucking home," Primo roared, the sound so loud it made me jolt, "and you dared to put your hands on my fucking woman?"

"Shit," Vissi hissed, and I was aware of his body coming down closer to mine just a second before his hands cuffed over my ears. "Hum with me," he demanded, even as he started to do just that.

Even with both of us humming. Even with his hands pressing down on my ears, the sounds of Dawson losing his life crept in, making me need to swallow hard to keep from getting sick as the man screamed and begged for mercy.

But Primo proved he had none right then.

It seemed like forever that he exacted his revenge on the brothers he'd thought had been loyal, who had proved to be anything but.

At some point, Vissi's hands dropped from my ears, and his humming stopped, even though I couldn't seem to stop my own, some part of me was terrified I'd hear even more of something that I didn't want to.

Behind my back, a key was put into the lock, and the cuffs loosened and were pulled off my wrists.

My arms fell limply for a moment until I managed to force them up, pressing them to my face as I pulled my knees up to rest my head on.

Shock and fear and whatever drugs were still lingering in my system seemed to assault me all at once, keeping me a prisoner in my own swirling mind.

"Isabella," Primo's voice said, low, soft. Soft for him anyway. He must have been kneeling in front of me. He sounded close. "Baby," he tried again, reaching out, pressing a hand to the side of my face. "You're okay," he insisted, fingers stroking back into my hair. "Talk to me, lamb," he demanded, worry seeping into his voice.

"I don't feel good," I admitted.

"What kind of not good? What did they do?" he asked, anger rising in his voice again, and I swear if he could resurrect his brothers to hurt them some more, he would.

"They... there was a needle," I admitted, holding out my arm. "I passed out," I added. "I feel sick." Though, admittedly, it might have been just as much from the sounds of torture and death as it had been from the drugs.

"Ketamine, probably," Vissi said. "That's what those bastards who ran me all the way to Italy were into dealing."

Primo cursed under his breath as his hands reached for me, pulled me against him, held me there like I was something precious.

"It will wear off in half a day," he promised me. "But we can get you home to try to sleep it off."

"No!" I shrieked, body jolting. "No, we can't go home."

"Why?"

"They said... they said there was going to be an ambush."

"Shh, baby, no there won't."

"No, they said it," I insisted.

"I know. It's okay. There will be no ambush. I called Lorenzo Costa myself," he said, meaning the *Capo dei Capi* of all the mafia. "All the Families are coming together on this. If any of them are still alive, they won't be by morning. It's over. It's all over," he promised, arms tightening around me, as he lifted my body while he got to his feet.

"Oh," I said, breathing a sigh of relief. "Okay. Let's go home then," I said, resting my head into his chest.

"You still want me?" he asked, voice vulnerable. "Even after all of this?"

"I can't help it," I admitted, taking a deep breath, catching traces of blood, yes, as well as his cologne, but also just... him, a smell I was getting a little addicted to, if I were being completely honest. "I think I might actually be falling for you," I admitted, wincing at how those words sounded, but knowing there was no other way to say them.

"That's convenient, lamb, because I fucking love you."

19

Primo - 1 day

It wasn't going to be easy.

There was no taking back the events of Christmas that year.

There was more death and blood and fear and anger and grief than I'd ever felt before in my life.

But underneath all of that, there was Isabella.

We'd gone back home and climbed in the tub together, just holding each other in silence, a bit in shock over the events of the last twenty-four hours.

She slept restlessly after, tossing and turning in my arms, crying out, plagued by things she couldn't un-feel, unsee, or un-hear.

Thank God for Vissi with his quick thinking to tell her to close her eyes, cover her ears, to make her hum, to dull the sounds of what was going on. I knew Isabella had very few illusions about the kind of man I was, and especially, the kind of boss I was. But I didn't need her witnessing it in action as I cut the tongue of a lying brother out. Or as I sliced the Esposito Family crest that all my men had inked on them when they got made off of his body while he was still alive. And I didn't need her to see or hear as I strangled him to death, watching the life drain from him minute by minute.

His fate would have been death no matter how his disloyalty came to light.

But the ferocity of it was due to Isabella.

I'd never felt panic like I'd felt when I knew she was taken, when I didn't have any idea what was being done to her, or if I would get to her in time.

It had been Vissi who had been able to remain logical while I spiraled out of control. He was the one to remind me that there was no way Dawson or Dulles could take Isabella to their apartments which were across the hall from each other on a high floor. There would be too many neighbors there.

"And it seems too personal for that," he'd reasoned. "What is more personal to you and them?"

Then it came to me in a rush of blinding realization.

Of course.

Of course they would take this back to where it all began for them.

The basement of the brownstone where all our childhood and adolescent beatings had taken place so the neighbors didn't wise up and call child services on my father.

I still owned the place. I made sure I had some men do upkeep on it to make sure it didn't crumble on me, but I hadn't stepped foot inside of it myself since the day I murdered the man who'd turned it into a house of horrors for all his sons.

That was where Dawson and Dulles would take her.

It brought everything full-circle.

They would hurt her there because they'd been hurt there.

And they blamed me for it.

Hell, I'd blamed myself for it.

But I thought we'd worked past all that shit in the years after our father's murder.

Clearly, I was painfully mistaken about that.

And who had suffered? Everyone else I cared about, who I'd vowed to protect.

Vissi had needed to leave his life behind.

Terzo had lost his.

And Isabella was hurt and traumatized.

Thankfully, I'd gotten there before they really did a lot of damage. Any damage was unacceptable, of course, which was why their deaths had been slow, painful, and terrifying. But aside from a bruise on her face, the knocked out tooth, and the after-effects of the drugs, she'd been okay.

She'd woken when I'd tried to quietly climb out of bed in the early hours of the morning. And while she didn't say it out loud, she clearly felt like she needed to be as close to me as possible. She was my shadow, right at my heels as I moved around the house.

There was shit I needed to handle.

But I'd brushed the responsibility off on Vissi who was understanding of my needing to take care of my woman.

"Primo?" Isabella asked from her position laying on my chest as I stroked my fingers through her hair.

"Yeah, baby?"

"Can we move?" she asked, surprising me enough to make me jolt. "Not right now," she rushed to add. "I just... this hasn't been a good place for us. We should start over somewhere else."

"If you want to move, we can move. I will look into it tomorrow."

"Vissi said the place... where I was taken... that was..."

"Yeah. That was my childhood home," I said, my arm tightening around her waist.

"You still own it?"

"Yeah."

"Why?"

"Honestly, I don't know," I admitted. It wasn't like it was cheap to own a brownstone. Sure, it wasn't as expensive as one in Manhattan would be, but it wasn't chump change I tossed at the place, either.

"Do you think a part of you wanted to go back?"

"It was a hell house," I told her.

"But you held onto it. It could have been someone else's dream house, but you held onto it. Do you think a part of you was maybe considering, you know, changing the narrative you had of it?"

"Honestly, I don't know, lamb. I haven't really thought about it."

"Do you want to think about it?" she asked. "It's okay if it is a no. I'm sure there are a thousand other places in the area that we could move to. But it seems significant that you held onto it. And we could, you know, gut the place. Make it have no traces of the past. Then raise healthy and happy kids there. Break the cycle attached to it."

"Kids?" I asked, hopeful.

"Well, Primo, my mother is expecting at least four grandchildren from each of her kids."

"Only four?" I asked, pressing a kiss to her forehead.

"Well, the number is negotiable," she said, turning her head to give me a soft smile.

Suddenly, I could see our kids running around the small, fenced backyard behind the brownstone as Isabella and I moved around the kitchen making dinner. I could see us decorating a big tree in the front window. I could see us shuffling up the steep stairs to the bedrooms.

I could see it all so vividly.

"Okay," I said, nodding. "Let's do it."

Isabella - 1 month

They needed to create a new word for how exhausted I was.

I'd been spending every spare minute of my day at the brownstone with the contractors and the designers.

When Primo had agreed to my slightly insane plan, I'd promised myself that I would remove everything from the house that could even, in passing, remind him of his father and his dead brothers.

That meant we were even redoing the layout of both upper floors.

The basement level, the one where one of Primo's men had worked tirelessly to remove blood stains and then paint the floor, was going to be a panic room. It was Primo's one bit of input. He wanted there to be somewhere safe where he could shuffle the kids and I into if something happened.

He was going to handle the plans for that since it wasn't my forte, but he left the rest to me completely. And I jumped in with both feet.

Sure, we'd hired a full team, and many of Primo's men had rolled up their sleeves as well, but I didn't want to stand by and do nothing. I was there, sanding, painting, and even ripping up all the awful cement in the back courtyard, wanting the space to have a lawn. For kids. Maybe even a dog someday.

I'd grumbled my way through a quick shower when I got back home, even though my mind was on food and sitting down for five minutes after being on my feet all day.

As I made my way down the stairs, though, the scent of sauce was already filling the apartment.

And there he was.

The man I'd been forced into marrying, a man I swore I would hate until the end of time, but had begun to love to a depth I didn't even fully grasp existed before.

He was the man who murmured to me through my nightmares, who always thought about me first, who was loyal and protective and incredibly giving.

"Hey," I said, giving him a smile. "I was going to get dinner started."

"Vissi said you've been busting your ass all day. I can handle dinner," he said, shrugging.

"What are you making?"

"Ravioli," he told me, gesturing toward the little puffs of dough already lined up next to the stove, waiting to be given a warm bath to cook.

"That sounds amazing," I said. "What's that?" I asked as Primo pulled a small box out of his pocket and placed it on the counter beside where I was leaning. "I don't think I trust that look in your eye," I added when he moved a little closer, something wicked in those dark eyes of his.

I wouldn't claim things had gone back to normal between us. Grief and trauma was still hanging around us, and likely would be for a good while yet. But we'd found our way back to lighter, easier moments, to finding joy and comfort in each other and the relationship that only managed to grow stronger each passing day.

And one of the things that had only gotten better and better for us was the sex. Now that we were done pretending we didn't want it.

In a way, having sex as a normal, healthy outlet kind of made all the other stuff easier to deal with.

So my body tripped into overdrive at the way he stalked even closer to me, a dark promise in those molten eyes of his.

"You're cooking dinner," I reminded him.

At that, he grabbed a hold of my pants and panties, and yanked them down off my legs.

"I just want a little appetizer first," he said, dropping down to his knees, and draping one of my legs over his shoulder, then wasting no time as he started to lick and suck at my clit.

But, like the monster he was, just when I was close, he pulled away, a wicked gleam in his eyes as he moved to his feet.

"Not yet," he told me as his hands reached out, turning me away from him, then bending me forward over the counter.

I was vaguely aware of him opening the box, and I guess I figured it was a vibrator or something. But my whole body jolted when something small and cold pressed inside of me, making my muscles tighten around it instinctively.

A low, rumbling sound moved through Primo as he started to thrust whatever it was in and out of me in slow, controlled motions until I was whimpering and wiggling my hips, needing more.

But then it slipped out of me for the last time, moving back and up, pressing against my ass as the realization finally dawned on me.

A plug.

It was a plug.

Even as I thought that, though, it was slipping inside of me, creating a new, unexpected sensation.

As soon as it was in, Primo moved back a step, reaching out with both hands to massage my ass cheeks for a second.

"Okay," he said, then turned and walked away.

He walked away.

"What are you doing?" I said, turning my neck to see him walking over toward the stove, mixing his sauce, and then pouring a little oil into his boiling water.

"Making dinner."

"You can't leave me like this," I said, a strange choking laugh escaping me.

"Sure I can. I just did, lamb."

"But..."

He turned toward me at that, his gaze slipping from my face to my plugged ass, and a low, primal growling sound escaped him that had me pressing my thighs together to ease the ache that was growing inside me.

"Come here, lamb," he demanded.

"What? I can't..."

"Come here," he demanded, tone a little firmer. And damn if my body didn't react to that authoritative tone.

I pressed up and turned, feeling the strange, full sensation as I moved.

The wicked smile that toyed at his lips said he knew the strange, forbidden sensation that was building in my system as I moved toward him.

"Be a good girl and make the salad for dinner," he demanded as I got close.

"What?" I asked, confusion and desire mingling in my system to wipe all rational thoughts away.

"Make the salad, baby," he said as his hand wandered down my spine to squeeze one of my ass cheeks. "And when you are dying for it and begging for it, then you can have my cock in your ass," he said, giving my ass a hard slap, then turning around and getting back to the ravioli.

Not entirely sure it was possible for me to want him to fuck my ass badly enough to beg for it, I decided to play his game, turning away, then getting to work on the salad.

By the time I had the veggies all chopped up, though, there was no denying the fact that my system was begging for him to fuck me.

The plug had somehow created this strange fullness that pressed against my inner walls, making my pussy ache with need.

I was so wet by the time I put the salad on the table that it was almost embarrassing.

"Done trying to pretend you're not dying for me?" Primo asked as he scooped the ravioli out of the pot and placed it on a platter.

"Yes," I admitted, placing my palm flat on the table as I took a slow, steadying breath.

"Say please, lamb," he said as he moved closer toward me.

"Please," I said immediately, without even a hint of hesitation.

That low growl moved through him again as he got closer.

"Turn around, arms on the table," he demanded.

I didn't even think. I just did what I was told. Because I knew it was going to be what put an end to the clawing need for release.

I heard the zipper sliding down, then felt the thick head of his cock sliding between my lips, grazing over my throbbing clit, then slamming inside my pussy.

Hard.

Deep.

And that little extra fullness of the plug had a loud moan escaping me, the sound ricocheting off the walls in the apartment as Primo started to fuck me.

"So fucking wet," he groaned as one of his hands squeezed my ass as he thrust before slipping inward to toy with the plug.

Just twisting it at first.

Then grabbing it and starting to thrust it in and out of my ass, each movement bigger as my comfort with the sensation grew.

Until, suddenly, the plug was gone, and his cock was pressing against me instead.

"Say it, Isabella," he demanded as the head pressed inward just ever so slightly.

I knew what he wanted to hear.

And what I needed to feel.

"Fuck my ass," I demanded just a second before I felt him sliding inside me.

He was unexpectedly slow and controlled at first, giving my body the time it needed to adjust, using small movements that had his breathing going sharp and shallow as he fought for control.

It wasn't long, though, before I was beyond needing him to be soft and sweet with me.

"Primo, please," I whimpered, wiggling my ass against him.

That was all he needed.

His hand reached out, fisting my hair at the nape of my neck, using it to drag me up until my back collided with his chest, then realizing to close around my neck instead, a hard hold that didn't bruise or cut off air, but was just the right amount of possessive.

"You're so fucking good to me, lamb," he murmured even as he started to fuck my ass. Harder, faster than I could have thought I would enjoy. But, God, was I enjoying.

I never felt a pressure quite like I felt right then, this deep, aching need for release that had my whimpers turning to loud moans, then even pleads for release.

On a groan, Primo's free hand moved between my thighs, two fingers thrusting into my pussy, turning, and stroking over my top wall as his thumb pressed against my clit.

Gone were thoughts, were words.

All that was left was sensation.

And this deep, primal moaning as he drove me closer and closer to that edge.

"Come for me, lamb," he growled, sounding close himself.

His cock thrust, his fingers stroked, and his thumb pressed.

And I simply… shattered.

I felt like I exploded in a million pieces as the triple-zone orgasm slammed through my system, stealing my breath—or maybe that was Primo's hand—and making my whole body shake as the waves kept crashing and crashing.

"Fuck," Primo hissed, pulling out of me, bending me forward, and coming on my ass as my orgasm finally waned. "Fuck, baby," he hissed, his hand slapping down on my other ass cheek as he let out a long, deep breath. "You're so fucking perfect," he added, making my heart flutter a bit, like it always did when he praised me. Which he did surprisingly often.

"Primo?" I called a couple seconds later.

"Yeah, baby?"

"Can you clean me up?" I asked. "I want some dinner now," I told him, getting a deep chuckle out of the man I'd swore I would hate forever, but couldn't deny that I was head-over-heels in love with.

Primo - 1 year

We'd pulled a rabbit out of our hats to get it ready in time for Christmas.

At the beginning of the plans, Isabella had been almost wholly in charge of the renovation of the brownstone.

It wasn't until about seven months into it that she declared, "I am too fat and tired to do anything but eat Milanos in front of the TV."

And so, me and my men took over, trying to get it done in time for Christmas.

Our son's first Christmas.

He'd been a Thanksgiving baby, born just a couple of days before so that Isabella's mom and sister could come over and cook us a whole Thanksgiving feast while we sat in bed, marveling at the life we'd created together.

Isabella had insisted that we had enough going on, that we could just let the brownstone be an ongoing project, but I knew how important it was to her to have our first Christmas as a family of three in the new house.

So I made it work.

And then as soon as I moved us in, she set to work decking it out for Christmas with her over-the-top but classy flair that had the whole place brimming with warmth and joy that I had to admit I'd never really gotten to experience myself growing up.

We'd spent the night before at Isabella's mom's house, letting everyone coo over our baby. She'd been hesitant at first because it was going to be "so loud and overwhelming" but I'd reasoned that the kid's whole life was going to be that way, so we'd gone. And despite all the noise, he'd slept like an angel most of the time, despite how many different arms he found himself shuffled into.

Christmas morning, though, that was at our new place.

Granted, the baby was only a month old, so it wasn't like we had any big Santa story to tell or wide-eyed-wonder to witness yet. But it felt right to cuddle up in front of a fireplace and our tree, listening to our baby coo at the twinkling lights on the tree as we got occasional drop-ins from Vissi and some of my more distant relatives, as well as some of hers.

Including Emilio.

The Woman with the Ring

Who, while he seemed permanently changed from the helplessness and rage he'd felt over the whole marriage situation, had become a doting and loving uncle.

He'd brought over what had to be the entire baby toy section for him, as well as spa gift cards and offers to babysit while she went for Isabella, and even a bottle of whiskey for me.

We would likely never be the best of friends.

But it was a start.

"Who the hell is that?" I grumbled when the doorbell rang for what felt like the tenth time that morning.

Before I could even get up to see who it was, though, there were footsteps in the hall.

And suddenly, New York's craziest sonofabitch was standing in my living room.

Holding a goddamn puppy.

"Hey there lil' mama," Brio Costa greeted Isabella who looked a mix of absolutely in love with the giant-eared, squat-legged puppy, but also concerned. Maybe that I wouldn't let her keep it. "Kids, they should have a puppy to grow up with," he declared as he reached out, tracing the garland over the doorway with his fingers. "Figured it would be a good first Christmas present. You got a yard and shit," he added, shrugging. "You got a yard, you gotta have a dog for it. It's a rule."

And with that, he dropped the dog into Isabella's lap, walked over to our son, and gave him a nod. "Merry Christmas, little man," he said. And then he was gone just as suddenly as he came.

"The fuck was that?" I asked, feeling a little whip-lashed at the whole situation.

"Yeah, ah, apparently, that is Brio's thing now," Isabella said, shaking her head at her distant cousin's strange appearance. "He just... brings people animals. Like he's doing community outreach for the local shelters or something," she added, smiling as she rubbed the puppy's head.

"Yes," I said, reading her mind. "We can keep him," I said, watching as she shot me a beaming smile.

It seemed right.

A house to build memories in.

A wife I loved more than I knew I was capable of.

A son who was just one of many, we hoped.

A yard.

And a dog.

It sounded like a great start to forever to me.

Are you CURIOUS about how:

Lorenzo Costa became *capo dei capi?* —> Then read "The Woman in the Trunk."

How Alessa Morelli got kidnapped and saved? —> Then read "The Woman in the Back Room."

If you liked this book, check out these other series and titles in the NAVESINK BANK UNIVERSE:

The Henchmen MC
Reign
Cash
Wolf
Repo
Duke
Renny
Lazarus
Pagan
Cyrus
Edison
Reeve
Sugar
The Fall of V
Adler
Roderick
Virgin
Roan
Camden
West
Colson

Henchmen MC Next Gen
Niro
Malcolm
Fallon
Rowe

The Savages
Monster

Killer
Savior

Mallick Brothers
For A Good Time, Call
Shane
Ryan
Mark
Eli
Charlie & Helen: Back to the Beginning

Investigators
367 Days
14 Weeks
4 Months

Dark
Dark Mysteries
Dark Secrets
Dark Horse

Professionals
The Fixer
The Ghost
The Messenger
The General
The Babysitter
The Middle Man
The Negotiator
The Client
The Cleaner
The Executioner

Rivers Brothers
Lift You Up
Lock You Down
Pull You In

Grassi Family
The Woman at the Docks
The Women in the Scope
The Woman in the Wrong Place

Golden Glades Henchmen MC
Huck
Che
McCoy

STANDALONES WITHIN NAVESINK BANK:
Vigilante
Grudge Match

NAVESINK BANK LEGACY SERIES:
The Rise of Ferryn
Counterfeit Love

OTHER SERIES AND STANDALONES:

Stars Landing
What The Heart Needs
What The Heart Wants
What The Heart Finds
What The Heart Knows
The Stars Landing Deviant
What The Heart Learns

Surrogate
The Sex Surrogate
Dr. Chase Hudson

The Green Series
Into the Green
Escape from the Green

Seven Sins MC
The Sacrifice
The Healer
The Thrall

Costa Family
The Woman in the Trunk
The Woman in the Back Room

DEBT
Dissent
Stuffed: A Thanksgiving Romance
Unwrapped
Peace, Love, & Macarons
A Navesink Bank Christmas
Don't Come
Fix It Up
N.Y.E.
faire l'amour
Revenge
There Better Be Pie
Ugly Sweater Weather
I Like Being Watched
The Woman with the Ring

Jessica Gadziala is a full-time writer, parrot enthusiast, and coffee drinker who has an unhealthy obsession with acquiring houseplants. She enjoys short rides to the book store, sad songs, and cold weather. She lives in New Jersey with her parrots, dogs, bunnies, and a whole flock of chickens.

She is very active on Goodreads, Facebook, as well as her personal groups on those sites. Join in. She's friendly.

Connect with Jessica:

Facebook: https://www.facebook.com/JessicaGadziala/
Facebook Group: https://www.facebook.com/groups/314540025563403/

Goodreads: https://www.goodreads.com/author/show/13800950.Jessica_Gadziala

Twitter: @JessicaGadziala

Website (and newsletter): JessicaGadziala.com

Amazon: https://amzn.to/3Cwa5ei

TikTok: JessicaGadziala

Discord: https://discord.gg/yXCvuWTJ

<3/ Jessica

Printed in Great Britain
by Amazon